I, PAUL . . . : THE LIFE OF THE APOSTLE TO THE GENTILES

I, PAUL . . . : THE LIFE OF THE APOSTLE TO THE GENTILES

Allienne R. Becker, Ph.D.

Writers Club Press
San Jose New York Lincoln Shanghai

I, Paul . . . : The Life of the Apostle to the Gentiles

Writers Club Press
an imprint of iUniverse, Inc.

For information address:
iUniverse, Inc.
5220 S. 16th St., Suite 200
Lincoln, NE 68512
www.iuniverse.com

ISBN: 0-595-21321-9

Printed in the United States of America

To Dr. Isidore H. Becker, Ph.D., my husband, my proofreader, and my best friend

Contents

CHAPTER 1

I, Paul, the least of your apostles, now in chains for the gospel, long for death and to be with you. I am alone now, except for Luke who is sleeping soundly in our prison here in Rome. Demas, loving this world, has deserted me for Thessalonica. Crescens went to Galatia and Titus to Dalmatia. No one came to my aid at my first trial. All of them abandoned me, but you strengthened me and delivered me that I might preach to the Romans so that they might believe in you. But now, the work you gave me to do is finished. I fought well, I believe. I finished the race set for me to run. I have kept the faith and given it to those that you have chosen.

Already, little by little, my sacrifice has begun. My books are gone and with them my parchments. I no longer even have a cloak to wrap around my old and aching bones. Soon it will be winter and Roman winters can get quite cold. The prison is damp, dug out of the earth beneath the Mamertine, and the incessant rain is sending rivulets into my cell. The pines that I can see above are bending slightly in the wind. All is quiet now except for the pelting down of the rain. With no one wishing to be out on a cold wet night, traffic has stopped on the Via Laurentia. Alone with my thoughts, I share them all with you.

I have heard that Peter, the big fisherman and my dear brother, has already gone before me into the valley of the shadow of death. As

I wait for my hour to come, my thoughts turn on a straight course to the God of my fathers, Abraham, Isaac, and Jacob, whom I have served diligently since my youth and to you, Lord Jesus, whose apostle I am and for whom I lay down my life as a witness.

You know well, Lord, that I am not worthy to be called your apostle. It grieves me to remember that I once persecuted your church. Like a thorn in my spirit is the remembrance of my part in the death of Stephen and in the persecution of other Christians whom I, in my misplaced zeal, even pursued to foreign lands to catch, persecute, and destroy. Although I was ignorant of what I was doing, I was, in fact, a blasphemer, a persecutor, a bitter adversary of yours. I can never stop praising you, Lord Jesus, for the mercy of God that saved me, the greatest of sinners, from destruction.

My parents were devout and holy members of the tribe of Benjamin. I am a Pharisee, a member of the strictest sect of our religion. I kept the law; I led a blameless life. In fact, zeal for the law of Moses consumed me and I must confess that I was proud that I was not like other men.

Your wisdom and your knowledge are of unfathomable depths. Your judgments are inscrutable; your ways unsearchable. I thought it was my duty to persecute your followers. Now your name is emblazoned in my heart, burnt there by the fire of the words you spoke to me when I was traveling to Damascus, looking for your followers to arrest them and make them denounce you, and throw them into prison as now I am in captivity for your name. Your name, may it be glorified forever, at the sound of which I kneel before you. Glory to the name of Jesus!

I am grateful for Stephen whose death I witnessed and sanctioned. I hope to meet him soon. As the stones were being hurled at him and he lay bleeding profusely from almost every part of his body, he cried out asking you to receive his spirit and not to blame those who were killing him. You heard his prayer. But I, still called Saul in those days, I persisted in harassing and persecuting your church, going into one house after another to find your followers and drag them out and throw them all—men, women, and even children—into prison. Most just are your judgments—my own days in prison for love of the gospel have been many.

In my extreme rage, I threatened your people with death for the sake of the law. Eagerly and of my own accord, I sought out the high priest and requested letters to the synagogues in Damascus that I might search there for your followers and bring them back in chains to Jerusalem.

Energized with great self-satisfaction, I set out on the road to Damascus, but I did not get very far with my plans. Saul, my old self, died that day. As I drew near to Damascus, it was about mid-day, when suddenly in a flash, in a twinkling, you were there and I beheld your glory.

"Saul," You said gently but firmly, "Why are you persecuting me?"

"Who are you," I stammered. I already knew.

"I am Jesus…"

O, Lord, I fell to the ground. My eyes were blinded by your glory, but my spirit beheld you as clearly as in the brightest day. In an instant, I learned to be true what I later heard from the lips of your beloved disciple, John. The law came from Moses and grace and truth come by Jesus, the Christ. At that time, I only had the law which served but to condemn me. I realized that I needed your grace and your truth and you filled me with them in abundance making my ignorance vanish. I knew in that moment that you are the hope of Israel. Setting me free from the law, you let me taste and see the goodness, the mercy, the love of God, the tremendous love of God that was poured into my soul by the Holy Spirit who was given to me. I perceived that you died for me, a sinner. I know now that love is the fulfillment of the law—you are the fulfillment of the law—bestowing justification on all who believe in you. Until I met you, I did not have love in my heart.

Having beheld you, I could no longer judge anyone. Consumed by your love, I could think of nothing else, but you. Filled with fear and feeling utterly weak, I asked with trembling "Lord, what do you want me to do?" Feeling a tremendous sorrow for my past life, I surrendered completely to you. In that instant, Saul died and a new creature with a quickening spirit was born.

You told me of your plans for my life, appointed me to be your minister and a witness to this heavenly vision and the future visions that you would grant me. You commissioned me to open the eyes of the people that they might turn from darkness to light, that they might receive forgiveness of sins and an inheritance among those sanctified by faith in you.

· You were more radiant than the sun! Fixing the gaze of my soul upon you, I wanted to behold you and remain with you forever! Even now as I remember the vision, my heart is overflowing with joy unspeakable and full of glory! I had found my hope, the hope of Israel. Since I was as yet unaccustomed to the life of the spirit, my mortal flesh could not bear the vision of you then as it can now. For three days I was blind. Seeing nothing, I was all absorbed in your glory. Neither could I eat or drink anything. If you had not commanded me to get up and go into the city where I would be told what to do, I would have remained there on the Damascus road. Although I was overwhelmed by the vision of you, the men who accompanied me saw a bright light, but did not see you.

With your words, "I am Jesus" emblazoned on my soul for all eternity, I arose and stumbling made my way to Damascus where I remained as you instructed me to do. The house I was directed to was on the street called Straight. I was on the straight way to God, I mused. As I was praying—and that was all I could do, or even wanted to do—Judas whose house it was—announced that someone named Ananias wished to talk with me. Although I could not see him, because of the blindness, I knew he was a kind, compassionate, humble man and filled with the love of God as he greeted me.

"Brother Saul, the Lord has sent me…Jesus…"

I bowed my head.

"…Jesus—who appeared to you on your journey—that you might recover your sight and be filled with the Holy Spirit." Approaching me, he laid his hands on my head.

"Brother, Saul, receive your sight."

Instantly I could see him. Rather anxiously, he was looking at me intently. When he perceived that I did in fact see him, his face burst into a smile that revealed his strong, straight, teeth. Falling to my knees, I waited for him to speak.

"You must be baptized washing away all your sins. Why wait any longer?"

"Will you baptize me?" My eyes held him fast.

His eyes were small slits as he asked, "Do you believe in the Lord Jesus?"

My glance was steady. "You know I do," I replied softly.

"Do you believe that he is alive?"

His eyes were intent and burned into my soul.

"I have seen him." My heart pounded at the memory.

"Do you believe that the Holy Spirit raised him from the dead and that he is the fulfillment of the law and the prophets, the Messiah, the anointed, Holy One of Israel?" His face was motionless; he was tense and so was I.

"I believe."

Relaxing a bit, he continued addressing me. "The God of our fathers has chosen you to know his will, to see his son, and hear his voice. You shall witness to everyone what you have seen and heard." Extending both arms towards me, his eyes sparkling with charity, he commanded: "Get up and be baptized and wash away your sins, calling on his name."

"I called on your holy name, Lord Jesus, and I was baptized into your death. I was buried with you in order that, just as you have arisen from the dead through the glory of God our Eternal Father, so

I might walk in newness of life. I was united with you in the likeness of your death and therefore I shall one day be united with you in your resurrection also. My old self was crucified with you and I died to sin. I died with you, Lord Jesus, and I believe I shall live with you for you are risen from the dead nevermore to die. Because of this, I await my death with great joy as I am incarcerated here in the Mamertine prison.

In the waters of baptism, I received your Spirit. As a son, I cried out, "Abba! Father!" The Holy Spirit revealed to me that I am a co-heir with you, Lord, and because I suffer with you, I shall also be glorified with you.

Your Spirit warned me in every city during my journeys of labor for the churches that imprisonment and persecution were awaiting me, but I fear none of these if only I accomplish the ministry you have entrusted to me. I am ready to die for your name, Lord Jesus. I know that all of the sufferings of this life cannot compare with the glory that will be revealed in me in the life that is to come. You have redeemed my soul and now I groan for the redemption of my body after death.

Actually, I have already died and my life is hidden with Christ in God and when you, my Life, shall appear, then I, too, will appear in glory with you. Living for me is Christ; dying, endless happiness and joy with you. I truly long for my departure from this life.

Humbly I ask you, Lord, to accept these meditations of my heart, made during my final hours before I am made like you in death, pouring out my blood for the city of Rome. I rejoice in what I suffer for your sake and for Rome, for I have grown to love this city. You will become the light of the Gentiles, as you are the glory of Israel. Although I am a Jew of the tribe of Benjamin, born in Tarsus, I am also a citizen of Rome. In your providence, you foreordained that I should be born a Roman citizen so that here in Rome I can unite my sacrifice to yours. Following your appointed plan, Rome shall witness my death and the shedding of my blood will give them life.

When Nero kills me, a million people will ponder the event in the secret recesses of their hearts, making my blood the seed of a great harvest. In taking my life, Nero will give you Rome.

While I wait in the silence of this rainy night, I remember the events of long ago as my life flows past my view like a river on its swift course to the sea. Recalling my conversion and those early days in Damascus as your follower, I remember how the Holy Spirit came into my soul at baptism and has been my faithful companion ever since to this very day. I became a Christian, but I needed time to understand what was happening to me. Realizing that I knew very little about you—and I wanted to learn everything I could—I prayed for light to comprehend the height and the depth and the breadth of your love.

After healing my blindness, Ananias, invited me to partake of your Body and Blood, but I was not yet ready to enter into your august mysteries. No man explained to me the mystery of our redemption, but you yourself revealed it to me. On the night when you were betrayed, you took bread, gave thanks, and broke it, saying that the bread is your body and you took wine and blessing it saying it is your blood. I knew I had to wait until your Holy Spirit drew me to partake of these mysteries.

When I felt that the time was right, I asked Ananias to take me to the assembly in the home of one of the Christians there in Damascus where the mysteries were to be celebrated. With a certain amount of apprehension, I entered the house, because I did not know how I would be received. When Ananias introduced me as "Brother Saul of Tarsus," smiles froze on the faces of the men and the women began scurrying around collecting their children and heading for the door; no doubt my reputation for persecuting the Church preceded me. When the men began talking among themselves in whispers in one corner of the room and it became obvious that everyone was terrified of me, I knew I had to do something. Rushing to the center of the room, I tried to explain.

"I have seen the Lord! I am one of you now!"

Obviously they did not believe me. When I showed them that I carried no weapons and when Ananias assured them that he, himself, baptized me, calm slowly returned to the assembly. The bread was broken and the cup of blessing extended to me. For the first time I ate your flesh and drank your blood, and your life became my life. I beheld you within me, not face to face, but as through a smoked piece of glass and I yearned to be transformed, to reflect your glory and be transmuted into your very image going from glory to glory. I put on Christ and was ready to suffer with you—yes, even to being handed over to death for your sake that your life might be revealed in my mortal flesh.

For love of you, I counted everything else as lost. I gave up all—parents, home, religion–everything that I might find you and be found in you, so that I might know and experience the tremendous power of your resurrection. And now, I embrace the fellowship of your sufferings and will soon become like you in death in the hope that I will behold your glory, face to face.

Your body and blood were to me like the coal of living fire that the angel took off the altar and placed on the lips of Isaiah, the prophet. That day in Damascus I was united to you; I was no longer a stranger or a foreigner, but a citizen and a member of your household.

Filled with your Spirit, I went to the synagogues of Damascus and preached loudly that you are the Messiah, the Holy One of Israel, that you are risen from the dead and alive for evermore—that I had seen you. To the Pharisees I was an abomination—anathema. Not sure if I was really one of them, the Christians were very cautious with me.

As I was becoming stronger in the ways of the Spirit, you were with me in power. One day, when I was in ecstasy, you appeared to me telling me to leave Damascus, which rejected me, saying that you were going to send me to the Gentiles far away. This time you did not blind me, for by now I was becoming accustomed to communing with you. I knew in my heart that you had set me apart for your service even when I was still in my mother's womb. Knowing that my mission was to non-Jews, I needed time to prepare for my ministry so I went toward the East and traveled about three days into Arabia and the desert. I wanted to meditate and pray and to ponder the eternal secrets that had been hidden since the world began and which had been revealed to me. I also hoped to visit Jerusalem—to visit the Place of the Skull and kiss the ground that had been drenched with your Holy Blood. I wanted to see with my own eyes the sepulcher that was unable to contain you. Yes, and I also wanted to meet Peter and the other apostles, but I knew that Saul would not yet be welcomed in Jerusalem. So I went into Arabia and preached Christ Crucified to anyone who would listen. As I lived alone and spent long hours in prayer, you revealed to me the mysteries of faith.

I was healed of my blindness, my own blindness and the blindness of the Pharisees. Isaiah wrote of the blindness of our people saying that our hearts were hardened, our eyes closed, our ears stopped up as we refuse to understand. Constantly grateful that you opened my eyes, I rejoice in your truth. In the Arabian Desert, I slept out under the stars where I felt close to you. Your Holy Spirit led me to sing the psalms of David in my heart, giving thanks for everything in your name. To learn more about you, I turned to the Sacred Scriptures, for I am a Hebrew of Hebrew parentage, a Pharisee of Pharisees, who began to learn the language of Scripture as a small child. When I attended the school of the Tarsus synagogue, I studied Hebrew and the sacred writings of our faith. In your Providence, you planned for me to go to Jerusalem when I was fourteen to study with the famous Rabbi Gamaliel. Although the Scriptures have been my food all my life, in the desert they were the manna that nourished me. As I imbibed the riches of my Jewish heritage in your holy word, my eyes opened to your truth and my heart was truly circumcised. I thank you that I was born of Jewish parents and know the prophecies of old that are even more meaningful for me now that I see their fulfillment in you.

I had the mind of a Pharisee and we Pharisees could not imagine that our Messiah would die on a cross. Did not the law say that everyone who hangs on a gibbet is cursed? Becoming accursed of God for us, you hung on a gibbet that we might be justified in his sight. This is the stumbling block of the Jews; they simply cannot understand it. In time their blindness will be completely healed, as was mine, and all Israel shall be saved. You redeemed us from the curse of the law by becoming a curse for us. No one could really keep the law and it serves only to condemn us by showing us how we totally miss the mark. With your death, you freed us from the law of sin and death by becoming our justification.

Having walked in spiritual darkness, I rejoiced in the light. Having dwelt in the shadow of death, I found the new light that arose in my heart. Because the prophet Isaiah told us that Messiah would sit upon the throne of David, we expected an earthly kingdom, picturing you coming as a great king clothed in purple and majesty with a flourish of trumpets resounding throughout all Jerusalem and Judea. Instead you came riding on a lowly donkey. But Isaiah also wrote that you would be a man of sorrows wounded for our iniquities and bruised for our sins. It was incredible! Isaiah had clearly stated that the Lord would place on you the sins of us all. When I read the passages of Isaiah that foretold your death, I wept, for I was pierced through and through and brought face to face with the reality of your crucifixion and the enormity of my sin. God, himself, died for my sins and for the sins of the whole world!

When I first encountered you, when I first began to have visions of you, it was my greatest regret that I was not allowed the privilege of conversing with you in the flesh as the other apostles had. On one occasion, I was in Jerusalem at the same time you were there, but I did not see you. When first I heard of you, I scoffed, as the rest of the Pharisees did, because you did not keep our law–the law the Pharisees and the Scribes overlaid upon the law of Moses. As I said, at first I was disappointed not to have met you in the flesh, but now I am very thankful that I was not in Jerusalem for the Passover when you were betrayed. I hate to think what would have happened, if I had been there. I would have howled for your blood. This thought fills me with fear and trembling. I can see myself coming to you and reproaching you disdainfully, with an arched eyebrow, because your disciples did not always wash their hands before taking food. I would have been one of the first to yell that you cast out devils by the prince of devils. I would have attacked you because your disciples freely ate and drank and I fasted twice a week. Making a great pretense of piety, I would have forced my way, with my long and costly robes billowing around me to the front of the temple to pray with my phylacteries very wide and my tassels as large as I could possibly have them. When I heard you call us Pharisees hypocrites and blind guides who have neglected mercy and faith, I would have breathed forth fire. When you said we were like whitewashed tombs that are full of death and filth, I would have seethed with anger and rage. Always ready for a fight when my beliefs are challenged and attacked, I probably would have been the most enraged of all, for I, Paul, am a true son of the tribe of Benjamin. No doubt I would have rushed to the High Priests and pleaded for your blood to be shed. And when Caiaphas said that it was better for one man to die than for the whole nation to perish, I would have shouted my approval. I can picture myself even going to Gethsemane with the soldiers, priests, Scribes and Pharisees to take you prisoner. I would have stood with the Pharisees outside Pilate's Palace—it would have made us unclean to enter it—when Pilate said he could find nothing wrong in what you had done and he was willing to release you after he had you scourged. Mercilessly, I would have yelled louder than all the rest: "Crucify Him!"

Crowned with sharp prickly brambles and wounded from head to foot, Luke, my very dear physician, says you were weak because of the blood you lost. Although according to our law, you as a prisoner were not to receive more than thirty-nine lashes, Luke told me that the scene of your scourging was too horrible to describe and that when he wrote his gospel a few years back, he passed over this scene in silence, for this very reason. As a member of the healing profession, Luke said he would rather not meditate too much on what happened to you at the hands of the Roman soldiers. You, Jesus, were tied to a post and beaten until your whole body was one open wound.

Beaten with lashes that had balls of lead on the ends of the thongs in order to tear your flesh until your very nerves lay bare, you fell exhausted to the ground. Draping you in scarlet, they mocked you for being a king. Kneeling before you, they jeered and rising spat in your face–the face of God–and struck you.

"Crucify Him!" the Pharisees shouted and I would have too, if I had been there. According to our law you were to be crucified because you said you are the Son of God. We Pharisees had all the answers. "Crucify Him! Crucify Him!" we shrieked. I could see the whole ghastly scene with myself in the forefront. O Lord, I thank you that I was not in Jerusalem when you were taken to the Place of the Skull and nails were driven through your hands and feet!

During the long nights in the Arabian desert, I had much time to ponder your dying and death realizing that it was because of love you died for me and for the whole world. Wanting to know all the details of the shameful event that purchased my salvation and, since I had no gospel to read, for these events had not yet been written down, I turned to the prophets of Israel who foretold your death just as it happened. As I beheld you on the cross in my heart, I whispered to you that I, Paul, a Pharisee, was ready to die for you, for your name, for your gospel, which I shall proclaim as long as I have breath. In the psalms of our father David who foretold that they would pierce your hands and feet and number all your bones, I found you, my dying Lord. The psalms even foretold that they would gamble to see who would get your garments. When the psalmist speaks of how all the earth would bow down before you and that men must proclaim you so that future generations will know and praise you, I was reminded of my calling. It seemed that these words were written especially for me, for by them I entered into your very soul and I saw the love that is there for me and for all people everywhere. It was because of love that you came to us so humbly.

With Isaiah, we prayed that you would rend the heavens and come down. The mountains, we said, would melt away at your presence. You came down and we nailed you to a cross of wood. You are the Life of the world, and we condemned you to death. You made the stars, the moon, the seas, hills and the valleys and we took your hands and nailed them fast. You are Love, and we hated you. In you is all benediction and we made you a curse. You became sin for us and you turned death into Life. I rejoice in you, and my soul is joyful in my God, for you have clothed me with the garments of salvation and the robe of justice.

Although my speech is blunt and brusque, nevertheless, you infused me with knowledge and wisdom, revealing to me hidden mysteries as the time passed quickly in the desert. To learn of you, Lord Jesus, I kept searching our Hebrew Scriptures. Although the other apostles had known you in the flesh, I know you in the Spirit and I consider myself in no way inferior to them, but I glory only in my infirmities.

From reading the prophets, I learned much about you, Lord. From the visions you gave me, I learned even more. Both the prophets and the visions told me that the Gentiles shall behold your salvation. Time was drawing near for me to return to Damascus and begin my ministry of reconciliation that would take me to the Gentiles in the far corners of the empire.

The prophecies of Joel were being fulfilled. The day had arrived that anyone who calls on your name shall be saved. Young men were seeing visions and old men, dreaming dreams. You were pouring forth your Spirit on all flesh and the sons and daughters were prophesying.

In reading the prophets, there was one thought that struck my attention and which I could not put out of my mind. Isaiah wrote that a virgin would conceive and bear a son and he would be called Emmanuel, which means, God with us. A virgin! You were born of a virgin! Who was this woman chosen from all Jewish maidens to be your Mother? I did not even know her name. She was of the lineage of David–that much I learned from the Scripture. For centuries women had anticipated that one of their number would be the mother of the Messiah. One thought especially intrigued me. Perhaps this virgin who had been the dwelling place of the Most High was still alive! Perhaps I could even meet her.

What was she like, this woman who gave so much of herself to you and who had carried the Messiah in her heart and in her arms? Did she sing to you and play games like other mothers do? What did she tell you about Yahweh? How did she pray with you? Did she share with you your passion for souls? Was she there when you died? Did she wash your body for burial? Did you tell her things that you told no one else? How did you fashion your mother when you created her? Is she the most beautiful of women? Is her soul more resplendent than the stars? Is she all fair and the glory of our people Israel? I hoped to have answers to these questions when I returned to Jerusalem.

Leaving my desert retreat, I returned to the ancient city of Damascus. On the Sabbath I went to the synagogue and preached with power that you were crucified for our sins and that you rose from the dead and that you are alive forevermore always interceding for us all. Because of this fervent sermon, Ananias cautioned me.

"Some of the Jews here have hatched a plot to kill you, my brother. The governor of the city under King Aretas is looking for you to throw you in prison."

Because I came to Damascus to persecute the church and instead became its chief exponent, certain of the Jews were extremely furious and determined to kill me. For this reason, Ananias and some of the other Christians hid me away until they could devise a plan to help me escape from Damascus.

One night when I was in the home of Ananias, some of the brothers came bringing a basket large enough to hide me in. After placing me into it, they put me on a cart pulled by a donkey. Very cautiously taking me to the old wall of the city, far from the gate where the sentinels watch, they lowered me down from the wall through a window where some other Christians received me and arranged a caravan to take me to Jerusalem.

This was the beginning of my life as a persecuted man. I bear your marks on my body, Lord Jesus. Five times have I received thirty-nine lashes from the Jews. Three times I was scourged. Once I was stoned and left for dead. Three times my ship wrecked and I was adrift on the sea for a day and a night. I have been in danger in the city, in the wilderness, on the sea. False brothers have tried to destroy me everywhere. Because you wanted me to stand before Caesar in Rome and proclaim you with my blood, you kept me always in your care and delivered me. Soon by Nero's command, and in accord with your loving Providence, I shall die by the sword.

The rain continues—a fine mist blown in the winds of autumn. Still no word from Timothy. I hoped to see my dearest son one final time before my blood is poured out by the executioner's sword. Certainly he received my letter entreating him to come before winter. Ah! There are many things I would tell him. I would not have him ignorant of the peace and joy that are in my heart as I prepare to die for you, Christ Jesus. I would strengthen him in the faith and prepare him to make this same sacrifice one day. Even now my eyes are searching the road in front of this prison watching for him to come—before it is too late.

From Damascus I traveled to Jerusalem, entering by the gate of Benjamin. When I encountered the familiar sounds and smells of the city, it brought back memories of the days I spent studying the law there with Gamaliel. No need to visit him, even if he were still alive.

The temple loomed ahead. I was a Jew and I had come home. Proceeding down the deep valley that divides the city in half, I found and entered a tavern where Roman soldiers were sitting around a large table drinking, jesting, and singing their vulgar songs. When I approached the proprietor, an old Jew with a mangy beard, I noted that he was stooped by the burden of many years and had doubtlessly seen many people come and go. He, if anyone, would know the people of the city. Clearing my throat to attract his attention from his pouring wine for his guests, I addressed him.

"Friend, I have been absent from this city for a long while. Would you be so kind as to direct me to the house of one called Cephas also known as Simon?"

Setting down the wine skins, he replied with an edge in his voice. "I don't want any trouble here. I am poor man trying to earn an honest living by running a peaceful establishment."

"I am not from these parts and I don't know of any trouble." I studied him closely, as he rubbed the large wart on his nose, glanced apprehensively at the Roman soldiers, and shrugged his shoulders.

"I don't want any followers of the Galilean in my tavern," he explained coldly, returning to his work.

"Peace be unto you. I mean you no harm."

I laid a few coins on the counter in front of him. Anxiously looking around the room as he grabbed the coins, he scribbled an address on a piece of parchment and handed it to me.

"Go! Go quickly," he ordered.

The house to which he directed me was in the lower city, an unpretentious house—like any other on the street. Boldly entering the courtyard, I strode to the door and began pounding vigorously. The late afternoon sun was shining in my eyes and I raised my hand to shield them when I heard someone coming to answer. Taking a deep breath, I waited, hoping that the person who answered would welcome me.

The man who answered was virile, of medium height, neither young, nor old. Leveling his black eyes at me, he greeted me.

"Peace be unto you."

"And unto you peace." I repeated the formula I learned in Damascus.

He waited for me to state my business.

"I come to share the fellowship of Christ with you," I told him with my warmest smile. I could see that there were many people inside the house looking at me, staring intently with curiosity.

"What is your name?" he asked, holding the door partway shut so that I could not enter.

"I am Saul of Tarsus, recently of Damascus and the Arabian desert." I saw his eyebrows go up at the mention of my name.

"Ah! I saw you," he exclaimed, rubbing his bulbous nose, "at the stoning of Stephen in the Kidron!"

When he started to close the door in my face, I pushed hard against it and said, "Wait! Let me explain!"

Inside the house, people were beginning to panic. It was no use. They would not even listen to me. I released the door, which slammed violently in my face. Turning, I began to walk away.

"Wait! Wait!" A young man came running out of the house waving his hands to stop me. "Wait, Saul! I will take you where you want to go. You are expected."

Bowing my head to the workings of Providence, I greeted the young man warmly and thanked him for his help.

"I'm Barnabas," he introduced himself with a boyish grin. He was even younger that I had originally thought. It was good to see young men like him in the service of the Lord.

Leading me to a nearby house that was very similar to the one we had just left, he knocked on the door. In a few minutes, a serving girl let us in and showing us to a large, but simply furnished sitting room, invited us to take a seat and wait.

"This is the house of James, the son of Alphaeus," Barnabas whispered as I heard someone coming toward us. Rising to my feet, I eagerly awaited my first glimpse of one of the apostles. As our host strode vigorously into the room, Barnabas fell to his knees and motioned for me to do likewise.

"May the blessing of our Lord Jesus Christ descend upon you both," intoned James lifting his hand in benediction.

When we rose to our feet, Barnabas excused himself and left me alone with the apostle.

"I am very happy to meet you," I said with sincerity. "I have heard the followers of Christ in Damascus speak of you." I really knew nothing about him except his name and that he was chosen as one of the twelve.

His smile was kindly and courteous.

"I, too, have heard much about you, Saul of Tarsus. We wondered what became of you after you left Damascus in such an unprecedented fashion. I hear you went out lowered in a basket from the wall!" He laughed softly. "Yes, we heard all about how you outwitted King Aretas escaping so cleverly."

Leading me across the room to two chairs, we settled down to get acquainted with each other. Resting his chin on his folded hands, he studied my face pensively with his quick brown eyes. Seeming to read my thoughts he asked, "You want to know about me, don't you?"

Silently I returned his glance and waited for him to speak. I noticed that his hands were thickly calloused. Nodding my head, I said, "More than that. I want to know about Christ. You knew him very well, did you not?"

"As far back as I can remember. I've known him all my life. You see, he is my cousin—the son of my mother's sister. He spoke very humbly. When I suddenly realized he was speaking of the virgin mother of Jesus, my heart beat a little faster.

"Your mother's sister?" I tried to appear casual.

"Yes, Mary, the mother of the Lord." He smiled not appearing to be the least surprised that I did not know these things.

"The virgin?" I asked. I had to know if it was really true.

He made no attempt to answer, so I decided to push the matter.

"It was as the prophet said?" My eyes probed his. "A virgin shall conceive and bear a son…"

He nodded. "It was as the prophet said. She and my mother are sisters—in the family, we knew." At the thought of this great mystery, he bowed his head and became silent. Shadows of night were now beginning to fall. Once the sun sets in Jerusalem, night comes quickly since they do not have the long twilight like we have here in Rome.

Rising, James lit the oil lamp that was hanging suspended from the ceiling of the room.

"It's getting dark," he murmured, picking up a small brass bell from the table that was between us. Ringing it three times, he waited for someone to appear in the doorway opposite me. Almost instantly a serving girl, the same one who let us in, stood before him.

"Supper, please," he ordered as he flourished his hand in my direction, "for our guest and myself." The girl bowed her way from the room.

Determined not to let the subject rest, I returned to our conversation where it left off.

"The mother of the Lord…she is still living?"

"Yes, we still have her with us."

Seeming to wish to change the subject, he toyed with the bell he still held in his hands and said, "I thought it was Cephas you wanted to see?"

"By all means! He is chief of the apostles, is he not?"

"He is all that!" James exclaimed enthusiastically.

When the serving girl returned with a tray of food, she put it on the table before us. Following the lead of my host, I made the customary ablutions and proceeded to partake of the thick vegetable soup that the girl served me in a bright blue pottery bowl.

Hardly noticing what I was eating, I observed that James' garments were well worn and patched.

"There is still persecution in Jerusalem?"

"Recently we have enjoyed a measure of peace, but," he shook his head sadly, "it is not an abiding peace. Strife could break out at any moment." A trace of worry flickered in his eyes and then gave way to confidence. "We are cheerful for we know that if Christ was persecuted we shall likewise be persecuted."

"Yes, I know!" I replied emphatically. "We apostles are doomed men."

"You are an apostle?" He looked at me incredulously.

"I have seen the Lord," I whispered softly, lowering my glance. It was not easy to speak about it. "He charged me with the ministry of carrying his light to the Gentiles," I informed him confidently.

"Brother Saul," he sighed, "if you employ the same zeal in preaching Christ that you did in persecuting him, the entire Roman world shall hear of him!"

"That is the vision I bear in my heart," I confessed.

When our supper was finished, night had fallen and somewhere in the darkness outside the city a hyena was howling. Stifling a yawn, James arose from the table.

"Brother Saul, or whatever you wish to be called…" He waited for me to answer.

"Paul," I replied at once. "Since it is to the Gentiles I must go, let everyone call me by my Roman name—Paul. I am a citizen of Rome, you know."

"No, I did not know." Looking surprised, he continued, "How did you manage that? Did you buy your citizenship?" he asked as he tugged thoughtfully at his short black beard. "I hear it can be done, if you can afford the costly fees."

"I was born a citizen of Rome. It is a long story and the hour is getting late. I really must be leaving." I walked towards the door.

Laying his hand on my sleeve, James restrained me gently. "Brother Paul you have a exciting life ahead of you. You have a great work to do. Now you must be tired from your journey. Come," he insisted, "let me show you to your room, for you are staying with me."

I started to protest. "Surely there is an inn…"

"You will stay with me," he said with an air of authority. "That is an order." He smiled and added by way of explanation, "I am the Bishop of Jerusalem."

I grinned at him and acquiesced. "By no means would I disobey the bishop of Jerusalem."

"Good!" Proffering his hand, he said, "I extend to you the right hand of fellowship." His clasp was warm and hearty. "Tomorrow you shall see Cephas. I personally will inform him that you are here and desire to see him."

I thanked him and followed as he led me out into the courtyard and around the house to the stairs that took us up to the second floor. After he showed me into a neat and tidy room equipped with the essentials, I knelt for a while at the window overlooking the courtyard. In the distance, I could see the temple. How much I desired to go there and preach Christ crucified. Desiring that all Israel be saved, I am telling you the truth when I say that I am sad and continuously sorrowful and even wish I could be anathema for the sake of my brethren, if that would bring them to Christ.

As I prayed for my people, my thoughts turned to the virgin who brought forth the Messiah. I fell asleep that night whispering the name of Mary into the night.

When morning came, a bright sunny spring morning, I arose early and quietly left the house, setting out to visit the places that the

Lord Jesus made holy by his dying. Leaving the courtyard of James' house, I glanced in the direction of the palace of Caiphas and Annas, recalling that it was there that he received the first blow of his physical passion, when the soldier struck him across the face criticizing him for the way he spoke to the high priest.

As I walked along the familiar narrow street that cuts its way through the southern quarter of the city, with the wall of the temple on my left, I noticed that Jerusalem was bustling with the business of beginning another day. Just missing me by a hair, a housewife tossed a bucket of dirty scrub water into the street from a second floor window. So far no one recognized Saul of Tarsus. A rat scurried down the gutter. When a camel came lurching down the narrow street followed by his owner, a nomad, I was almost flattened against the wall. Up ahead I could see the golden pinnacles of the temple shimmering in the morning sunlight. It was good to be a Jew and to be in Jerusalem once more.

Slipping into the temple unobtrusively, I gave thanks unto the Father of the Lord Jesus for all his great and manifold mercies. We have a God who is rich in mercy! Then, from the gate, just below the temple, I left the city with the Kidron valley extending before me. Beyond I could see the tombs of the prophets and further still lay the tomb of Absalom. By a narrow path, I descended a slope and crossed the stone bridge over the Kidron that was quite dry. Once across the bridge, I followed the road that was flanked on the right by a low stone wall and a hedge of cactus. Ahead up the hill, there was an olive grove. I climbed up the road about two hundred yards and then stood for a few moments at the gate of the Garden of Gethsemane before entering.

Glancing up to the top of the Mount of Olives, I saw the place from which the Lord ascended to his Father and our Father, to his God and to our God. Slowly I entered the grove of silver-leaved olive trees, sank to my knees and recalled what I knew of the night of agony Christ spent there. Luke later explained to me how he sweated blood that night. So great was his anguish that he actually sweated blood, a phenomenon, which Luke says is very rare in the annals of the medical profession, but which does occur, when anguish is very intense. His clothing was soaked with this bloody sweat. So profuse was this shedding of his blood that it trickled down on to the ground. Reverently, filled with awe, I pressed my lips to the dust of Gethsemane.

I was on holy ground. It was here that the Lord took on the burden of my sins. It was here that he saw each one of my sins and felt the guilt of each of them as if they were his own. The iniquity of us all fell upon him and he was bowed with the weight of sin into the dust. Every sin that every son of Adam ever committed or would commit down to the end of time lay bare to his gaze.

Leaving Jesus alone to endure his agony, the apostles slept. The worst agony was in knowing that some souls would be lost forever even though he poured out every drop of his blood, because they refuse to accept the love and salvation he offers them. This was the bitter chalice. Some will reject him—some will refuse to love him. Some want no part of his inheritance; for this, I, Paul, try to console him.

Judas was the first of those who refused his love. I pictured him stealthily walking up to this garden with a mob of men armed with swords, clubs, and staves. And I could see the Lord, leaving the sleeping apostles and going alone to the gate to meet them saying, "Who are you looking for?"

"Jesus of Nazareth."

" I am the one."

He gave himself up to them and still Judas drew nearer and kissed him. Did he get blood on his lips when he placed them on his cheek still damp with the bloody sweat? Did a few drops of blood cling to him in that embrace? Down through the centuries there will be many who will drink his blood unworthily and be guilty of his death.

I rose to my feet and started back to the city. From this garden they took you to the palace of Annas and Caiphas near the place where I spent the night in the James' home. It was in this palace that Jesus proclaimed officially to the priests of Israel who he is. When Caiphas, the high priest, adjured him to tell him if he was the Christ, he answered very plainly without the slightest hesitation, "I am." With their ears greedy to hear him say this so they could condemn him, they pronounced the death sentence.

Brutality, such as the world had never witnessed before nor since, was unleashed with demonic fury. Spitting in his face, they mocked him. Buffeting him with blows, they made fun of him. Wrapping a blindfold around his eyes and striking him, they commanded him to prophesy who struck him.

As I returned to Jerusalem that morning, I reflected that it appeared to be a civilized and peaceful city. How had it witnessed the death of its Savior? Realizing that the evil that was unleashed that unholy night could break forth again at any time against the Church and me, I beseeched the Lord to strengthen me in the might of his power.

Even now at this very hour when I am in chains here in Rome, I beg you, Lord to clothe me with the armor of God that I may resist the attacks of the evil one, for my wrestling is not against flesh and blood, but against the world rulers of this darkness, against the spiritual forces of wickedness in high places. O Lord, put over my heart the breastplate of justice, and gird my loins with truth, put the shield of faith in my hand, and may my feet be always ready to follow the gospel of peace. Let my head be crowned with the helmet of your salvation. Place in my hands the sword of the Spirit—your Holy Word.

Continuing to visit the holy places of Jerusalem, I walked the deep valley that divides Jerusalem and proceeded north, going through the bazaar where the early morning shoppers were haggling over the Roman goods that had been brought into the city from the far reaches of the empire. Rome had not built fifty thousand miles of roads over the length and the breadth of the world to let them be idle. Caravans daily poured into Jerusalem and trade flourished.

With the wall of the temple on my right, I continued walking northward. When the street veered sharply to the right, I saw in front of me the barracks of the Roman soldiers and the tower on the fortress Antonia. Stone stairs led up to the Governor's Hall. It was here on this very spot, on these steps, on a morning not too different from this one, that Jesus encountered Pilate. He was bound and led to the top of the steps where Pilate was forced to come, because according to our law to enter the dwelling of a Gentile would have made the Jews unclean for the space of a day. Since the Passover was at hand and there were ceremonies to be performed, one could not become unclean at such a time. Such was the law. Jesus was blood stained and besmeared with camel dung that someone had thrown upon his pure white robe as he, a prisoner, walked through the city streets with his face bruised and swollen. While the mob waited, Pilate took Jesus into his palace and from his exalted throne questioned him, and sent him on his way to Herod, since he was a Galilean and as such was under Herod's jurisdiction.

Herod did not keep him long. He thought Jesus was mad, just as Festus thought me mad. He dressed him up to look like a fool and paraded him back to Pilate who had him scourged. Down these very steps he came, bleeding profusely from the thorns that were piercing his head. Right here on this very spot he was given the wood of the cross to carry. Since Calvary was about half a mile away, I walked along the north wall of the temple, the way Jesus walked with the cross on his shoulder. Down into the Tyropoeon valley I went and up the street that has so many steps and on through the bazaar. The tower of David rose before me. As I walked along the way of the cross, I pictured myself, in some future time, being led to my execution. Later when the Roman soldiers were planning to take me out from the city of Rome to execute me, I kept remembering Christ's final trip out from the city of Jerusalem.

When I left the city of Jerusalem by the Gate of Ephraim, I was but a short distance from the very spot on which Jesus was crucified and died. An execution was actually taking place at the very instant that I arrived on Golgotha. Some strange magnetic force impelled me to draw near the cross of the dying criminal. A sign over his head informed me that the man who was hanging there was a thief. Although I was repelled by what I saw, the very horror of the scene drew me on. I had to see just exactly what Jesus suffered for love of me. The sun was hot, blazing down directly overhead, for it was about noon. A sudden weakness swept over me. As one who is spellbound, I had to see every hideous and vile detail of the sufferings of the poor wretch in the throes of agony before me. Suffocating, his face was purple, his eyes bulging from their sockets. Because his chest was bare, I saw that it was expanded with breath that he was unable to expel. With his hands nailed to the cross and his body sagging beneath them, he was unable to breathe. With the small amount of strength left to him, I saw him rear up, putting all his weight on the nail that was piercing his feet. By pushing up against the nail in his feet he was able to relax the constriction of his chest enough for him to exhale a little air and gulp in a few gasps of fresh breath. With the influx of fresh air into his lungs, the purple of his face turned to red and then to ashen gray. Unable to support himself any longer on the nail in his feet, he sagged again. Once more asphyxia began to overcome him. Flies were crawling on him, stinging his flesh. None of the people who were passing by on the Joppa road paid any attention to what was taking place.

The soldiers in charge of the execution were sitting at the foot of the cross, quietly discussing some sporting event they had witnessed. The dying man moaned. He gasped for breath to no avail, for his lungs were already filled to the bursting point with air he could not expel. I later learned from Luke that crucifixion causes intense pain in the heart. You, Lord Jesus, died with your heart consumed with intense pain and anguish.

Like a worm, the man squirmed and writhed. The wound in his feet was torn and very bloody from sustaining his body the many times he pushed against it in an effort to suck in a little life-giving air. He sagged. The purple deepened on his face. He could struggle no more.

"No more kicks left in this one," remarked one of the soldiers.

"Stick a spear in the pig and finish him off," commanded the soldier in charge of the execution.

A third soldier took his lance and stuck the man on the cross between his ribs. Blood gushed forth. The smell of blood and the stench of death rose to my nostrils. My head reeled as a wave of nausea racked me. Leaning against the city wall, I relieved myself. A wild dog was at my feet lapping up my vomit. I bolted and, turning my back on the ghastly scene, I ran down the Joppa road to the garden that I knew lay just beyond.

Once inside the garden, I composed myself. To forget what I had just witnessed, I busied myself with examining the tomb that had not been able to hold the Lord of Glory. Stepping inside it, I saw that the chamber of the tomb, hewn from the rock, was about eight feet square, eight feet wide, eight feet long and eight feet from floor to ceiling. On one side, I observed a ledge carved into the rock where the broken and tattered body of Jesus was laid to rest from the demoniacal fury that was unleashed against his chaste and holy Person. The horror of it all! Suddenly, I realized the Virgin watched him die, just as I watched that criminal die a few minutes before. She had come here with him into this tomb and held his blood-smeared body in her arms. Reverently with my hands, I caressed the place where the body of the Savior once lay and kissed it. Back outside in the fresh air once more, I noticed that a large boulder of rock stood beside the entrance. Without doubt this was the stone that the soldiers used to seal Jesus' tomb. It would have taken quite a few men to move it.

Rejoicing, I recalled that he remained in this tomb for only a few hours. After having been placed there in dishonor, he rose again in glorious triumph on the third day. Weakness was transformed into power. Death itself was consumed in victory, losing its sting forever. He is risen! He is risen! I have seen him. He is the first to rise from the dead, and all those who believe in him will also rise.

Overflowing with faith and hope, I made my way back through the city. I rejoiced exceedingly for I knew that we have a great high priest who is at the right hand of the Father in glory, having compassion on our weaknesses, tried in all things as we are, except sin. He himself is both the priest and the victim whose blood has won our eternal redemption and everlasting life.

Recalling the things that I learned from Rabban Gamaliel, I thought of how God chose Israel to be his peculiar people and made a covenant with us that had its ritual and a sanctuary. There was a tabernacle in the outer part in which were the lamp stand and the table with the shewbread. Beyond the second veil was the second tabernacle, the Holy of Holies, with the golden censer and the Ark of the Covenant covered with gold on every side. In the ark was a golden pot containing the manna and the rod of Aaron that budded and also the tablets of the covenant. Overshadowing the mercy seat were the cherubim. Oh how we struggled with the law of the covenant that served to remind us of our sins! But praise God, Jesus came and made a new covenant—a covenant of grace and truth.

Although various priests went into the first tabernacle to perform the sacred rituals, only the high priest was permitted into the Holy of Holies, the second tabernacle, and only once a year when he offered blood for his sins and the sins of the people, following the example of Moses who after reading every commandment of the law to the people, took the blood of calves and goats and sprinkled it on them saying it was what God commanded.

He also sprinkled the tabernacle and all the sacred vessels with blood showing that there is no remission of sin without blood. I could see that this was a foreshadowing of the new covenant. Christ canceled out the old law by sanctifying his people through the offering of his blood. Having offered his one sacrifice for sins, he now sits forever at the right hand of the Father as a faithful high priest expiating the sins of his people.

We have been sanctified through the offering of Christ's blood. Having offered one sacrifice for sins, Jesus has taken his seat forever at the right hand of God; he is a priest forever, living to make intercession for his people. He is the King of Justice, the King of Peace who is holy, undefiled, and higher than the heavens.

As I rejoiced in the hope of our calling, Christ revealed to me the mystery that had been hidden since the world began–Christ is within us! And this is the hope of our glory! He lives within me. I am his hands and feet. I am his voice in this troubled world. He lives and Paul is lost in him to be found in him forever. Through my lips he preaches his gospel of peace. In a blaze of light on the road to Damascus, he called me, asking why I was persecuting him. He identifies himself completely with his followers, his apostles, his priests, and his Church. I have been called to share in the one high priesthood of Christ in his ministry of reconciliation and to carry his light to the Gentiles. This is an honor that no man takes upon himself, but only the one who is called by God assumes it. Christ is my life and he is priest of the Most High God and mediator of a new covenant and I share in his priesthood and mediation. Until this time I had not thought of myself as a priest, but now I knew that with all my soul I hungered for the day when I could hold the cup of blessing up for all the faithful. Offering myself to be a living sacrifice that is both holy and pleasing to him, I returned to the house of James, son of Alphaeus.

As I was mounting the steps to my room, someone called from below,

" Brother Paul!"

Turning, I saw James standing beside a large date palm in the garden. He was beckoning to me.

"Come, we have a visitor," he said enthusiastically.

I understood Cephas was waiting. Boldly I walked down the stairs and entered the sitting room. Cephas, Peter as he is known here in Rome, was standing before me. He was tall, a head taller than I. His hair, dark and wavy, was like a crown upon his high well-arched brow. I noticed that his robe was spotlessly clean, but very much worn and patched. Warm and friendly were his dark brown eyes as he stretched forth both arms towards me. Taking my hands in his, he said in a deep, husky voice, "Welcome, Brother Paul…welcome to Jerusalem!"

"Thank you," I responded. "I am very happy to be here once more, but I do not plan to stay very long at the present time." I thought of my mission to the Gentiles.

Excusing himself, James left to visit an elderly widow.

Curious about my plans, Peter inquired, "You are leaving Jerusalem soon?"

"Yes, by all means. Too much time has passed already and I have done so little."

Pensively Peter tugged at his ear and then, looking straight into my eyes, came right to the point.

"What do you plan to do?"

"I want to do the will of God." I returned his smile.

The answer I gave seemed to please him. Without hesitation he asked, "You have seen the Lord?" As he waited intently for my answer, I noticed that he leaned forward slightly in his chair.

"I have seen Him and have lost everything to follow him. I, too, am an Apostle, commissioned with the ministry of taking the gospel to the Gentiles. Already I have been preaching to anyone who would listen, but I have no reason to boast about that because I have to preach. Woe is me, if I don't."

"I quite understand. I also know," he spoke slowly and deliberately while observing my small stature, "that it will take great strength to evangelize the Gentiles." Pausing a moment weighing his words carefully, he said, "You will face persecution. I have already been arrested and scourged for the name of Jesus." He rubbed his shoulder with his hand, remembering the pain of the lash. "You will have to endure similar treatment—sleepless nights, fasting, possibly even shipwreck."

I was quick to reply. "My bodily appearance is weak and my speech is of no account, but I can do whatever he calls me to do with the strength he will give me. I am glad to be weak, because the strength he will give will be greater than my weakness. I am happy to endure all the things you mentioned for him—infirmities, insults, hardships, persecutions—for when I am the weakest, he gives me the most strength."

Peter smiled and commented, "Brother Paul, are you preaching to me?" He chuckled and exclaimed, "By the marvel of God's grace the zealous Pharisee has been transformed into a fearless apostle!"

I glanced at his hands. Although they were big and clumsy, he had adroitness in dealing with souls such as I have never seen in anyone else. He had an instinct for going to the heart of people and events.

"Brother Paul," he continued, now, quite seriously, "you are a dear brother for you cost the Lord a great price. But don't worry; he paid a heavy price for me too. You persecuted him without having known him. I, who knew him, denied him." Peter's eyes grew somber and very sad. "I even boasted that I was ready to die for him." He hesitated, looked at the floor an instant, then raising his glance, stared me straight in the eyes and said, "I denied Him. I denied him three times. I said that I didn't even know him."

I could see he was still haunted by the memory of his betrayal.

"You and I, Brother Paul, have much in common. He has forgiven us both much. He would have forgiven Judas too, but Judas wouldn't let him."

Peter grew silent at the thought of Judas. He rubbed his hands together absent- mindedly as his memory turned to events long past. Finally, he said, "Judas was sorry. He was contrite, but he despaired, because he didn't think that he could be forgiven…that made his case hopeless."

"Yes, I know Christ. He would have forgiven Judas. He is rich in mercy and his love is everlasting." I paused a few moments, and then asked, "Whatever became of Judas?"

"Judas? Poor Judas." Pain was written on Peter's face. "He hanged himself. He burst open in the middle and his insides poured out all over the place."

I shrugged. "You chose someone to take his place?"

"Yes, Matthias, a great lover of God and an apostle eager for the spread of the gospel." He smiled broadly and exclaimed, "And now we have you, Brother Paul, as one of us. The Holy Spirit inspires me to know that you are truly an apostle."

Glad to know Peter welcomed me, I said, "I am thankful that he called me and I want to be all things to everyone so that they might come to know his love as I do."

"You have truly seen the Lord. I know it," the chief of the apostles stated it as a matter of fact. "Your instantaneous conversion is proof of it. I am equally certain that the Lord has chosen well in calling you. I have heard much about you." He paused as if trying to recall what he had been told of me. "Although you come from an affluent family of Pharisees in Tarsus, you know how to relate to all kinds of people. Your education is far superior to mine. I am just an ignorant fisherman and you are a doctor of our Jewish law. You speak Greek like a native of Athens." He ran his hand through his thick bushy hair. "I approve of your project officially in my position in the twelve and I approve of it unofficially as, Cephas, your friend in Christ. Now, would you like for me to lay my hands on you and seal your soul with the priesthood of Christ in all its fullness? You have been baptized and you have received the Holy Spirit, have you not?"

"I have been immersed in the waters of baptism and I have received the Holy Spirit by the lying on of hands," I replied.

"Good. As our Lord instructed me, I shall lay my hands on you and you will become a priest forever according to the order of Melchizedek. Is that what you desire?"

I looked deep into his eyes.

"I desire to receive the fullness of the priesthood of Christ to be an apostle on equal footing with the rest."

Peter was not one to waste time. He pointed to the floor. I fell to my knees. When I arose a few seconds later I was a bishop in the Church of God.

The next morning, I was present when Peter offered the Holy Sacrifice. Closely I observed Peter, for soon I, Paul, would offer up the chalice of salvation. Together we shared your Body and Blood. The thought of being able to turn bread and wine into the Body and Blood of Jesus caused me great joy, but also, I confess profound awe.

The following days I spent in prayer, sometimes in the temple, but most often in my room. I rejoiced in the Lord and tried to prepare my soul for the most momentous event in my life, the event by which Christ was to become present in my hands for the first time.

Carefully observing my hands, I noticed how calloused they were from my work at the loom. Remembering all the evil that these two hands had done, I marveled that Christ Jesus, the Son of God, would come and rest in them as often as I took the bread and broke it and the cup and blessed it, following the formulary revealed to me. These hands would carry Christ far across the sea and give him to the Gentiles who would also come to know the joy of his salvation.

To make them as clean and beautiful as possible, I scrubbed my hands performing more rigorous ablutions than I ever did before. As a Pharisee, I had excelled in keeping clean, but now my justice must exceed that which I had known. The kingdom of heaven would soon lie in my hands. Christ, whom I had seen and loved would give himself completely to me.

The high point in my daily routine was when Peter would come in the evenings to share our meal with us. Sometimes our conversations were heated, always fascinating. In Peter, I saw the same love and devotion for you that are in my own soul. As we ate our frugal supper, we would talk of Christ with Peter and James speaking of the things that they heard Jesus say or seen him do, each of them remembering different things and seeing things each in a different light.

"Do you remember his eyes, how engaging they were? He just seemed to hold you with his eyes. And do you remember how he could look right into your heart with them and read your secret thoughts?" James sighed as he recalled Jesus.

"Ah," exclaimed Peter, "do you remember the light that was in his face—the radiance, the joy—when he spoke of His Father?"

"Our hearts were ablaze with divine love when he spoke." replied James falling into reverie.

"I, too, know the fire of his words," I joined in. "He is a devouring and engulfing fire."

"Would that I could be completely enveloped in those flames!" sighed Peter.

We were all silent for a few minutes, and then looking at James who was seated across the table from me I asked, "Does he resemble his mother?" I was determined to see her before I left Jerusalem.

Both Peter and James nodded affirmatively, but said nothing. As I looked from James to Peter and then back again to James, they were preoccupied with the business of eating supper and doing their best to ignore me, and I got the feeling that there was a conspiracy to envelop Mary, the mother of Jesus in silence.

"What became of her?" I persisted. "You are her nephew, James, tell me about her." I was not going to be put off.

"When Jesus," James bowed his head at the mention of the holy name, "when Jesus was hanging on the cross he gave his mother to John, because he had no brothers or sister to take care of her after he was gone. You know, John was the only one of us men who stuck with Jesus through it all. The rest of us ran and hid, such was our confusion and cowardice, but John was on Golgotha right until the end. Jesus gave Mary to him, saying, son, this is your mother and to Mary he said John is your son. She has been living at John's house ever since." Dismissing the subject with a wave of his hand and turning to Peter, he said, "A large number of Hellenists arrived in Jerusalem today from Alexandria, I am told."

Refusing to give up, I asked insistently, "Will you take me to see her?"

"She lives a secluded and a hidden life, a life of silence and of prayer," answered James. "We try to respect her desire for seclusion."

It was Peter's turn to speak. "She prays for us and our labors with the gospel, interceding constantly. You see, she is very much with us and we ask her prayers for everything."

At last I was getting the answers I wanted. Because I had unloosed their tongues, I kept quiet for now they were eager to speak.

"She was with us in the upper room," commented James, "when the Holy Spirit descended upon us all. We were all praying together when he came. Consequently she has a very great love and devotion for the Holy Spirit."

I returned to my original question. "Does she resemble Christ?"

"In what way?" asked James.

"In all ways—physical and spiritual," I replied eager to learn all I could of the woman who had given birth to the Savior.

"She resembles him in all ways," answered Peter reflectively gazing into the flame of the oil lamp that flickered on the table before us. "He took his physical appearance from her and in return he endowed her with his grace and radiance."

"She is all fair," remarked James "there is no stain in her."

"She is our joy and our glory," Peter sang her praises.

"I must see her!" I persisted.

"We will have no peace in this house," commented James, smiling at Peter, "until you do."

"Yes," agreed Peter. "Take him to see her tomorrow." My heart beat faster as I listened to his words. He continued, "Our mother will be happy to see and become acquainted with her new son from Tarsus."

"You call her mother?" I asked.

"Yes." explained Peter as he folded his hands on his breast and leveled his eyes on mine. "She is truly mother to us, for the church is Christ and she is the mother of Christ."

"Yes," James concurred. "And we are the Church and therefore she is our mother."

I sighed and confessed, "I sensed this mystery—intuitively. That is why I said I had to see her. Christ who is within me cries out Abba, Father to God and Mother to Mary, we being sons by adoption like John who stood by her on Calvary."

"It is easy to see that the same Spirit lives in us all, for we are of one mind and heart in the Lord," Peter concluded as we ended our evening meal. Our spirits were more closely united the next morning when Peter offered the chalice of salvation and broke the bread of heaven. So great was my happiness that I was like one drunk with new wine when Peter gave Christ to me under the form of bread and wine. When the ritual was completed, we parted from one another in silence. Still in ecstasy I went to my room to spend the morning in adoring prayer, rejoicing in the Lord and in the hope of glory. The Holy Spirit was praying within me with unutterable sighing, making me burn for the accomplishment of God's will.

Outside the door of my prison cell, I can hear my jailer making his rounds. Perhaps even now he is coming for me. When my sacrifice will take place, I do not know. Any minute the door could swing open and you, Jesus, would beckon me to follow you in drinking the bitter chalice to the dregs—but whether I live or die I am yours. None of us lives to himself and none dies alone. If I live—I live in you; if I die—I die in you and I will be blessed, for the psalmist says that our deaths are precious in your sight.

How happy were those days in Jerusalem while I awaited offering up the mysteries of our redemption for the first time. James was faithful to his word and as he had agreed we set out the next day to the house of John to satisfy my great desire to see Christ's mother. The sky was cloudless—the day, warm and clear. The air was balmy and delightful with the fragrance of the flowers that were blooming everywhere. Exclaiming that the Lord is great and worthy of all praise in the city of Jerusalem, I began singing one of the psalms. Experiencing the same joy as I, James took up the psalm and replied that your holy mountain is the joy of all the earth. We walked through the city streets in the shadow of the temple praising Christ and glorifying our Heavenly Father in the Holy Spirit.

Ten minutes of chanting the psalms brought us to a house with a very lovely, little garden secluded in its courtyard. His face fully teeming with joy, James rapped softly on the door that was answered by a serving girl who took us into a pleasant, but simply furnished room.

"The apostle is not at home," she informed us politely. She looked to be no more than twelve years of age.

"We wish to see the mother of the Lord," James told her almost in a whisper. He was the very picture of reverence.

The girl asked us to be seated on the hard wooden chairs in the corner of the room. Nervously, I tapped my foot and kept glancing in the direction in which the girl had gone. Upon hearing footsteps approaching, we rose to our feet and James strode across the faded blue carpet calling, "Mother, I have brought someone to see you."

Suddenly she was standing before me, smiling at me with an air of expectancy. Her beauty was breathless with an ethereal quality that can only be explained by the great purity of her spirit.

"Welcome, my son," she said slowly. He voice was like the music coming from a stringed instrument—a harp or a lyre. Speechless, I drank in her radiance, trying not to stare.

She repeated her greeting. "Welcome my son." Then she laughed and said, "don't just stand there staring at me, do sit down and tell me about yourself. I want to know all about you."

I fumbled for a chair. I was at a total loss for words. Seeing my plight, James came to my aid, saying, "This is Brother Paul, a very learned doctor of the Jewish law, who has been converted to the Way. When he was traveling in a caravan on the road to Damascus, right there in the road, he saw Jesus."

At the mention of her son's holy name, the mother's face glowed with love. "You have seen my Jesus?" She studied me with interest. Lowering my gaze from her face, I noticed that she was dressed immaculately in white garments with a touch of temple blue at the waist. In being near her, I felt some of the same joy that I experienced in being near to Christ.

"I have seen him and I am ready to die for him and for his Name," I confessed to her with tremendous joy. When she looked at me and nodded her head slightly, I caught a glimpse of her burnished golden hair. She spoke softly, almost whispering, "I hope to see him again soon, myself."

I knew she spoke of heaven. Because she was so radiantly alive, it was impossible for me to conceive of her dying. As I looked at her, waiting for her to explain, I am sure my bewilderment was obvious.

Folding her hands in an attitude of prayer and glancing upward, she confided in us her yearning to be with her son.

"I am sure the day is drawing near when he will take me where he is. He said there are many glorious dwellings in his father's house and that he is preparing a place for us all."

Caught by surprise at the thought of her leaving this world, James protested. "No! No, mother, you must not leave us yet. We need your prayers."

Smiling at him tenderly the way one does at a little child who doesn't understand, she explained, "Dear James," she spoke very patiently, "I shall not forget you in heaven, I shall pray all the more for you there."

In the pale light that filtered through the shaded window her eyes were the color of the sky at dawn. Looking from James to me, she peered into the depths of my spirit and asked, "Paul, what are you going to do with your life?"

"To the Gentiles far away I must go. Jesus commanded me to go and preach his gospel of salvation to all the world."

As if searching in her soul for words to express something she wished to tell me, she remained silent a few moments. At length she said almost inaudibly, "You will suffer much, Paul. You will go hungry and thirsty. You will lack proper clothing. You will buffeted, spit upon, reviled, and persecuted, just as Jesus was. You will have no fixed abode. You will be maligned, even stoned, and you will become as the refuse of this world. And finally," her eyes saddened and she was pained, "finally you will face the sword." Softly in a whisper she asked, "Can you bear it all, my son?" "All this and more—if you will pray for me—during all my hours of trial." I looked at her hopefully.

"Know this, my son. You will not see me again in this world, for when you next return to the house of John, I shall be with Jesus." Her smile was full of love as she assured me, "l shall always be with you in the Holy Spirit and I *shall* pray for you always until that day when once again I shall look into your face and you will behold the face of God."

Her words caused a sweet joy tingled with sadness to well up in my soul. "Mother," I stammered. I was on my knees at her feet, looking up into her face. She was the most beautiful woman that I have ever seen—ageless, young in appearance, but with a spirit mature beyond her years.

"Yes, my son?" Just to hear her speak filled my heart with great peace. "Give me your blessing on my life and on my work," I implored her.

"I give you a woman's blessing," she said and then taking my face in her hands and looking into the depths of my being she whispered, "Go, now, my son. Jesus be with you."

Taking her hands in mine and still kneeling, I kissed her fingertips lightly. "Jesus be with you, mother," I whispered.

"He is, my son," she said and with a smile playing across her face. "He is!" My heart pounded with happiness as I rose to my feet. Keeping my eyes on her face, the chaste and holy face of Mary, I stored up the memory of her beauty for the rest of my life, until I see her again in heaven.

When James and I left John's house, we decided to go to the temple to pray for a while before we returned back to his house, because I wanted to give thanks for giving me the grace of seeing the mother of the Lord. No sooner had we entered the temple than James directed my attention to a group congregated in one corner.

"They are the newly arrived Hellenists that Peter spoke of at dinner," James explained. "Let's stroll over and hear what they are disputing with the local Jews."

As we drew near them, one of the Alexandrine Jews was speaking rather heatedly. Because he was speaking very loud, I had no trouble in hearing what he was saying.

"I recently arrived in Jerusalem," he announced "and I hear all kinds of tales about a prophet who reportedly arose from the dead." Because he was very expensively robed, very self confident, and in the middle years of live, he was well respected. Although many listened to what he was saying, nevertheless, one of the local Pharisees interrupted him and taking the center of the circle cried, "It was a fraud! Nothing but a fraud!" The rest of the Pharisees nodded in approval.

"His followers stoled his body and then told everyone that he had risen from the dead.

I didn't see him, nor did any of my friends see him. In fact I don't know any one who did—for the simple reason that it was all a fraud."

Cheers rose from the circle of Pharisees. Unable to constrain myself, I felt impelled to speak out. Before James knew what was happening and before he could stop me, I was in the midst of them ready for a fight like a true son of Benjamin.

"I have seen him," I cried.

Silence fell like the blow of a sword. Disbelief was written on all the staring faces that surrounded me, waiting for me to speak.

"Men of Israel…I must bear witness to what I have seen." I spoke with boldness for all to hear. James was at my side tugging nervously at my sleeve, but the Spirit in my soul quickened and I had to speak out. "Jesus, who was crucified, died, and was buried," I said with fervent and impassioned enthusiasm, "is risen from the dead and is alive forevermore seated at the right hand of God!"

"He blasphemes!" screamed one of the Alexandrines incensed with my proclaiming that Jesus is at the right hand of the Father in glory. "Death to him!" shouted another of them.

"Death to him!" the Pharisees took up the chant.

Realizing that I was in a very precarious situation, I prayed for inspiration as to what I should do. When someone lunged at me, I jumped aside and then saw that it was Brother James whose fast thinking saved my life. Raising his hand, he gave a signal and in an instant we were surrounded by a mob of men that came from all parts of the temple, creating a terrible disturbance by rushing in and out of the mob of Alexandrines.

"Come on," cried James pulling on my arm "let's get out of here while we still can."

Later I learned that the men who created the disturbance so that we could escape were fellow Christians who were observing what was transpiring and at the command of their bishop came to our aid.

"That was close!" exclaimed James. "I could just picture them dashing you to bits over the temple wall."

When we reached James' house, Peter was waiting for us. After he heard what happened in the temple, Peter shook his head sadly and placing his large burly hand on my shoulder said, "Paul, dear brother, you must leave Jerusalem. Those men with whom you disputed will seek to kill you. The Lord Jesus has need of you, so you must prepare to leave. I cannot permit you to stay here and be stoned to death." He was adamant that I go. James' brow was deeply creased. Anxiously he looked for a time and then stating his case directly said, "For the safety of the followers of Christ in this city, I urge you to leave. You must leave the first thing in the morning."

The next morning when it came time for Peter to offer the sacrifice of our salvation, he turned to me and handing me the bread and wine said, "Paul, we are waiting." He nodded towards the holy table and at Peter' s bidding; I broke the bread and blessed the wine. You came to us, Lord Jesus. I cradled you in my hands, partook of the sacrifice. Once again, I was absorbed in your glory—for a few moments. I could not linger. I would have prolonged my thanksgiving all morning, but my things were packed and Peter was eager for me to leave.

CHAPTER 2

$\mathcal{A}$s my ship approached the Cilician coast of my native land, Tarsus—no insignificant city for it fairly bustles with trade and culture—was sparkling like a sapphire mounted on the horizon. Ahead I could see the estuary of the Cydnus river with its brackish yellow waters mingling with the clear water of the sea as my ship glided swiftly and noiselessly over the dark, ink-like waters of the Mediterranean. Along the coast, the quays and docks came in to view. In the far distance, the Tarsus Mountains, mauve in the morning haze, rose four thousand feet like a bastion or rampart behind the city.

For a thousand years people had flocked to Tarsus, among them Assyrians, Persians, Syrians, Jews, Greeks and then finally the Romans. When Julius Caesar came to Tarsus, the city promptly renamed itself Juliopolis—for a time. When Anthony came, Cleopatra, visiting him, sailed up the Cydnus with purple sails and silver oars gleaming in the sunshine and the inhabitants of the fashionable villas built by wealthy merchant families, such as my own, on the foot hills of the Tarsus range came out to goggle at Egypt's queen.

As we dropped anchor, my thoughts were mixed. Although I had not been home for several years, I did write to my parents, explaining briefly to them, what happened to me on the road to Damascus and of my conversion to Christ. Plainly they did not understand, and

I knew that I would be faced with the task of trying to share with them my newfound faith, as soon as I arrived home.

Because there were so many different religious groups in Tarsus, a tolerance existed there that was unknown in Jerusalem and the people were broad minded to such a degree that I felt confident that my family would give me a good hearing. I couldn't have been more wrong.

When I arrived at my family villa, it was mid-afternoon. Even more beautiful than I remembered, the orchard was in bloom and my old friend the fountain that was shaped like a seashell still bubbled and gurgled in the gardens before the house. Many hours I spent splashing in that fountain when I was a child. Bougainvillea covered the entire front wall of the house with a frock of magenta flowers. The lemon tree along the entrance walk had grown taller and a songbird was perched in its branches singing out its heart in the praises of its Creator. After I pulled the bell cord and waited for the slave to answer, I was surprised when the door opened and I saw my mother.

"Saul! Saul!" she cried, "it is good to see you, my son."

When she embraced me, I caught the scent of the jasmine blossoms she grew and pinned to her gown that was made of some silver fabric that must have cost my father a great deal. Her hair, beautifully combed and arranged, had a silver cast to it that was very becoming. Because she was always well and healthy her entire life, she looked young and vibrant.

"You are beautiful, mother, just as beautiful as ever," I exclaimed holding her at arms length and gazing into her face.

Laughing, she remarked, "Your father and I have missed you very much. Come," she beckoned let's go onto the patio to see him. He will be so surprised." As we made our way through the house she called out, "David, Saul has come home!"

My father, whom I could see through the open doorway, dropped his accounts, which he had spent hours studying as long back as I can remember, jumped to his feet and energetically bounded towards me with his toga almost falling from his shoulder.

"Welcome, son," he boomed as he took my hands in his. "Glad to have you with us again. Things have not been the same since you left—nothing like having your own son in the business. No one can take your place."

Wanting to be agreeable and reestablish my filial relationship with my parents, I tried to show enthusiasm for his business affairs. He spoke of a new breed of goats that was being raised nearby which produced a superior grade of hair so that he was weaving better fabrics than ever before and getting a higher price by far than the weavers from other cities. Tents made from his stuff were the best in the world, he boasted, and being shipped throughout the empire. Although I tried to appear interested and share his enthusiasm, there was only one thing I was interested in exporting and that was the gospel of Christ.

Even though my father was a Pharisee, he had not taken the interest in the law that I had. He was primarily a businessman who knew his duties and obligations under the law and tried to fulfill them as best he could. Because he was a practical man, concerned with everyday affairs, and he did not have a religious or philosophical mind, the subject of religion was slow in being broached.

My mother's time was taken up with her friends, social events, and flower growing. Rachel, my sister, who was visiting with relatives in Alexandria at the time, shared all her interests with her and together the three of them were a very happy family.

At dinner that night, I observed that both my mother and my father were being overly courteous and polite to me. At first I thought it was because I had been away such a long time.

"Here, Saul," mother said motioning to a slave to serve me," have some more lamb. You look a bit thin." "No, thank you, mother," I refused as politely as I could. I don't eat much. You know how my stomach is nervous and easily upset."

"You look a bit pale," observed mother as she looked at me anxiously.

My father squinted his eyes and looked at me the way one does at a child when he expects to find him covered with rash. "Are you feeling better now Saul?" he asked.

"Sick? Me?" I stammered. "No. I've been very well."

As both of them smiled at me with a certain amount of condescension, my mother reached over and patted me on the arm and patronizingly said, "Of course you are, dear." "The sun *was* hot, you probably had a sun stroke," my father commented flatly as if that settled the matter.

"Sunstroke?" I was bewildered.

"Look, Saul," mother exclaimed shaking her head, "you *were* seeing things." Her eyes avoided mine.

"So that's it," I cried. "You think I am sick and you are trying to pamper me."

"Normal people just don't see things that aren't there," my father remarked laconically. "Why you even fell down on the ground," he added shrugging his shoulders.

"You never had the falling sickness before, dear," worried mother.

"Look, I protested. "I really did see someone." I could see it was not going to be easy to convince them.

"Did the other people who were with you in the caravan see anyone?" my father asked.

"No," I replied truthfully, "but that doesn't mean that I didn't."

"Of coarse, not, dear," mother said in soothing tones, "We understand."

"No! You don't." I sounded rude and at once apologized for my discourteousness. "But I did see him," I persisted. "He rose from the dead."

My father shook his head sadly and looked at my mother and gasped, "He rose from the dead? That is impossible! Look Saul, I can tell you for a fact that I have never met anyone yet who rose from the dead," he announced sarcastically "Furthermore, I have never seen anyone who was invisible to my associates," he snorted. "I will have my own personal physician prescribe for you." Then more gently and paternally he added, "He will have you well in no time at all."

"Yes dear," mother agreed, "You'll see." She smiled at me sweetly the way she did when I was a boy and had taken sick."

"Let me explain," I insisted. "It was the Messiah! I saw the Christ. The high priest and the Scribes and the Pharisees turned him over to the Roman governor and saw to it that he was crucified!"

"The Messiah?" my father sneered. "Put to death by the cooperation of the high priest and the Roman governor? Preposterous!" He threw up his hands in a gesture of despair. "If he had been the Messiah the high priest would have recognized him and they would have put a crown of him and he would now be our king!" he proclaimed with certainty, thrusting forth his lower lip in defiance.

"They killed him just as the prophets predicted and he arose from the dead and is alive forevermore! I saw him myself." I witnessed to the faith within me.

"So he is in Jerusalem now upon a throne?" he demanded.

"He went out on the Mount of Olives and disappearing into the clouds, he ascended into heaven."

"Enough!" my father interrupted. "You expect me with my intelligence to believe that?" An ironic laugh punctuated his words.

I went all the way. "It is true. He is at the right hand of the Father in heaven." These words are blasphemy to a Pharisee.

"Hush! You'll get stoned!" Mother shrugged.

"Nonsense!" My father smashed his fist on the table. "We will hear no more of it. You will forget all these wild imaginings when I put you to work again." He rose from the table and with finality charged out of the room.

Christ said that a prophet is without honor in his own country; I failed miserably in mine.

Because the idea my father had of my going to work seemed to be a sound one and I needed money to undertake my apostolic labors to the Gentiles, I put on a toga once again and went to help him in the business where I came in contact once more with the friends of my youth and I began telling them about the tremendous world-changing events that happened in Jerusalem when Christ was crucified and rose from the dead. Although they were interested—religion made good conversation—my Jewish friends were satisfied with their way of life and could not conceive it possible that the Messiah would hang on a cross and die. The young Gentiles I spoke to privately thought that it was nonsense.

At home my parents assiduously avoided the subject of religion, but we went to the synagogue for Shabbat. The second Shabbat that I was there, I was invited to address the assembly and I knew at once what I was to say. "This is Saul, one of our doctors of the law, who studied with the famous Gamaliel in Jerusalem and who has recently returned to us," one of the members introduced me.

Rising confidently to my feet and filled with the Holy Spirit, I preached with fire. "The God of our Father's Abraham, Isaac and Jacob exalted our people when they were held captive and repressed in Egypt," I began. "With a cloud by day and a pillar of fire by night he led our people out of their bondage, destroying seven nations in Canaan so that we might have our promised land. Then the judges kept us from all harm until the Lord sent us a prophet—Samuel. We were given a great king—Saul ben Kish of the tribe of Benjamin. You know well the glory of King David and his son Solomon. Now, I announce to you that as a fulfillment the prophecies of old, the Lord has sent us a Savior from the root of Jesse—Christ Jesus."

Every eye in the synagogue was upon me. Boldly I continued.

"Before he came, a man called John preached from one end of Judea to the other, calling people to repent and be baptized, telling them that the kingdom of heaven was drawing near. The Messiah came, being born in Bethlehem as was prophesied, but the inhabitants of Jerusalem and its rulers did not recognize him, even though the prophets predicted his death. They sentenced him to die by crucifixion. On the third day after his death, he rose from the dead! Many people saw him—five hundred people at one time saw him. I, myself, have seen him."

A rumbling murmur broke out through the entire assembly. Fearlessly I pressed on. "I bring to you the good news that the Lord is faithful and fulfills all his promises. The Messiah is come. If you only believe in him, you are forgiven of all your sins. I, Saul, am sent by him to baptize you and all men with water and the Holy Spirit in the name of the Father, and of the Son and of the same Holy Spirit. To God be praise, glory, honor, forever. Amen."

When I returned to my place, no one else rose to address the synagogue. My father, seated beside me, rubbed his nose nervously and hurried me out to the carriage, looking furtively in all directions. Mother was not with us, because she felt ill that night. At his command, we hurried to our villa by the sea.

"I told you," he thundered, "that I would have no more of that nonsense. I command you to be silent in the synagogue in the future! A fine thing, I pay to send you to a famous rabbi for your education and you come home and publicly disgrace me." His face was livid with rage. I had never before in my life seen him so furious.

"I cannot be silent," I told him passionately.

"When I saw the Lord Jesus, he commanded me to preach to the Gentiles. I am his priest and I am ready to die for his name. I am going to proclaim the new covenant that he inaugurated."

"I am quite well satisfied with the old covenant!" he cried waving his hands. "If you persist in this unheard of behavior I will be forced to ask you to leave my house. You will renounce this folly immediately!"

"Father," I said calmly, "I am no longer a child. When I was a child I thought as a child, but now that I have become a man I have put childish things away." As the carriage stopped in front of the villa, I surveyed him in the moonlight that brightened the night. Dead serious, I continued. "Christ is my life. He, himself, said that if I were not willing to leave mother, father, house, wife, or children for his sake, that I am not worthy of him." I knew what I had to do. Very softly I said, "I shall leave immediately."

There was joy in my heart once more. Turning away from me, he replied bitterly, "I no longer have a son." He strode towards the house. I could see that I had inherited my stubbornness from him.

I went to my room, packed my few belongings, looked in on my mother who was sleeping and without awakening her, I went to the stable, mounted my horse, and headed for Tarsus, going to a large inn that was situated near the docks. Trusting in divine providence to lead me, I paid my money for one night's lodging and gave my name to the innkeeper, not having any idea of where I would go from there.

"Well this is a coincidence," asserted the innkeeper as he gave me change for the money I had given him. "Someone was just looking for you. A stranger—a foreigner. He is staying the night. I will locate him and send him to you.

"What is his name?" I asked, my curiosity aroused as to why a foreigner came to Tarsus to see me.

"Just a minute—I have it here some place" the innkeeper replied shuffling through the accounts on his desk. "Ah, yes. Here it is—Barnabas." "Barnabas," I repeated under my breath.

The name sounded familiar. As I walked briskly across the large dormitory of the inn and proceeded to settle down in one corner away from the large majority of travelers, I searched my memory trying to recall the identity of the man who was looking for me. Just as I was beginning to give up, I saw a young man strolling over to where I was reclining. When he came closer, I recognized him immediately as the young man who first took me to the house of the apostle James the day I arrived in Jerusalem. "Brother Saul!" he greeted me with open arms.

"Welcome, welcome to Tarsus, Brother Barnabas."

Looking at him expectantly, because I knew that there was something providential in his coming, I waited for him to speak.

"Peter sent me," he explained at once. "He wants you to come with me to Antioch." He grinned at me boyishly and in his eyes I could see the stamp of holiness. I studied his face. His high forehead, well chiseled nose and keen brown eyes spoke to me of nobility of spirit. He was a very personable young fellow sure to do great things for the Lord.

"So, Peter remembered me."

For a few moments I contemplated what it was that was being asked of me, and then declared. "It is providential, Brother Barnabas." I told him of the circumstances of my leaving my parental home. We both marveled at the workings of providence in my life and then with great curiosity about the future I asked, "Are there many followers of Christ in Antioch?"

He sat down beside me and answered, "Many, by the grace of God. You see, when you went to the high priest years ago and asked for authority to exterminate the Christians in Damascus and other places, many of them fled. Some went to Cyprus—some to Cyrene, others went to Antioch and have succeeded in converting a good number of Gentiles in the city." He grinned at me again and concluded, "You and I are to take charge of the church in Antioch. Peter remembered your mission to the Gentiles and so he sent me to recruit you."

"Well, I have failed to make any head way here in Tarsus," I sighed sizing him up, noting that he was quite a bit younger than I. "Your home in Antioch?"

"No. I was born in Cyprus," he replied. "I am a Levite."

"You are a priest of Jesus Christ," I corrected him.

"And you, Brother Paul, are his bishop and you are needed in Antioch to lay your hands on the converts so they may receive the Holy Spirit."

Seeing the Lord's will in the events that were transpiring, I replied without hesitation, "We shall leave in the morning." I smiled and added, "It just so happens that I am all packed and ready to go. There is nothing to hold me in Tarsus. I believe, there is a caravan that starts at dawn."

Because the inn was noisy and crowded, I got little rest that night. I awoke long before dawn only to discover that Brother Barnabas, an early riser, was already dressed and waiting for me.

"Here, have some bread," he proffered, tossing me a small loaf. Extending to me a flask he invited, "Here's some goats' milk to wash it down. I just bought these things from the innkeeper who tells me that the caravan is beginning to assemble.

Just as the dawn was beginning to break over the sea, we left Tarsus, winding our way over the foothills, as the first rays of the sun burst forth. Slowly we began our ascent of the four thousand feet high mountains we had to cross before we could enter Syria. By chiseling out the rock on the mountainsides, Roman ingenuity had built a carriage road. With cliffs dropping down on either side a sheer six hundred feet, as the road snaked upward, I tried not to think what would happen, if the camels were to loose their footing. Higher and higher we climbed up to the bleak and barren regions where there is no vegetation at all. On the crest of the range we rode past salt encrusted lakes. Before long we were faced with the perilous task of descending which is more treacherous even than ascending, especially because of the falling rocks. From time to time a giant boulder would work its way loose and fall in the road, forcing the caravan to stop so we all could work together to push, shove, and heave the boulder over the cliffs. One day followed another. On and on we rode until my bones ached and we arrived in Syria.

Then one day, the city of Antioch lay before us in the distance. Antioch, the third largest city in the world, was a city of splendor. When we arrived in the late afternoon its broad avenues were thronged with people. Magnificent buildings lined the streets and statues of people I did not know were everywhere. Lovely refreshing groves of trees invited us on every side. Gleaming porticoes boasted of sumptuous frescoes. We passed libraries, schools and a pagan temple. It was a lively city, Antioch in Syria, for it had an hybrid population with a seething lower class that was always ready for a riot. From the surrounding towns and villages, trades people, artisans, and people of leisure, and scholars, came to Antioch. Every sort of religion found a home in the city and many adherents to Greek oriental paganism were active there.

I grew to like Antioch. The climate was superb, the air, bracing, and the scenery beyond compare. Best of all, there was a thriving community of followers of the Way there, where they were known as "Christians," for it was in Antioch that this appellation was coined and from there spread to the entire empire.

When I went to the people of Antioch, I did not go with lofty speech or erudition, but rather I was determined not to know anything among them except Jesus Christ and him crucified. And my speech and my preaching were not in persuasive words of wisdom but in manifestations of the Spirit, so that their faith would not be based on human wisdom, but on the power of God. When I planted the seed, the Lord made it grow so that the Christians of Antioch became like a seal placed on my apostleship, fulfilling my vocation. Trying to be all things to everyone, a Jew for the Jews, as one without the law to the Gentiles, I became the servant of all, that I might win more converts to Christ, doing all things for the gospel. A minister of the new covenant, not of the letter, but of the Spirit, for it is the Spirit that gives life, while the letter kills, I discharged my ministry, showing mercy, as I have known mercy.

Fearing that having preached virtue to others, I might fall into sin, I disciplined and castigated my body. I can honestly say, thanks to the grace given me, my conscience is spotless and above reproach. Not wanting to be a burden to anyone, nor desiring that anyone should have to feed me, I worked day and night, whenever I could to support myself.

Despite my youth, I tried to be an example of charity, faith, and chastity to all. Diligently I read the Scriptures, exhorted the people of God, and preached frequently. My conscience was unimpeachable. I engulfed myself in Christ, imitating him in all my actions, letting him live in me, seeing everything with his eyes, letting his mind replace my own so that only he lived and acted in me. Thinking his thoughts, I became one with Christ who dwells within me. He is the Good Shepherd who tended the flock in Antioch. He is in all; I am nothing. Through my lips he preached his gospel and drew souls in the Holy Spirit, washing away their sins and reconciling them with the Father.

From the many Gentiles who came to me seeking the faith, I learned that, for the most part, the Gentiles had a consciousness of sin and were burdened with feelings of guilt. For this reason they were much easier to convert than my fellow Jews. On many occasions, I told them the parable about the Pharisee and the Publican, making it obvious to them who is the most justified.

Barnabas and I worked side by side. Then the Lord sent us Lucius of Cyrene to help us. Dear old Lucius—a faithful friend he was—but we had to watch him for he would give everything we had to the poor including my only cloak.

We had a glorious year in Antioch. We did your will, the church grew and flourished, and we rejoiced. The thought of leaving the city never occurred to me until Agabus, a serious looking fellow with a hump on his back, came knocking on our door one afternoon. Once more providence was taking over my life. Seeing in him only the brother for whom Christ died, we welcomed him, overlooking his physical ugliness, as he, leaning on a home made staff, introduced himself.

"Agabus—Agabus of Jerusalem, I am."

"You are most welcome, Brother Agabus," I greeted him.

Barnabas who had an excellent memory said, "Once when I was in Jerusalem, I believe I met you.

"How is the church in Jerusalem?" I inquired anxious for news of Peter and James.

Agabus scowled and shook his head. "Not so good, we are threatened by famine. Peter wants you to come at once and bring relief."

Immediately, we scraped together all our resources and set out with Agabus on the road south to the holy city, glad that we were going to have the chance to be in Jerusalem once more for the upcoming Passover in the near future.

Very insistently Agabus told us that he was instructed by Peter, himself, to take us to the home of someone called John Mark, which I soon learned was hidden away in the southeastern quarter of the city, not far from the pool of Siloam. We arrived under cover of night, because Agabus explained that the political situation was very hot with both Jewish and Christian pilgrims pouring into the city for the Passover.

When we arrived at John Mark's house, the maid Rhoda seemed to be expecting us for she greeted Agabus with recognition and eyeing me aloofly said, "You are welcome—come in."

Because a prayer service was under way, we slipped unobtrusively into the rear of the gathering and knelt down giving thanks for the great blessings of God. At the conclusion of the prayers, Peter, head and shoulders taller than most of the people in the room, came striding towards me. With the passing of time, he had grown mature, confident.

"Brothers Paul and Barnabas," he extended his hands to us, "it is good, truly good to have you both with us once more. I am sure Agabus explained our great need to you, and we appreciate your coming so quickly to our aid. First, I want you to meet some holy people, true saints of God. As I glanced around the room, I saw that there were many that I did not know. Leading me across the room to where two men were seated and talking to each other in subdued tones, he said, signaling out the younger of the two:

"I want you to meet your host, John Mark. Mark this is Paul from Antioch."

By way of introduction Peter added, "Mark is planning to write the story of the life of our Lord, once he has collected all the facts. Of course, you know Matthew has already written one and I shall see to it that you have a copy to take back to Antioch with you."

That was news. I had not dreamed that anyone had written down the drama of our redemption.

"I will look forward to reading both Matthew's and Mark's accounts," I said glancing at the other man to whom I had not yet been introduced.

"This is Brother James whom the Lord called a Son of Thunder," explained Peter.

There was power in the glance of this man, James, the brother of the apostle John to whom Christ entrusted his mother on Calvary. He was animate, bubbling with life and enthusiasm. He smiled up at me and said, "This Son of Thunder hopes to make a loud crash over the far stretches of the Orient preaching the gospel of Christ to Susa and Persepolis."

"Let's go together," I grinned back at him.

We all laughed and Mark, jumping to his feet, said, "I'm a poor host. Here, you must be hungry. Let me bring you some supper. Surely you must be hungry"

"Nothing, please except perhaps a little wine for my stomach's sake. It's a bit unsettled from the two weeks we just spent in the caravan coming from Antioch."

When Mark excused himself to fetch the wine, James and I settled down to a long conversation, for we were immediately attracted to each other since he shared with me my enthusiasm for converting the Gentiles to Christ.

"Nice young follow, that John Mark," I observed to James.

"They say he fled stark naked through the streets of Jerusalem the night our Lord was betrayed," remarked James by way of making conversation. He laughed and then began to explain. "You see he had just…" James stopped talking and began listening to the sound of someone making a good bit of noise in the street in front of the house. With a look of alarm coming into his eyes, he jumped to his feet and ran to the window. Instantly I was behind him. Through the open window I saw four soldiers bearing down on the house. Within seconds they were beating loudly on the door and shouting at the top of their lungs,

"Open up, open up! In the name of King Herod…open!"

So, King Herod Agrippa was taking a hand in the affairs of the church! It could mean nothing but bad news. He was in Rome when his mad friend Caligula became emperor and bestowed on him the title of "King" as well as the estates of the dead Tetrarch Philip northeast of Galilee. When Herodius, the wife of Herod Antipas, who had John the Baptist beheaded, protested about his making Herod Agrippa king, Caligula took their lands away from them, and giving them to Herod Agrippa, made him even more powerful. Then when Caligula was assassinated, Herod Agrippa was instrumental in helping Claudius become emperor so that he stood in great favor with him. Now he was in Jerusalem flaunting his authority.

"Open, open up, in the name of King Herod!" the soldiers yelled a second time.

Undaunted Peter rose to the occasion. A giant of a man, he walked slowly and deliberately to the entrance door. I admired tremendously the big fisherman that Christ chose to lead the Church. The Lord must have been pleased with him that night as, he boldly threw open the door and rising to his full stature looked down at the soldiers and asked, "Who are you looking for?" This was Christ's response when the soldiers came looking for him in Gethsemane.

"Cephas, sometimes called Peter," the first soldier proclaimed officiously.

"You are looking at him." Once more Christ was being arrested.

"Also," proclaimed the soldier, "we seek one called James, the son of Zebedee."

"That's me," announced James who was standing beside me with a sound of triumph in his voice.

As Peter stretched out his hands to make the task easier for them, one of the soldiers tied a rope around his wrists, while the largest of the soldiers struck James brutally across the face, for no reason at all, causing him to stagger and wipe away the blood that was trickling from his left eye. So awesome was the appearance of Peter that the soldiers did not touch him and when the soldier raised his hand to strike James again, one look from Peter caused him to stop his hand in mid-air.

Turning to the flock of God that was witnessing his arrest, Peter raised his bound hands in blessing, and then quietly permitted the soldiers to lead him and James away. It all happened so suddenly that it was hard to believe it really took place. At first dead silence seized the assembly with people just staring at each other dumbfounded. Then they all began to talk at once.

In the hope of giving them all some consolation, the Bishop of Jerusalem, my old friend James, the son of Alphaeus, silenced the group that encircled him and began addressing them, holding his hands over his head, imploring them to listen. With great assurance he started to speak.

"When trials, persecutions, and even imprisonments happen to us, count it as a great joy. Peter has been taken from us and with him our beloved Brother James. God has permitted this so our faith might be tried that we might learn patience. Be patient therefore until the Lord returns in glory."

I glanced around at the circle of faces that were turned towards James as they listened to the words of their shepherd.

"We have to be like farmers who plant the seed and then wait patiently for it to bear fruit as it drinks in the rain. We must likewise be patient. Rain is falling on us in the form of persecution. Let us receive it in patience as coming from the hands of Christ himself. Let patience have its perfect work in us and it will bring forth great fruit. We must not complain, but accept the trials and persecutions as coming from the all-merciful Lord whose coming draws near. Let us strengthen our hearts and follow the example of the patience of the prophets of old. Let us recall what they endured. Let us remember the heroic patience of Job whose final state was more blessed than what it was before his trials began. We know that the Lord is merciful and compassionate and he blesses those who endure temptation with the crown of life that God promises to all who love and serve him.

"Let us not be concerned about our lives—they are but a mist that hovers over the earth for a brief time and vanishes in an instant. And when they vanish from the earth we shall all behold the face of God. In our time of trouble, we must draw near to God who will then draw nearer to us.

"Now let us all pray for the strengthening of Peter and James that they may bear witness to the truth without fear and that they may be safely delivered. We know that our constant prayer is of great importance to them. We recall that Elijah prayed that it would not rain and it did not for three and a half years, but when it did the earth produced its abundant harvest. Let us ask with faith, without any hesitation, for Peter and James to be restored to us."

When James fell to his knees, the rest of us knelt with him, continuing the entire night in prayer. When day broke the next morning everyone in Jerusalem was talking about what happened to Peter and James the son of Zebedee.

Herod, basking in the favor of Emperor Claudius, was in Jerusalem for the Passover, bringing with him his entire entourage of attendants, courtesans, and a large number of soldier-body guards. Although he was more Roman than Jew, supporting anti-Christian forces for political reasons, he seized the apostles and imprisoned them. Since it was the ninth anniversary of the resurrection of Jesus, there were many Christian pilgrims in the city as well as Jewish ones. When a rumor came to my ears that a mass movement was afoot among the Christian, who made a sizeable mob, to storm the palace of Herod and demand the release of the Apostles, I was worried that warfare might break open between Christians and Jews causing blood to run in the streets.

When, in fact, a mob did begin to gather not far from Herod's palace, I went at once and joined it, determined to use all my strength to keep peace. It was an angry and insistent mob that stood before Herod's Jerusalem residence stamping their feet and yelling,

"Give us our apostles!"

"Give us Peter!"

"Give us James!"

"Peter!"

"James!"

Clapping their hands and shouting, they said they intended to do as their ancestors had done at the battle of Jericho, continuing the demonstration until Herod freed the apostles Peter and James. Because of the restless throng that kept pushing at the gates of Herod's palace, the kings guards were becoming tense and on edge.

When I saw the numbers of anti-Christian Jews swelling, I too became apprehensive. At any moment, a spark could ignite the hatred that burned in their hearts and start a conflagration that even the Roman soldiery would have extreme difficulty extinguishing. It was with mixed feelings that I witnessed Herod Agrippa's sudden appearance on the balcony of the palace. Surrounded by his body-guards, the short fat King Herod Agrippa peered over the balcony, sneering at the crowd below. Contemptuously he spat into the upturned faces of the incensed mob that was screaming more vehemently now that Herod stood before them.

"Give us the apostles," the mob roared with one voice.

Holding up his hands and calling for silence, Herod faced the agitators. When a hush fell over the milling throng, Herod stood posed
with his fleshy, ring-encrusted hands folded over his distended belly
and roared, "I'll show you what it is to antagonize King Herod!"

"We want Peter and James," someone cried out from the mob. It
was echoed from every side in a deafening roar.

Standing akimbo, head cocked jauntily to one side, chin thrust
forward, Herod arrogantly surveyed the crowd signaling for them to
get quiet. When they did, he bellowed, "I will give you James, right
now."

A cheer arose from the throng that stared tensely at Herod. "But
you'll have to wait for Peter," he added slyly. A rumble of disapproval
marked these words. All eyes, including mine, were glued on Herod
as he turned to his bodyguard and muttered a command. Instantly
the bodyguard turned heel and rushed into the palace. Dead silence
fell over the crowd. I heard a baby wailing. Slowly the minutes
dragged past while Herod stood posing grandiosely on his balcony,
occasionally parading back and forth so that everyone would have an
equal chance to view him. When some of the Roman Governor's soldiers arrived on the scene, I felt relieved that they were evidently
there to ensure the peace. Thank God there would be no riot. As
Herod moved his hands dramatically, a fanfare of trumpets ruffled
the air and the doors of the palace burst open as we all waited
expectantly for James to walk out of the palace. Instead a soldier
came charging out of the palace, brandishing his sword high in the
air for every one to see, bearing on it the bloody severed head of
James! Barely able to recognize the features of the son of Zebedee
who had such a short time before told me of his dream to carry
Christ to Susa and Persepolis, I stared in horror. Blood was gushing
from the stump that was his neck. When his mouth gaped open and
his tongue fell out, I gasped. I saw Christ crucified once more in his
apostle. He was dying afresh in the city of Jerusalem on the very
anniversary of his death. The vision faded. Then to my terror I saw

my own face in the features of James. It was my own head that I beheld on the sword held high in the soldier's hand.

Herod laughed a high-pitched, shrill, strident laugh that chilled me to the core. With mock bravado he grasped the sword bearing the bloody head and flourished it triumphantly over his head and then with a flick of the wrist tossed the head like a cabbage into the crowd of Christians below. Still he was not finished. Looking out over the horror stricken crowd, he yelled, "Today I have given you James as I promised you I would." He swaggered to and fro on his balcony then stopped and with both hands on his hips, hissed, "Now hear this, I will give you Peter—three days from now on the first day of the coming week." He sneered, spat into the crowd again, turned his back, and stormed into the palace.

Although my weak stomach was jumping, I overcame my weakness, and running to the place where James' head fell on the earth, and taking off my cloak, I put it over the precious relic, which I picked up, kissed and began to carry in mournful procession to the tombs outside the city wall near the tomb that could not hold Christ. We were reenacting Christ's death. Although I was too stricken with shock to preach to the people, I blessed them after we laid the head of James in the tomb of one of our Christians. Then I asked them all to disperse quietly and to return to their own homes and pray for the deliverance of Peter who was being guarded day and night in Herod's palace by four soldiers.

When I returned to the house of John Mark, it was filled to over flowing with people who were being led in prayer by Barnabas. I was happy to throw my soul into the prayers that were being said. Christ within me was reliving his passion. Everyone in the house seemed to sense the nearness of the Lord in our hour of trial. The death of James and the promised doom hanging over Peter served to draw us all closer together so that we prayed continually, hoping against hope, determined to pray constantly until Peter was sent forth from Herod's palace in safety.

In fasting and in prayer we kept the Passover. Night fell, still no news about Peter. As the night wore on, the anniversary of the night in which Christ came back from the dead, our hearts were quickened to pray especially fervently. When someone knocked on the door, Mark motioned to Rhoda to answer. When she approached the door, instead of answering it, she came running back to us, yelling,

"It's Peter! I heard his voice!!"

"Silly girl, you are mistaken," Mark replied.

"It is him," she insisted. "I know his voice!"

"Perhaps it is his angel come to tell us that he is dead," Barnabas ventured.

"Enough! Enough! I will go myself," I announced exercising my authority. Nervously I walked to the door.

"Hurry! Hurry! Open the door quickly," someone whispered from the other side. I threw the door open. It *was* Peter!

"Peace be unto you," he greeted us all.

"And to you peace," I replied.

I had never seen him look better.

"Christ has raised him from the dead!" a woman yelled wildly.

Peter strode confidently into the assembly and motioned for everyone to be quiet.

"No. I have not come back from the dead. Something strange, but very wonderful happened. Someone came and tapped my side while I was sleeping between two soldiers in the prison. At first, I thought I was dreaming, for the chains fell off my hands. The one who woke me up told me to get up, dress, and follow him. Amazingly, we just walked right passed the sleeping guards! The iron gate of the palace opened all by itself and we walked into the city street. Suddenly the one who rescued me vanished! At once I knew the Lord sent an angel to deliver me." At the memory of his miraculous deliverance, an ethereal smile came to Peter's face.

"Now, I must go somewhere to disappear for awhile."

He raised his hands in blessing and in the twinkling of an eye he was gone.

The next day Herod Agrippa publicly killed his guards who slept while Peter escaped. In fury, he departed from Jerusalem going to Caesarea. A short time later, I heard that he fell ill and died, his living flesh being consumed by worms.

Since we had no more business in Jerusalem, Barnabas and I headed back to Antioch taking with us John Mark and a copy of Matthew's gospel, which I was very eager to start reading.

Lucius, with the help of a convert named Simon Niger, managed very nicely during our absence. The church in Antioch was flourishing and as we discovered, able to thrive without us, so I began to dream and to plan a missionary journey for the purpose of establishing churches among the Gentiles, similar to the one in Antioch.

In preparation for the journey, I prayed, fasted, and read the copy of the gospel which Matthew had written in Aramaic and which Peter had arranged for me to have. This book was my one material possession, if you could call it that. How I grew to love those parchments that depicted Christ's life and death! Unfortunately they got left together with my cloak in Troas with Carpus. If only Timothy would come soon and bring it and my cloak–I could use them both. The heavy felt cloak would keep out the dampness of this prison so that I would not ache so much.

As I readied myself to set out to convert the Gentiles, I meditated upon Christ's ministry and public life, reading the instructions he gave the apostles and learning how he gave them power to cast out unclean spirits, together with the power to cure every kind of disease and infirmity. I reasoned that he had bestowed, or would bestow these powers also on me, once I embarked on my mission.

Bearing in mind all the Lord told them, Barnabas, his cousin John Mark, and I set out from Seleucia with clear skies and calms seas, and headed for Cyprus, which is not too far distant, being clearly visible on the horizon from the mainland. It soon became apparent that it was a mistake to bring Mark with us.

We went directly to Salamis for Barnabas had relatives there that he had not seen for some time. They received us warmly and hospitably giving us meals and a place to stay. When we preached the word of God in the synagogue in Salamis, many people responded by coming privately to us afterwards asking about the forgiveness of sins. However, we did not remain there very long, because I was anxious to press on to regions where the name of Jesus was still unknown.

We crossed the island, reaching Paphos, the seat of the Roman government for Cyprus, then under the jurisdiction of Governor Sergius Paulus. Here our preaching was powerful in the Holy Spirit. Even Sergius Paulus, a man of great discernment and learning, became interested in us and sent for us to come to explain the word of God to him. His palace reminded me of the homes of the wealthy that I knew in Tarsus with gleaming white porticoes, sumptuous frescoes, trellises hanging with grapes, and located nearby the dark blue waters of the sea. Getting an audience with the Roman Governor was much more than I had anticipated. Obviously it was time for me to wear the Roman toga again. It is a difficult garment to wear properly—a troublesome garment, a length of fabric skillfully arranged over a tunic. No one but a citizen of Rome is permitted to wear one and no one but a citizen or his slave could possibly drape it properly and correctly. It is easy to understand why most Romans remove the toga in the privacy of their homes and relax in their tunics. As I dressed, I mused that my toga would surprise Sergius Paulus and I was not disappointed.

Accustomed, as I was, to the social life of my parents in Tarsus, the Governor's palace did not pose any problems for me. Ah! But Sergius was really taken back when I entered his home wearing my toga! His own toga was luxurious white linen edged in crimson and he cut a handsome figure in it. In the prime of life, he was a virile man, sophisticated, a charming host.

I greeted Sergius as a fellow Roman. I was no longer a Pharisee, and for some time I had been entering freely and quite naturally into the homes of the Gentiles and even ate with them, contrary to my former religious convictions and all without any scruples. I even drank milk and ate meat at the same meal, but I will never be able to stomach the flesh of swine, which is abominable to me with the very smell of it making me nauseous. How people eat it, I will never understand. The night I had dinner with the Governor of Cyprus, to be courteous, I even ventured so far as to eat a little of the shellfish he had served.

Cordially, Sergius Paulus welcomed us, escorting us into a magnificent room with a terrace overlooking the sea. As he lead us out onto the terrace, I noticed that Barnabas and I were not his only guests, for a short fat man wearing Jewish robes arose from his chair where he had been admiring the vista of sky and sea, and stepped forward to meet us.

Quick with the introduction, Sergius said simply: "I want you to meet a great Jewish prophet, my good friend Elymas."

Arrogantly eyeing us, Elymas grunted a greeting. This was an unexpected turn of events. I began to realize that Sergius was one of those men who like to dabble in various religions. In my ministry so far, I had not encountered any dilettante, and I was determined to win the soul of Sergius and through him all Cyprus for the Lord. Immediately declaring war on the so-called Jewish prophet, I planned my strategy.

"A Jewish prophet?" I asked in surprise with a lift of my bushy brow. "I am well informed about Jewish affairs. I was recently in Jerusalem and I was not aware that there was a great prophet on Cyprus." I deliberately emphasized the word great and intently studied the face of the self-styled prophet. Obviously disapproving of my appearance, he regarded me coldly, saying, "I am Elymas and I have never heard of you." He spoke with a definite edge in his voice.

The battle was on. Picking up the challenge, Barnabas remarked in a very calculated manner, "You will hear more, much more, of Paul in future." With seeming great courtesy, Barnabas smiled at our fellow Jew. Oblivious to the undercurrents of our conversation, Sergius jovially led us to the nearby dining room where a splendid table was spread. After a slave removed our sandals, we reclined to a regal banquet of shellfish, as I said before, and a roast of lamb, olives, and fruits of all kinds in abundance. Displaying a great liking for anchovies rolled in sprouts of some kind, Sergius urged us to try them. They weren't bad, but they weren't good either. A slave served me some kind of vegetable with which I had no familiarity. The wine was a local vintage sweetened with honey in the way the Romans prefer it. Mulsum, I believe, it is called.

Since Elymas was too busy eating, he pretended to pay no attention to us. So, never timid, I decided to attack head on.

"What does the 'great prophet' prophesy, Elymas?" I peered at him as he reclined directly across from me.

"You have not heard of the new religion I founded?" As Barnabas and I exchanged glances, he feigned surprise and continued speaking. "Judaism is only for Jews. I am going to give the monotheism of the Jews to the Greeks and Romans without giving them the burdens of Judaism, such as the dietary regulations." He stuffed a large piece of roast lamb into his mouth. "Why, I have discovered," he informed us, wagging his finger almost in my face, "that the meat on the hind quarter of animals, which Jewish law forbids us to eat, is the most succulent of all. And as for snails, and shellfish, and cold ham…! The Scribes just don't know what they are missing!"

Giving me a knowing look, Barnabas winked his eye, all unseen by Elymas who was devouring his shellfish. Sergius was the one to speak.

"Elymas has the most wonderful ideas. He wants to combine all the best of the Roman way of life with the Jewish. Since you, Paul and Barnabas, appear to be wishing to incorporate the Romans and Greeks into your new way, I thought it would be an excellent idea for you to come and meet Elymas and learn about the religion of which he is the prophet."

Aghast, I was at a loss for words. Sergius Paulus was trying to convert me! Barnabas shrugged and asked point blank, "What does the Roman Governor have in mind?"

"Yes?" I questioned while stalling for time in which to plan an attack. "What do you have in mind?"

Carefully rearranging the folds of his fine white toga, Sergius answered slowly. "I would like to see you preach the new religion of Elymas. Your reputation as a preacher is unsurpassed. We have raised a lot of money and will finance your preaching, generously supplying everything you need. You see," he paused and nodded at his "great prophet," "Elymas is divinely inspired. What he wants to do, to put it quite simply, is to eat like a Roman and pray like a Jew."

Surveying the self-styled prophet, I observed that he was munching on a bowl of cherries that he moved from the center of the table to a spot near him. In a few minutes, the silver dish was empty and he was reaching for the grapes. Since the governor was talking for him, he had no need to say anything.

Like a flash of lightening, inspiration flooded my mind. Fastening my eyes on Elymas, I asked, "Elymas, if I were to translate your name into Hebrew, your name would signify 'sorcerer.' Tell me are you a magician?"

Arrogantly cocking his head and continuing to eat, he replied with his mouth full. "To be totally frank, I *have* dabbled in that art."

"How very interesting," I countered, "I would enjoy seeing some of your tricks." There was a faint touch of sarcasm in my voice.

"Yes!" boomed Sergius Paulus with delight, "I had no idea that you did tricks." Like a petulant child he demanded, "Do something right now!" He clapped his hands together with enthusiasm. "Do something to amuse us, I command you."

Obviously novelties intrigued Sergius. Fixing my gaze intently on Elymas, I urged, "Yes, Elymas, let us see what you can do."

Since he was now the center of attention, Elymas, pleased with himself, arrogantly looked from me to Barnabas and then to Sergius and waving his hand before our faces, dropped a chameleon on the table before the astonished and delighted governor.

As the little chameleon turned from bright green to brown, Elymas purred with honeyed tones, "You may keep him, my dear Governor. He will be a good house pet, for any insect that dares cross your threshold, he will devour."

Staring in amazement, Sergius picked up the chameleon and gave it to a slave to have it removed to the inner courtyard of the palace.

Fire burned within me as inspiration came to me. I let the Spirit speak through me with power.

"You, son of Satan! You are the enemy of truth and justice. Twisting and confounding the ways of the Lord, you are deceitful and insidiously crafty."

The atmosphere of the room was charged with tension as when lightening begins to strike. Sergius Paulus stared at me in open-mouthed and wide-eyed amazement. Even Barnabas was surprised. He had never heard me attack anyone the way I had Elymas. But I was not yet finished with that imposter. "Elymas," I pointed my finger directly in his face. "The Lord's hand will strike you. You will be blind for a time, even unable to see the light of the sun!"

In utter panic, the would be prophet let out a terrifying shriek and jumping up and rubbing his eyes, stumbled into the furniture in his confusion. When he fell with his face pressed to the floor, Sergius Paulus signaled for the slaves to carry him away to his sleeping quarters.

Apprehension and fear were plainly visible on the handsome and regular features of the governor, as he sat toying with a silver spoon trying to comprehend what had happened. Seeing that I had frightened the governor, I hastened to reassure him by saying, "Don't worry. The blindness will go away as quickly as it came in just three days time."

With perplexity showing in his eyes, Barnabas blurted, "We would not harm anyone." He looked at me questioningly.

Relaxing a bit, but still very pensive, Sergius waited for me to speak.

"You invited us here because you wanted to hear the word of God. That is the only reason we came."

Sergius nodded. "Continue."

Rising to my full stature, I proclaimed, "I will promise you life eternal, in the name of Jesus of Nazareth, if you will believe in him and be baptized in the name of the Father, the Son, and the Holy Spirit."

"Yes, life—that's what I want. I want to live forever. I want life," he stammered nervously with his tanned brown face now red and flustered.

Slowly, point by point, I explained to him the creed that the apostles had composed.

"I believe in God the Father Almighty maker of heaven and earth." That presented no difficulties for Sergius. "And in one Lord Jesus Christ, his only Son our Lord." We spoke of Bethlehem and the birth of Jesus. When we came to the end of the creed, Sergius said with conviction, "I believe! I really do believe!"

"Will you be baptized in this faith?" I asked softly.

"I will," he replied firmly.

We baptized Sergius Paulus, the Roman Governor of Cyprus, successor of Cicero in that office, and we were confident that we could leave the church in Cyprus secure and certain of unbounded growth in the future. Rejoicing over what the Lord accomplished in Cyprus we set out to conquer the world, the entire world in Jesus' name and to lay it at his feet.

Setting sail on a sea-worthy vessel bearing a cargo of corn from Egypt to Asia Minor, we were headed for Perga in Pamphilia. Since the seas were calm, the roll and pitch of the ship were restful. What a beautiful sight were the snow-white gulls soaring with wings outstretched over the blue waters, rising and falling with the breeze. With the taste of salt air on my lips, I found the sea air invigorating. However, John Mark, I noticed was not enjoying the crossing, for he was restless and had practically nothing to say. When I spoke to him he would merely nod his head or mumble a few words. When we drew near the coast of Asia Minor, he finally broke his silence and bluntly told me what was troubling him.

"I have decided to leave you at Perga."

Since Barnabas showed no sign of surprise, I imagined that he already received his cousin's confidence. Determined to go right to the heart of the matter, I leveled my eyes on him and asked, "Do you want to tell me about it, Mark? I know something has been troubling you."

He sighed. A frown creased his furrowed and well-tanned brow.

"I—well, I—just don't feel right about entering the houses of the Gentiles and eating their food. It's unclean."

Nervously pacing to and fro on the deck and glancing out to sea before he spoke, he finally said, "You frighten me, Paul. Why you are more Roman than Jew!" He looked disdainfully at my toga.

"I belong to Jesus Christ! I follow my convictions!"

"Oh, Paul, look—I would just be out of place in Asia Minor." He threw out his hands apologetically. "I'm going to return to Jerusalem—that's where I belong." He heaved a big sigh of relief, as if a great burden had been lifted from his shoulders.

Because I realized that we were dealing with a question that would have to be faced many times in the growing church—a question that could not be denied or put aside—I knew I had to be very tactful in discussing it.

"Does it disturb you to hear me say that the Gentile Christians need have no connection with the synagogue?"

He shifted anxiously avoiding my eyes that were on his.

"Yes—very much—but I really must return to Jerusalem. My mother is worried about me. She really didn't want me to come. She said I would probably catch some strange fever or get beaten up by robbers or stoned like Stephen or murdered in an inn. I want to go to my mother. She needs me."

Once I saw what I was up against, I made no further comment. He left—deserting us as soon as we docked in Pamphilia. With no further ado, Barnabas and I set out at once on the road to Psidian Antioch, one of the cities on the great Asia Minor trade routes, where I knew there were a good-sized Jewish community and a synagogue that would assure us of a hearing. Although they might drive me out of town, it would be only after they had the gospel preached to them.

Having been established by Augustus to bring law to the lawless highlands of southern Galatia, Psidian Antioch, the military capital of the Roman province of Galatia, had been a Roman colony for about fifty years, although the city itself is much older. Established by Seleucus Nicator for his father Antiochus, it was situated on a magnificent site, overlooking a rolling plane beyond which lay the snow covered mountain pinnacles. Coming down off the mountain road from Perga, we entered the city where I noticed at once the Latin inscriptions on the buildings, reading them with interest. Although I had never yet preached in a Roman colony, I told myself at that time that I would go to Rome some day and preach so that even Caesar would hear of Christ. Soon I hoped the soldiers of Psidian Antioch who were speaking the Vulgar Latin tongue, would hear of the Lord Jesus.

Wearing Jewish attire once more, I went with Barnabas to the prosperous synagogue that had more than its share of proselytes from the pagans. Sickened by the Roman hero gods and equally repelled by the Oriental cults that made a religion of sex and indulged in unbridled orgies, many people in the empire turned to Judaism in their search for truth and good moral living. Looking back now over the years, I recall one city that had male sex organs carved in stone and placed in conspicuous places. When crossing a street in the city, I shuddered to see the stepping-stone on which I was standing resembled a giant erect male organ. As I said, many people revolted by such things had become converts to Judaism and I felt that these people would respond to the gospel. Later events proved I was right.

After taking our places in the synagogue, we heard the reading of the law and the prophets, with happy hearts. It was good to be once more in the assembly of the people of God. Perceiving us, the rulers of the Psidian Antioch synagogue invited us to speak to the people. It was the moment I had been anticipating. Motioning for silence, I rose confidently and began.

"Listen, Israelites," and looking then at the many proselytes, "and you who fear God, and I will tell you of the wonderful things that have occurred in Jerusalem."

With an eloquence that was not mine, I preached words of flame. When the assembly later dispersed many of the Jews and the proselytes came and talked with us and were so impressed with what we told them that they begged us to stay over and preach the following Sabbath.

Because a large crowd of Gentiles, wishing to hear me preach, had gathered in front of the synagogue the following Sabbath—not being again permitted to enter the synagogue—I decided to preach in the open air so all alike could hear. Infuriated by this, the rulers of the synagogue interrupted my preaching with screams of "Blasphemy!"

"Go away from our synagogue," their chief rabbi yelled.

The time had come for me to speak plainly and not to mince words.

"The word of God was preached first to you Jews, but because you reject it and make yourselves unworthy of eternal life, we turn to the Gentiles."

Amid great cheering of the Gentiles present and surrounded by them, I walked to a safe distance away from the synagogue and resumed my preaching and then continued my homilies daily thereafter as we watched the crowds continually increase from one day to the next. Taking the word of God into their hearts, they responded to the Holy Spirit and began spreading the news of salvation far and near over the whole countryside.

Infuriated all the more by the success of the gospel of Christ, the synagogue officials were determined to put an end to my preaching, but could not take the law into the own hands. However they persuaded a number of wealthy influential women of Antioch, who were converts, into nagging their husbands to have us driven from the city. Stamping the dust from our feet, we left while we still could peacefully, and with much satisfaction, because we had sown the mustard seed of faith in Psidian Antioch and knew that it would grow. Walking out under the aqueduct we turned and looking back over the city, prayed for the people there, and bade them a joyful farewell, but I was already planning to return there again at a later date.

Our next target was Iconium, sixty miles distant to the southeast. Just as we were arriving at this democratic Greek city—we were traveling on horseback in a caravan on the Royal Road—much to my surprise, a Greek who appeared to recognize me flagged us to a complete stop.

"Paul? You are the Apostle Paul, I believe!"

Amazed, I looked at him, a prosperous, well dressed, and educated man. As I peered at him waiting for him to state his business, I recognized the hand of providence at work.

"You're an easy one to spot," he exclaimed with smiling eyes. "My relatives in Psidian Antioch sent me word that you were headed this way, I've been watching for you. They told me to be on the lookout for a small man with crooked legs"—squinting, he looked at my legs as I stood in front of him and then continued—"with eyebrows that come together over a slightly hooked nose." As he looked at my nose, I found myself running the tip of my index finger up and down the bridge of my nose.

"Is that all they said about me?" I laughed noticing that Onesiphorus, as he introduced himself, had a nice straight Greek nose.

"They said that sometimes you look like a man and at other times you have the face of an angel."

"Why do you wish to see me?" I asked.

Still staring at my crooked legs, he thrust forth his hands in a gesture of warmth. "I wish to extend to you the hospitality of my house during your stay in Iconium." He smiled and waited for us to reply. Glancing at Barnabas, who had a big happy grin on his face, I accepted his invitation.

"We shall be happy, most happy, to be your guests."

He led us to his house, a charming place on one of the narrow lanes of the town. With child-like exuberance our host spared no expense at making us at home. A successful businessman, he welcomed the opportunity to repay the Lord for his many blessings.

Staying with Onesiphorus was a pleasant experience. His wife and children couldn't do enough for us to make us comfortable. Even his neighbors welcomed us and tried to lavish gifts on us. I especially recall one neighbor in particular. She lived in a house on the other side of the street from Onesiphorus. Because the street was so narrow, I could almost reach out and touch her house from my bedroom window on the second floor. According to Onesiphorus, it was the home of a wealthy widow, Theocleia and of her eighteen-year-old daughter, Thecla.

Often as I sat in my room reading or praying, I could hear laughter coming from Thecla's home. Observing that a handsome youth was a regular caller, I decided that the beautiful young Thecla must have a suitor.

Onesiphorus also had a daughter, Sappho, who together with her father, received baptism from my hands. Being much concerned about the welfare of his daughter, he often asked me my advice about his plans for her future.

"What shall I do with Sappho? Shall I let her marry a pagan?" With his chin in his hand he pondered the problem of his daughter's future as we sat after dinner one evening in the garden behind his house.

"In my opinion, I told him, "if she remains unmarried she will be free to occupy herself with the things of God. If she were my daughter, I would like to see her free from the cares that marriage imposes on women so that she can be busy with the things of God and become holy in both body and spirit."

With troubled gray eyes Onesiphorus asked, "Would it be a sin if I married her to some nice young fellow?"

"By, no means!" I was quick to assure him.

"Let her marry whom she pleases but don't let her marry a pagan. Her husband should be a Christian."

We sat in silence for a minute or two, enjoying the evening breeze and the setting sun. I wanted him to know the full truth in the matter, as I see it. "In my judgment, she will be more happy, if she remains a virgin."

"I think she will marry." He fidgeted nervously in his chair.

"See to it, my son, "—I called him son, although he was far older than I, because I had begotten him in the gospel—"see to it that she marries another Christian."

He shook his head sadly "There aren't very many Christian young men in Iconium." Then breaking into a smile he commented, "We will have to get busy, you and I and Brother Barnabas and convert some so Sappho can marry."

Truly eager for the spread of the gospel, Onesiphorus invited many people to his home to hear us preach. Before we were driven out of town, we baptized quite a large number. We even had the joy of seeing Sappho become betrothed to one of them.

One night I heard quarreling coming from the house of Thecla and her mother across the street. Soon thereafter, I began to notice that Thecla was sitting near her window watching each time Onesiphorus brought friends to the house to hear me preach. When the Spirit is upon me, I do get rather loud. Gradually it became obvious that Thecla was sitting close to her window in order to hear what I was saying. When I first arrived in Iconium, I met her mother who was not at all interested in hearing the gospel preached and so I was pleasantly surprised to learn that little Thecla was drawn to Christ. Whenever Thecla noticed that I was observing her, she would always shyly withdraw from her window.

When as I was in the courtyard of Onesiphorus' house one day, the serving girl informed me that I had a visitor, which was not an uncommon occurrence, for the house frequently overflowed with Gentiles who wanted to know how to have their sins taken away. Naturally I was quite surprised that the beautiful, but shy, young Thecla was waiting to see me when I entered the courtyard where I usually received guests.

"O Paul! You must help me!"

Her face was tear stained as she threw herself on the mosaic floor at my feet.

"Child, what is it?" I asked in alarm. "What can I do for you?"

With a finger, I wiped away a tear from her cheek. The amber of her eyes glistened behind fresh tears. On her knees, pleading up at me, she sobbed, "My mother wants me to marry Thamyris!"

"Well," I sighed in relief, "marrying a handsome young man like Thamyris is not the worst thing that could happen to a lovely Grecian girl. I met him once. He seems very nice."

"Oh, no! You don't understand. I have been listening to you preach. I've been listening from my window." Considering what she was going to say to me, she grew silent.

Smiling at her pretty upturned face, I gently urged her to explain.

"Ever since I first heard you speak of Jesus—I no longer love Thamyris." Sighing deeply and brushing away her tears, she whispered: "My heart beats only for Jesus. Him only do I love!"

I patted her on the top of the head paternally, and whispered gently: "I understand, little one. I understand."

"I think about him all the time—all the time."

"That is a very great grace."

Amazed at the wonderful thing that I was privileged to behold, I asked, "And Thamyris?"

"He pursues me constantly and mother wants to give me to him."

Softly she began to cry again.

"Perhaps your Thamyris will become a Christian. If you are baptized, perhaps he might be baptized also. I will talk to him."

Wanting to be absolutely sure that I understood her, I pretended to comfort her with these words.

"No! You don't understand." She spoke with much determination.

"What is it you want, little one?"

"I want to belong only to Jesus. I want to remain a virgin."

Lowering her large amber eyes she explained.

"From the window I heard you preach about the holiness of a virgins. That is what I want."

"You are a beautiful and a rare flower. Give thanks to Jesus for the grace he has given you. I will speak to Onesiphorus, he will—we will find a way. Now go in peace."

"Please," she begged. "Please baptize me, now right now in the garden pool where I have seen you baptize others."

"How can I refuse?" I asked, beckoning her towards the pool in the center of the garden. Never have I seen anyone else rise up from the waters of baptism with as much joy and happiness as Thecla did.

Knowing that I had not heard the last of the matter, it was a great joy for me to be able to send her back to her mother's house strengthened with the life and grace of God.

That night I had another visitor. Demanding to see me at once, Thamyris, stormed angrily into the house. Having lost his bride, he had come to do battle with me.

"You have stolen my Thecla," he thundered at me with the impetuosity of youth as he stood towering over me. He was a full head taller than I and very muscular.

"She is in her mother's house," I replied calmly trying to quiet his rage.

"She says she is betrothed to someone else. She says you betrothed her to someone else this very afternoon." Menacingly he came towards me. "She says she will have Jesus Christ for her bridegroom and no one else."

Pacing in a state of profound agitation and shaking his fist, he yelled obscenities at me. When he vehemently kicked his foot against a chair, wincing from the pain he caused himself, I tried to find some way to pacify him.

"Someday I think you will understand what has happened."

"I don't want to understand!" Shaking his fist in my face, he continued his tirade, while I, at any moment, expected him to take a punch at me. "My family is powerful in Iconium. I will have you run out of town."

Before I could say another word, he rushed out of the house, slamming the door. I didn't need any more problems in Iconium. Among the local Jews, I had plenty of enemies already. Because I had converted many Jews from my preaching in the synagogue, the rulers there were anxious for me to leave the city. Yes, Iconium was getting too hot for me.

Naturally when Thamyris burst upon the town with his story, the Jews did everything they could to stir up trouble against me. The wheels of Iconium's democratic government began turning against me. When Onesiphorus told me of a plot that he discovered in which certain people planned to stone Barnabas and me, I decided the time had come for us to say farewell to our newborn Christian church in Iconium and move on—for the time being.

Once more kicking the dust from our feet, we moved on to another town. I will always remember Lystra for it was there that I worked my first miracle or rather I should say Christ worked a miracle through me for the first time. I'll never forget that. It caused no small amount of trouble. The man we healed was a Lycaonian, a member of one of the native tribes of Asia Minor that has its own language. In the social strata the Lycaonians were on the bottom. In fact the Roman colony considered them rabble, but I learned to love the outcasts of society. So when I saw this poor wretched man, as a brother for whom Christ died, crippled from birth and dragging himself about on the rocky ground, I felt great compassion for him. Recalling that Christ commanded us to heal the sick, I sensed the Holy Spirit within me inspiring me to cure the man. Looking into the eyes, I sensed that he had enough faith to be healed. I looked at him steadfastly and said simply, "Stand up!" Then, just as Christ healed the paralytic at Capernaum, he healed the cripple man in Lystra. Although Pilate crucified Christ, he is living in me and will continue to live in his priests, working miracles of conversion and forgiving sins—down through the ages until time is no more.

"Getup! On your feet!" I commanded with authority. Immediately the man stood and laughed until he cried. Jumping up and down on his strong straight legs that had been twisted and lame, he raced all around Lystra, shouting for joy, telling the people of the town what happened.

From all directions, people came running to see us and marvel at the miracle of healing. I was pleased because there was going to be a large crowd to hear my preaching. In the wild confusion of the crowd milling tightly around us, I could hear two names repeated over and over—Mercury and Jupiter—as they spread from the mouth of one to that of another, making so much noise and confusion that I could not even begin to preach.

When Barnabas nudged me, I looked at him in a puzzled manner. Just then the crowd seemed to split apart to let someone come through, as Barnabas called my attention to the man who was approaching. "Look, here comes the priest of Jupiter with oxen and garlands. What are they going to do?"

I knew what they were going to do and had to stop it.

"They think we are their pagan gods! They are going to sacrifice the oxen to us." I was aghast. Horrified I shouted at the top of my lungs for them to stop. Undaunted by my protests, they continued making the preparations for the sacrifice.

"No! No!" I yelled. "Why are you doing this? We are also mortals—human beings just like you are."

Waving my hands for them to be silent, I finally quieted them enough so that I could speak.

"We are here to tell you about the true God who healed the crippled man." Seeing that I was getting their attention, I continued: "It was not I who healed the crippled man, it was Christ Jesus—I am merely his priest."

Finally after I repeated this a number of times, I got their complete attention. With profound interest they listened while I preached Christ's gospel of love and reconciliation. Just when I felt that I was starting to convince them, someone on the fringe of the crowd shouted,

"Blasphemer!"

Looking closely, I recognized the man as being the ruler of the Iconium synagogue. He was accompanied by a large number of his congregation who came all the way from Iconium to persecute me and take turns shouting.

"You preach blasphemy!"

"Death to the blasphemer!"

One of the Iconium Jews rushed at me, shaking his fist savagely. Another tried to grab me, but I slipped away from him. When the pagans of Lystra saw that we were so bitterly hated, they joined ranks with the Iconiums.

"They tried to make us believe they were our gods Jupiter and Mercury!"

"Deceivers," yelled the Lycaonians.

"Blasphemers!" shouted the Jews.

A stone whizzed past my ear. Another struck me on the leg. Bleeding and dazed from a blow on the head, I tried to dodge the stones that were pelting down on me from all sides. Sinking to the ground with my legs folding up under me, I prayed earnestly.

"Father, forgive them…. Father, into Thy hands…"

I don't remember anything else, until I regained consciousness sometime later outside the city wall where they dragged me and left me for dead. When I opened my eyes, my head was throbbing with pain and my vision blurred. Nevertheless through the haze, I thought I could recognize a familiar face smiling at me. It was the crippled man that Christ healed. The wonderful providence of God!

"You will be all right," the crippled man, or rather I should say the former crippled man assured me. "You healed me—now I will heal you."

When he saw that I was glancing around to find out about Barnabas he added, "Your friend—he will be all right too."

When I tried to move, pain shot through my body. Because I was bruised, bleeding, and sore all over, it took all the strength and perseverance I could muster, to get on my feet, even with the help of the Lycaonian. Leaning against wall, I watched Barnabas inch his way to a standing position.

"I'm Claytus," the Lycaonian informed us with an eager smile. I will take you home with me.

Since I was in no position to refuse his hospitality, as soon as we had the cover of the darkness of night, Claytus led us back to Lystra and to his house that became our home for the night. Although it was a small house, it was filled with hospitality and love. As Claytus' wife prepared a modest meal for us, the house was soon swarming with relatives of Claytus and his family who had come from the surrounding area anxious to hear about Jesus who had worked the "beautiful miracle," as they referred to it. Before the night was over, we baptized the entire family of about one hundred members. Brought forth with much pain and labor, the church of Lystra was born.

As soon as my injuries and the few that Barnabas received were healed, I wanted to travel to Derbe, which is only a relatively short journey from Tarsus. When we were finished in Derbe, I hoped to visit my parents again before sailing on to Antioch. However, I changed my plans, because I felt strongly inspired by the Holy Spirit to return to Iconium and appoint a priest in each church to minister to my spiritual children.

Before leaving Lystra, I ordained Claytus a priest and entrusted him with the spiritual welfare of the church there. Filled with zeal and enthusiasm, Claytus was an admirable priest. In his desire to tell everyone about the wonderful miracle of his healing, he became a great preacher of the gospel. Never have I seen any one else so thankful for strong healthy legs. With Claytus in charge of the church in Lystra, I knew it would flourish.

When I returned to Iconium, I fell ill with my usual stomach ailments. The people there could not do enough to help me. So great was their love for me as their spiritual father that they would have given me their very eyes! I was pleased to learn that Onesiphorus converted Thecla's mother and restored them to harmony. It was he, of course, that I chose to be the priest in Iconium. He was a good choice, because all the reports I have had of him have been very favorable.

As for Thecla, she had grown even more beautiful in virtue. When she greeted me, the love of God shone in her face. How happy it made me to know she had consecrated her life to Christ and dedicated herself to serving the Iconium church with her works of mercy and love.

When we reached Perga, I decided to go over to nearby Attalia and preach there before sailing from that port back to Antioch. Our return to Antioch led me to deal with a problem that was beginning to foment in the Church. John Mark was not the only one who had difficulty understanding the nature of the Church that the Lord was establishing all over the empire and the world.

Shortly after our return to Antioch, some Christians came from Judea and began preaching in our assembly that the Gentiles would have to be circumcised, as are the Jews. At once I saw that I was going to have to fight for the freedom of the church to keep it from becoming enchained with the very chains Christ came to destroy. Realizing that I would encounter the disfavor of men—good men, who failed to understand—but no longer caring about displeasing men, I knew what I had to do, because the Holy Spirit revealed it to me.

With Barnabas and Titus accompanying me, I went up to Jerusalem to confer with Peter, James, and John on the gospel that I preach to the Gentiles. As a result, Titus, Gentile though he was, was not forced to be circumcised.

Peter, James, and John agreed that Barnabas and I should go to the Gentiles, while they would preach to the Jews, provided only that we should be mindful of the poor—the very thing I was eager to do.

Later when Cephas, or Peter, as he is also called, came to Antioch, I faced him, stood up to him, and corrected him, because he was in the wrong. For a time, contrary to the old law, he did eat with the Gentiles, but after he met with certain people that had been with James, he began to withdraw and separate himself from the Gentiles because of fear of what the Jews would say. Barnabas was even persuaded to agree with them and their practices. I was especially disturbed that they were trying to make the Gentiles convert into Jews.

Finally, one day in front of the entire group of them, I challenged Peter, because they all were not walking uprightly according to the truth of the gospel.

"Why compel the Gentiles to live like Jews?" I inquired.

Patiently I explained my belief that we are no longer under the law, that our faith in Jesus Christ is our justification. Because we are all one in Christ, there is no distinction between Jew and Gentile, male and female, slave and freeman.

Wishing that those who were unsettling my spiritual children would mutilate themselves instead and leave my converts alone, I grew restless to leave Antioch and return to the churches I had established, to make it clear to them that, they were not expected to become Jews and keep the law of Moses. They had become very dear to me. I wanted to labor and expend my energies on them until Christ was formed in them. When I was with them previously, I could not address them as spiritual men, since they were still little ones in Christ. I had to feed them with milk, instead of solid food, for they were not ready for meat. Not wanting them to be ignorant about various spiritual things, I prepared to return to Asia, inviting Barnabas to accompany me.

When he insisted on bringing his nephew John Mark with us, I refused to hear of it, because he had deserted me previously. Quarreling over this with Barnabas became intense and heated, causing Barnabas and me to go separate ways. When he decided to go with Mark to Cyprus to visit their families, I chose Silas to go with me into Asia.

CHAPTER 3

*B*elieving that we could work together compatibly, Silas, or Silva-nus as the Romans call him, came to Antioch from Jerusalem, hoping to join me on my missionary journeys. Since we had much in common—we were both Pharisees and Roman citizens, I welcomed him warmly. After I had known him but a short time, I became convinced that I wanted him to accompany me on my forthcoming journey to Galatia and to wherever the Spirit might lead me to preach the gospel.

Providing us with the money necessary to begin our trip, the growing church in Antioch gave us a great celebration before we left. We set out in a caravan headed northward to Tarsus, where I learned from the old slave, who had tutored me when I was a child, that both my parents had died, victims of some strange plague that rampaged through the city. My sister, I was told, had married an influential Jewish merchant who was a member of the Sanhedrin and they were raising a family in Jerusalem.

After visiting the tombs of my parents where I prayed fervently for their souls, I set out with a heavy heart for Derbe. If only mother and father had died in the Lord, I would not have felt so sorrowful at their passing from this world. As we drew near Derbe, I began to feel anxious about my spiritual children there who were now my family.

My heart longed to see them and to know that they were walking with God.

"Perhaps," I worried to Silas, "the converts promptly forgot what I told them as soon as I left."

"You sound like a mother hen fussing over her chicks," Silas observed as he scanned the landscape for some sight of the town.

"Well if they have forgotten, we will stir them up and recall to them what they received in baptism."

As we rounded a curve in the road my heart beat a little fast because I could see the gates of the city. When we finally were within the city walls, I quickly learned that all my fretting had been useless—my converts received me with open arms.

"I promised you I would return," I said addressing the Christian community that had blossomed in my absence and was gathered in the home of the young Jew I made their priest.

"I have returned and I have brought with me someone who can tell you about Jesus. This is Silas, my co-worker and fellow priest of Jesus Christ." I called Silas to come and stand with me before the assembly. "Silas heard Jesus preach and saw him many times. He has been a disciple from the beginning."

With the same Spirit burning in his soul that flamed in mine, Silas began telling the Christians of Derbe about Christ. So beautifully did he speak to them about their Savior that I was deeply touched by his preaching. He spoke of how Jesus had gone about doing good to everyone and of how he was meek and humble of heart. He told them that Christ has compassion on human misery and suffering and is always quick to forgive if there is sorrow for sin in the heart of the sinner. Jesus came to love, and men hated him, and would hate them for loving him. He came to give life, and they killed him. When he talked of Christ's scourging and death, the people of Derbe wept and my own eyes were wet.

"Keep the faith," Silas exhorted them. "Avoid the immorality of the pagans society in which you live. Stay away from the synagogue and avoid persecution, so that the seed of faith will have a chance to grow into a mighty tree that cannot be chopped down. Learn from nature. You know how a little seed grows hidden in the ground, protected from the birds that would eat it, until it sends up green shoots into the light of day. Then it has a good strong root system and if it gets trampled on, the roots send up more green shoots until there is a vigorous plant."

What a great joy for me it was to see that Christ was dwelling in their hearts, that they were no longer pagans, but children of God. How sad they were when they begged me to remain with them, after I told them I would soon be leaving again. When I explained to them that I had other children to beget in other places that they would all meet in heaven one day, they were very generous in supplying the things we needed to proceed once more to Lystra.

Eagerly I looked forward to seeing Claytus and having Silas meet him. I was curious to see if the miracle was perfect, if he had been completely and permanently healed. I still have a scar on my arm from a stone that was hurled at me the day Claytus was miraculously cured. As we drew near the city and I saw the place where I had been left for dead, I told Silas about the experience and how Christ gave Claytus new legs. Since the people who had led the persecution against me in Lystra were Jews from Iconium, naturally they were no longer there and we had no reason to expect a recurrence of violence against us. As soon as we set foot inside the city wall, one of Claytus' relatives spotted us and came rushing to greet us.

"Father Paul! Our father in Christ! You have come back!" Although I embraced his as a spiritual son, I must confess that I did not recognize this child of God. He was probably one of the members of the Claytus' big family of cousins, nephews, uncles, and so forth.

"How is Claytus?" I asked him as he took my few possessions to carry them for me.

"Claytus! He's a holy one now. He preaches and many come to hear him and receive from his hands the body and blood of Christ. The church is growing fast—there must be five hundred of us."

"Have any of them lapsed into their former pagan ways?" This was a question that I was very anxious to have answered, but our guide did not hear what I had asked because we had arrived at the home of Claytus and he went bounding into the house announcing our arrival for all to hear.

"Paul is here. He has come back!"

Appearing instantly and kneeling at my feet, Claytus took my hands in his and before I could stop him covered them with kisses. Straightaway the house was thronged with the children of God of Lystra. Smiling I looked at all the happy faces and extended my hand in blessing. There would be a large number for me to lay my hands on in order that they might receive the Holy Spirit.

Overwhelmed by the large gathering of people Claytus had brought to Christ, I motioned for him to stand, for he was still kneeling before me. All this was the fruit of my having been stoned!

"Rise, my son. Meet Silas who saw Jesus and heard him preach." Silas greeted Claytus. "I am very happy to meet you and to extend to you, my brother priest the right hand of fellowship."

As I surveyed all the converts, Claytus was bursting with pride.

"Father Paul," he began, "there is someone I want you to meet." He beckoned to a lad in his late teens that came quickly to his side.

"This is Timothy, my helper in preaching the gospel. His preaching is responsible for gaining many of these converts to Christ."

I looked at the boy. He was straight, tall, and handsome with friendly brown eyes that were vivacious with truth and sincerity.

"That is wonderful, Timothy, my son. God is pleased with you. You have the appearance of a Jew, am I then correct in assuming that you are Jewish?"

"My mother, Eunice," he beckoned to a woman in the gathering who was obviously a Jewess "is Jewish. My father is a Gentile." Eunice made her way towards us and I greeted her cordially.

After Claytus blessed the people and dismissed them, we settled down to discuss affairs pertinent to the administration of the church in his care.

"What did you think of Timothy?" Claytus asked me as we talked that night after the evening meal.

"A fine young lad. Perhaps you can train him to take your place here when you become too old to preach and minister to the church."

"Timothy wants to go with you," Claytus told me softly. "He wants to preach to people in far distant cities so that churches like ours might spring up where now where are idols and pagan temples."

"That is a very laudable desire, but does it come from God?" I already had experience with young men who thought they wanted to travel to far away places only to desert me. I wasn't going to let that happen again.

"I feel he is very sincere," Claytus replied thoughtfully. "Quite honestly, I would hate to lose him, for he has been a great help to me."

Because I wanted time to consider the matter, I changed the subject. "How are those legs of yours? They look normal and healthy in every respect."

"Perfectly normal, thanks to you," he exclaimed looking at me with gratitude.

I corrected him. "Thanks to Jesus!"

For the joy of seeing my children walking in the truth and in the light, I continually praise God. It was a great joy the next afternoon for me to lay my hands on them and give them the Holy Spirit. Afterwards, when I preached to them, I informed them that I would be leaving the following day. Although they were sorrowful to hear me speak of leaving so soon, they took up a collection to speed us on our way.

Coming to see me that night, Timothy pleaded with me to take him with us. "What would you do if you came with me, Timothy? You are so young," I wanted to test his character.

"I'm not so young, I'm almost twenty," he replied standing up as straight and tall as he could. "I will preach and give the faith to many people."

"You will get stoned, like I did, right here in Lystra." I showed him my scars.

"I am not afraid of stones," he countered with his eyes showing intense passion. "They cannot kill my spirit. I am not afraid to die for Jesus Christ." He spoke more calmly and with profound conviction.

"What about your mother? She will not let you go." I remembered how John Mark's mother did not want Mark to leave her.

"I am no longer a child, sir." He spoke without a trace of emotion.

"You will get homesick."

" I will get used to it."

"What would you do? You would just get in the way." I was sounding him out. "My preaching carries me into the synagogues. Your father is a Gentile and you were not brought up a Jew, but I am sure you know that no uncircumcised Gentile is allowed in the synagogue. They would kill you on the spot and they would make me suffer for it."

"I understand." His eyes were saddened. He thought about it a few seconds and suggested. "Perhaps I could wait outside the synagogues for you."

"What good would that do?"

"Circumcise me! That's the answer. You circumcise me and then I can go wherever you go." Hope blazed in his eyes.

When I determined that Timothy had a true calling from God to be a missionary such as I am, I agreed to what he proposed. He has been my dearest son ever since. If only I could see him once more! If only he would come as I wait in this prison for the shedding of my blood. Timothy! Timothy! Where are you? O Lord, send him to me…let me see him, and then I shall be ready to die.

Although not without tears, Eunice turned Timothy over to me, and we set out to preach the gospel to the entire world. First we went to Iconium where we learned that Onesiphorus had done every bit as well as Claytus. Many received the Holy Spirit there with the laying on of hands.

When I heard Timothy preach for the first time, I was quite pleased with him. He did admirably well. The Greeks of Iconium liked hearing the gospel preached by a Galatian missionary—a Greek like themselves. We made quite a team—Silas, the priest who saw Christ in the flesh, I, Paul, the apostle who encountered Jesus on the road to Damascus, and Timothy, half Greek, half Jew, a native of Asia.

We advised the church in Iconium to keep apart, to remain aloof from the pagan society in which they lived and also from the synagogue, telling them that pagans would corrupt them and the synagogue would persecute them and I wanted them to grow unspotted from the world and from harm. I gave the Christians of Psidian Antioch the same advice. Satisfied that the churches we established were thriving, it was now tine to reach out and start more churches. Since Phrygia seemed to be a likely place, we went there. However, because once we were there the inspiration to preach was completely lacking and I was utterly devoid of words, we determined that the Lord had other plans for us.

"The Holy Spirit does not want us here," I told Timothy and Silas.

"Where shall we go?" They asked in unison.

"Let's head northward," I directed.

Although I had planned to go to Bythnia, we only went as far as Mysia, because I was constrained by the Holy Spirit. Turning completely around, we headed towards the Aegean. When we arrived in

Troas, we had covered many miles and had not even begun to establish a church. To make matters worse, I was ill, because the combination of bad food and water in our fruitless travels made my stomach rebellious. Since I could do nothing until I recovered, Silas and Timothy, not wishing to begin preaching without me, scouted around and found a doctor who could come to the small house we rented and prescribe for me. Although I did not want to be bothered by the medical profession, I consented to see him with great reluctance and that only after I was sick for a week and did not show any signs of getting better.

As I sat delighting in the sea air at the window of my room overlooking the Aegean, Silas announced that the doctor was there waiting to see me.

"Come in," I grumbled.

Turning my gaze toward the door, I set my eyes on Luke for the first time.

"Pretty as a picture—the view from your window. If I had time I would sketch it."

"You are an artist as well as a doctor?"

He nodded. I surmised from the jovial way he greeted me that Silas told him of my aversion to physicians.

"Make yourself at home. I would be happy to have you paint here if you choose but I must confess, I am not eager for medical treatment."

He had a kind face with large gentle gray eyes that seemed to smile even when he was serious.

"I understand how you feel." he replied sympathetically, "but I do think I can help—if you will let me."

He was trying to coax and cajole me into letting him treat me the way doctors always do with petulant children. Suddenly, he pointed out the window.

"Look there is a stork starting to build a nest on your house. They say that is a good omen."

Glancing out the window, I spotted a huge bird flying by with its long red legs tucked up under its body. "I don't believe in omens. I'm not superstitious."

"Neither am I." Luke smiled at me.

We both broke out laughing.

"You are a Jew aren't you?" he inquired. It was obvious he loved people. "I have admired the Jewish people ever since I went to school in Athens."

He took the chair I offered him opposite where I was sitting.

"Of all the philosophies and religions that I encountered in Athens, I learned that only the Jews have a concept of holiness. It is very beautiful. I envy those of you who were born to your way of life. It has a moral beauty that no other religion has."

Beginning to get interested in my physician, I explained to him my reason for being in Troas.

"It is my mission to give the light of Israel to the whole world. The doors have been thrown open, the heart of the God of Israel is open for you and all the world to come in!"

Since he was attentive to what I told him about my mission, I pressed on hoping I could give him the light of Christ.

"God, himself, took on human flesh and invites all the peoples of the world to receive forgiveness of sins and eternal life."

As he listened, very tactfully he began to examine me and I was so engrossed in preaching to him, I made no protest. By the end of the medical examination, we were friends. I liked him. After giving me some medicine to take, he told me he would return the next day and that he might just bring his paints and sketch the view from my window while we had a long conversation about ethics and philosophy.

Luke came the next day as he had promised, and the next and the next. We became very close. Because he has a quiet mind that goes right to the quintessence of everything, his observations on the Graeco-Roman culture in which we live were of the greatest interest to me and were helping me to understand the culture of the people I wanted to convert.

"I have never found a faith I could embrace," he confided to me. "The ideals of Judaism appeal to me, but I feel that it is a religion only for Jews. And as for paganism, well, I don't see how a man in his right mind could worship an idol made of wood or stone. And the stoicism of the philosophers appears so cold and indifferent to me."

I had to agree with him on all counts. Judaism is for Jews and pagan religion and philosophy fail to satisfy the human heart.

"It seems preposterous that a man created with a spirit, a soul, and a mind and intelligence can prostrate himself before some statue made of inert materials and call it his god."

"Yes." He laid aside the sketch he was making. "I was in Ephesus and saw the temple to Diana. It is really a magnificent piece of architecture. Larger even than the Parthenon." Luke looked at me questioningly.

Reading his thoughts I replied, "No, I have never been to either Ephesus or Athens."

"Well," he continued, "I was curious, so I entered the temple of the famous Diana to see for myself. There was an altar and before it a statue of the goddess. Sometimes they have a veil hanging before the statue, but the day I was there I got a good look at it. She was made of wood, possibly cedar or beech, I could not tell. Her lower parts were wrapped up like those of an Egyptian mummy. She had the upper parts of a woman—that is the hands and face of a woman—and they were decorated with jewel-like bee's eggs or something made to look like bee's eggs.

"Bee's eggs? I knew practically nothing about the cult. "The bee is the symbol of Ephesus, isn't it?"

"Yes, you see, Diana is the Queen bee. Her priests are called drones and they dress like women. There are also a swarm of priestesses called Melissai, they are her worker bees."

"Quite a hive they have! They got Diana from the Greeks, didn't they? Don't the Greeks call her the goddess of the chase—hunting and so forth?"

"Exactly! In Ephesus they really do put on a tremendous show. You should see the dancers, acrobats, musicians and the athletic games that they stage in her honor." He touched his fingers to his forehead as if remembering.

"People come from all over for the festival. No one works for a month." Luke tossed his artist's quill on the table, looked steadily at me and concluded: "I was completely disgusted by the whole thing."

Everything he told me touched my soul deeply and set me to thinking, pondering it all as I sat there watching the ships passing by in the sea in front of our house.

"Someday I will go to Ephesus and declare war on Diana." Luke did not hear me. He was pursuing his own thoughts.

"When I was a student in Athens, I dabbled into the philosophies. They failed to satisfy. Philosophies change. Today one is fashionable—tomorrow another takes its place—the next day, still another."

"Jesus Christ never changes. He is always the same today as he was yesterday, and he will always be the same forever!"

Feeling the Holy Spirit leading me to bring Luke into the light of Christ, I waited for him to make some response to what I said. I prayed—the Spirit prayed within me. As I sat quietly biding my time, pretending to look out the window, all the time I was studying his face.

"Forever?" He sighed.

"Forever!"

"If you baptize me, do you mean to tell me, that I, Luke, would become the temple of the living God? That Jesus Christ would come live in me together with his Heavenly Father and his Holy Spirit?"

I could see that he had understood what I had been telling him these past days about the faith.

"Yes" I whispered waiting for the Holy Spirit to act in his soul.

"And someday—after death, I will know him even as I am known by him?

"Yes." My heart was praying.

"Paul, will—will—will you baptize me?" His voice was barely audible.

"Come!"

It was the Holy Spirit who invited him. I motioned and he followed me. We walked down to the water's edge and taking off our outer garments we stepped into the warm Aegian in our tunics. When I baptized Luke in the name of the Father and of the Son and of the Holy Spirit, it was one of the happiest events of my life.

After the divine life came into Luke, we became even closer friends and our minds shared a greater intimacy. I told him of how I had seen Christ on the Damascus road. I spoke to him of the beautiful mother of Jesus whom I hope to see one day soon in heaven. I know she will be praying for me at the hour of my death, as she promised.

I also plied him with questions about Macedonia, for his parents were living in Philippi. Finally I told him of a vision I had since my arrival in Troas in which I had seen a Macedonian standing before me pleading with me to come over into Macedonia to help his people.

Upon hearing this, Luke thought it was a great idea for me to go to Macedonia.

"I feel that our fellow Macedonians will receive and embrace Christ as completely and as quickly as I have."

"Christ wishes for me to leave for Macedonia soon."

I spoke with a touch of sadness, because I hated to say farewell to my son, friend, and physician. Since I was in the best of health, there was every reason for me to hurry on my way.

"You might get sick again, Paul. "You might have a relapse, old fellow. Perhaps I should just pack up and come with you to Macedonia.

I could introduce you to many people there and help get a church started."

Luke had truly found Christ Jesus and never more wanted to be separated from him.

"Silas! Timothy!" They came running to my call. "Pack your things. We are sailing to Macedonia and my good physician is coming along."

The ship sailed a straight course across the strong current that was racing to the Hellespont. Once freed from the cross currents we picked up speed. Then Samothrace loomed up out of the sea. On the far horizon, mountainous islands rose stark and brooding over the waters of the Aegean like sentinels on guard.

Luke, very happy to be going home once more, had traveled extensively and enjoyed sailing immensely. As we sat on the deck, we drew up our plans for the future. Since illness and disease are not common to any one geographic area, as we well know, Luke said he could practice medicine anywhere.

After we docked in Neapolis, a village poised on the rocky sea coast with towering mountains behind it, we took the Via Egnatia and headed for Philippi, nine miles distant but separated from Neapolis by Mount Symbolum of the Pangean range, famous for its silver mines, one of which, Luke explained, his family owned. When we reached the summit of Mount Symbolum and stood looking down to the plane about seventeen hundred feet below, Luke announced with a trace of pride in his voice, "Philippi!"

It was an impressive city, named after its founder Philip II of Macedon. After Macedonia was conquered it became subject to Roman rule and eventually became a Roman colony, subject to Roman law. The Via Egnatia led us right through the center of the city where not far from the forum, we stopped at a imposing house of large proportions—the home of Luke's parents. They welcomed us heartily and made us very comfortable—too comfortable. I was glad when a few days later we baptized a woman called Lydia, who invited us to share her more modest dwelling.

Because there was no synagogue in Philippi, when Shabbat came, I asked Luke to take us to a place that would be conducive to prayer. He took us to the river that flowed about a mile north of the city where there was a tranquil place that had much to recommend it. Apparently the pagans used it as a place to pray for there was a large group of women praying on the banks of the river, when we approached. A ready-made congregation, I said to myself, as I hurried to make our arrival on the scene known to them. I wasn't going to miss a chance like that to preach the gospel.

At the close of my sermon, when I said that any one who wished to embrace faith in Jesus Christ should come forward and be baptized, Lydia came at once, visibly moved by the Holy Spirit. After we baptized her, other women began to follow her into the water. The church of Philippi was born.

We had nothing to fear from our usual Jewish persecutors in Philippi, for as I said there was no synagogue in that city. There seemed to be no possibility of trouble of any kind. At least so I thought. I was mistaken—terribly mistaken.

I experienced suffering and shameful treatment at Philippi. Amid much anxiety, I preached the gospel to them. So eager were they to receive truth and light, I would gladly have imparted to them not only the gospel, but also my very soul.

When we came to Macedonia we had no rest. We had troubles on every side—conflicts without—anxieties within. I believe that the Lord sent us Apostles forth as men doomed to death! I myself have been made a spectacle to the world—to both angels and men. I am a fool for Christ with no honor of my own. To this very hour, I hunger and thirst and am beaten around and have no fixed home. Working with my hands, I am reviled and I bless. Persecuted and maligned, I bear it all. I have become like the trash or junk of this world—even up till the present moment.

The trouble in Macedonia started so innocently. As I was walking from Lydia's house down the Via Egnatia with Silas, Luke, and Timothy on the way to the river to preach, I saw a very unfortunate child. She appeared to be, I would say, about twelve years old. She might have been older because her body was thin and undernourished. As soon as I saw her, I was moved with pity. Because something was wrong with her mind, she babbled incoherently, for the most part. Occasionally, she would say something rational. Her master, who was leading her on a chain, yelled for everyone to hear that the child was a soothsayer—an oracle—a teller of fortunes. For a fee he would interpret her babbling to any one who would ask her a question. With all the money he was making from the crowd they drew, it seemed he at least could have afforded to buy her some sandals for her feet that were bleeding from walking barefoot on the stone streets. The child reminded me of the people Christ healed of devils that possessed them. It grieved me to see that she bore many scars and bruises on her frail body. When her master struck her, if she failed to answer any question asked her, I shuddered with compassion.

The child must have noticed me the day I passed her in the street. Perhaps the way I looked at her attracted her to me. I don't know what it was that drew her to me, but one day when I unwittingly passed by the house where she lived with her master, she came running from the house and stood in the middle of the street staring at me. Turning toward her, I waited for her to approach me.

"Who are you?" she asked with a vacant stare in her eyes.

"We are servants of God on high and are announcing his way of salvation to the people of Philippi," I answered.

Satisfied by my answer, she smiled at me—a silly half-witted smile and picked up her heels and ran into the house. The next day she followed us again for a short distance. The following day she accompanied us as far as the river. It became a daily occurrence. She would trail behind us singing in a monotone that was very disconcerting to me, "These men are servants of God on high announcing his way of salvation to the people of Philippi."

Grieved by the pitiful state of this child, I became more and more convinced that she was in fact possessed by a devil. When I felt the inspiration of the Holy Spirit within me leading me to cast out that devil, I said with authority, "In the name of Jesus Christ I order you to come out of her." Immediately the unclean spirit vanished. As Christ healed the demoniac in the country of the Gerasenes, he healed the demoniac child in Philippi.

As an oracle she was finished. Since she no longer raved, her usefulness to her master was at an end. Because the avaricious people who owned her—she was a slave—could no longer exploit her, their wrath descended on me for her healing came through my ministry.

One day when I was preaching at the river, I saw her master and another giant of a man heading towards me. Sensing danger, I called to Luke. "Take Timothy and go. Here comes trouble and I don't want the boy Timothy to be involved."

It was a command and Luke obeyed. Silas stayed with me, determined that we would face any trouble that might befall us together. Because I did not wish to cause a big disturbance in front of the people I was in the act of preaching to and risk losing their confidence and respect, when the girl's master insisted that we accompany him to appear before the magistrate, we went. We had done no wrong and I felt certain that as Roman citizens Silas and I would vindicate ourselves.

As it turned out, the magistrate was just as annoyed by the whole affair as we were. He resented being disturbed and twisted anxiously in his chair and asked, "What is the charge?"

The master of the slave girl leapt to the attack.

"These men are making a great disturbance in our city. They are Jews and they are advocating practices which it against the law for us to adopt since we are under Roman law." He sneered at me contemptuously. I could see he was out for blood.

We must have been a terrible sight. We were wearing Jewish garments for they were more suitable for baptizing and we were soaking wet. A crowd began to gather in the market place to see what was going on. People are always ready to enjoy some amusement at someone else's expenses. The magistrate, a petty Roman official, was obviously anxious to be finished with us. Without interest, he inquired, "Are you trying to convince our people to abandon the worship of our beloved Emperor Claudius for your religion?"

"I heard him myself," howled the slave girl's master. Raising his fist menacingly, a Roman soldier standing at arms length from me yelled, "He is a traitor to our Emperor!"

"Traitor!" The crowd took up the cry.

Philippi, a Roman colony founded by the legions of Anthony and Octavius to celebrate their victory over the armies of Brutus and Cassius less than one hundred years before, was pledged to uphold the Roman way of life, as the seat of the Roman government. When the magistrate heard that we were indeed trying to convert the people, he came bounding toward Silas and me and violently ripped our robes from our backs. Screaming with delight at the show, the crowd went mad, making so much noise that no one could hear us yelling that we were citizens of Rome. They flogged me right there on the spot, beating Silas and me with rods. Gleefully the old Roman soldiers, the veterans who had nothing better to do, counted out my stripes. Christ was being scourged at the pillar once more by the authority of Rome. They beat me mercilessly. In a sea of pain that reached from head to feet, I fell limp and lost consciousness. I still bear the scars on my body of that flogging.

When I awoke I found myself in prison. Silas was with me and he had already rallied for he is stronger and bigger than I. When the jailor saw that I was regaining consciousness he put my feet in the stocks as he had already done to Silas. Silas—wonderful Silas! He was singing. He had found joy in suffering for Christ. Joyfully he cried out, "Sing, Paul, sing with me a new song unto the Lord."

Rejoicing that I had chosen him to accompany me, I responded with the next line of the psalm which we finished singing together. Without intending to do so, we attracted the attention of all the prisoners in the Philippi city jail. About two dozen of them were pushing around us, gaping at us and making wild guesses about our identity. Looking into their faces, I saw only an audience I could preach to about life in Christ.

"You are a fool," a tall lank herdsman flung at me.

He had probably been jailed for stealing someone else's sheep. Slowly I cast my eyes on the herdsman. The fisherman in me was delighted. I had a big fish on my line and I was determined to reel him in.

"Yes," I agreed with him pleasantly, "I am a fool. I am a fool for Christ," my eyes burned their way into his soul. "Christ's love for me brought him to what you Gentiles call the folly of the cross. He loved me so much that he allowed the Roman soldiers to scourge him until he almost dropped dead."

I surveyed the rest of the prisoners. My eyes came to rest on a boy who looked to be about fifteen.

"Why are you here, son?"

"I stole a loaf of bread." His eyes avoided mine.

"And you, old fellow," I called to a gnarled old man leaning on a cane. "Why are you here?"

Scratching his chin under his thick white beard and looking at me curiously, he replied he couldn't pay a debt he owed. "Look!" He thrust out his hands that were all twisted and bony, "my hands won't work any more and I can't make sandals. I can't pay my bills." In despair he flung his hands behind his back.

I looked into all the faces and souls that surrounded me. They all shared the same despair.

"Pray with us," I invited them all. "What have you to lose? Nothing but the bondage of your sins."

"The only thing I am willing to pray for," sneered the tall lank herdsman contemptuously as he spat on the floor, "would be for the doors of this prison to fly open and set us free. Since I know they aren't going to do any such thing, I won't pray." He looked at me defiantly.

The gnarled old sandal-maker sighed deeply. "I'll pray with you for that.

"Good," I replied, we will pray for just that—for the doors of the jail to fly open." I shot a glance at the herdsman, "Will you believe in Jesus Christ if the doors fly open?" I asked.

"Let's see what happens. I'll decide then." He shrugged his shoulders and spat again on the floor.

"I will believe in him," the boy decided, "if he opens the doors."

Murmuring, the rest of the prisoners were making their decisions about what they would do if the doors of the jail flew open. Many souls were at stake. I knew what I had to do. Nodding to Silas to do likewise, I knelt to pray.

"Anyone like to lay a bet on this?" scorned the herdsman.

In a few minutes the jail began to shake. The arrogant look vanished from the herdsman's face when he had to sit to keep from falling down, because the jail was shaking so violently.

"The whole earth is trembling!" screamed the old man. "It will swallow us up!"

"Make it stop!" the other prisoners joined. "Stop it!"

The shaking ceased. Everyone in the jail, including the herdsman, was on his knees.

"Look," shouted Silas. "Look! The door of our prison has flown open. It really and truly has!"

The stocks had fallen from my legs and I noticed that Silas was also free.

"My chains have pulled lose from the wall!" The herdsman was elated. As he rushed toward the open door, I jumped in front of him. I couldn't let him get away until he heard about Christ.

"Wait," I yelled blocking his way. "The Lord Jesus has freed you from your chains now let him free you from your sins. Then you will be truly free."

Silas was helping me block the doorway.

"In your Greek religions you speak of Nemesis and Erinyes," I continued," who are what you call your goddess of justice and the avenging spirit. Your religion teaches you that they will pursue and punish you even if you do run away from this prison. You have done evil and it will weigh heavily on you no matter where you go." I saw that I had aroused his interest and that of the others as well.

"Nemesis and Erinyes are your conscience. They will speak to you of your sins until you die or go mad running from them. Let Jesus make you really free. He can take away your sins just as easily as your chains." Suddenly I was interrupted by a high-pitched shrill scream that pierced the night like a sword.

"By Jupiter, come back!" It was the jailer. "They will kill me if you don't. Come back!"

Turning around I saw his sword gleaming in the moonlight. In horror I realized that he was just on the point of running it through his belly.

"Stop!" I commanded. "We are here." Because he thought we were gone, he had decided to take his own life. "Don't harm yourself. We are all here."

"Light! Light!" he called. His wife came running with an oil lamp. Seeing that we were indeed all still here, he threw himself at my feet. On his knees before me he said, "You could have escaped and you did not. I heard you speak of Christ. I heard you pray for the doors to fly open. Open they are. Yet you are still here." He began to tremble. Suddenly he asked, "What must I do to be saved?"

"Believe in the Lord Jesus."

"I do believe. I've seen what he can do with my own eyes."

"Then let us baptize you and make a Christian of you." Silas spoke up. He was grimacing so great was the pain from the wounds on his back–the open cuts and welts that the lictors of Philippi had given him. My own robes were glued to the bloody stripes on my back. I thought of how the soldiers had ripped Christ's robe from him after he was scourged, shuddering at the thought of it. The skin must have come of his back when they tore his robe to prepare him for the cross. I was hoping for water to soak my robe off.

"We need water for the baptism to wash away your sins."

"Come, my house is adjoining the jail."

Silas and I promised the other prisoners that we would return to them. Closing the door of the cell behind us, we followed the jailer to his house. When we entered, his wife was still trying to comfort their four children who were frightened by the earthquake.

"Helen," he called "Bring water." Looking compassionately at Silas and me he added, "I will wash your wounds, sirs."

A motherly looking Helen came back. "Is this enough water, Alexander?" She set the basin on the table.

"We will need more later." He poured the water on my back. It stung as if it had been wine. Helen returned bringing two of Alexander's tunics under her arm. In exchange for them she took our bloodstained clothing that she promised to wash. Quietly we talked to Alexander answering all his questions about Christ and the new life he bestows on all who believe in him. When he finally ran out of questions I said to him,

"Alexander, you washed me. Are you ready for me to wash you in the waters of baptism?"

By the flickering light of the oil lamp on the center of the table, I could see his face as he replied eagerly, "I am ready. I desire it for my entire family—wife and children. Baptize us all at once."

"Can we go now and take the children to the river?" I asked.

"We must go to the river?" I could see that he was bewildered.

"I will immerse you in the waters of the river three times. When you come forth you will be a new man in Christ Jesus. The old Alexander will die–die to sin, and the new Alexander will emerge to walk in newness of life. Christ will come into your soul and you will belong to Him."

He listened very attentively to every word I spoke. A look of dejection swept over him. With sadness in his voice he asked, "How can we pass through the city gates? They will be closed for the night." He threw up his hands in despair. If we don' t go tonight I'm afraid we won't have another chance."

After thinking about the matter for a few moments, I looked at Silas who was seated in the corner and I perceived he had the same idea as I.

"Look, Alexander, I am sure an earthquake as severe as the one we just had has broken open the city gates." I felt positive of this.

Joyfully Alexander sent his wife to bring the children. Silas carried one of the little ones—a boy of about six years old—in his arms very paternally out through the streets of Philippi. I carried a sleepy-headed little fellow with black curly hair who nestled snugly in my arms as we made our way towards the city gates. The mother, Helen, followed behind with the two year old Alexander in her arms. When we got to the city wall it was just as I expected. The severity of the earthquake had toppled large sections of the wall so that we had no trouble leaving the city. When we reached the riverbank, I tickled the little sleepy head under his chin. Softly I called his name. "Alcibides, wake up, little one." The child smiled up at me. "We are going in the water to get cooled off a bit." The night was hot. Children naturally love water and Alcibides was no exception.

After we splashed in the water a few minutes, and I saw that I had won his confidence, I baptized him. Silas did the same with the child he had carried. Then we baptized the rest of them. They were a beautiful Christian family, I thought to myself as we sat on the riverbank quietly talking into the night.

"What shall we do now that we are Christians?" asked Alexander bouncing his two-year-old son on his knee.

"Love one another—walk in love. Walk in love and you will walk straight into heaven."

I could hear the frogs croaking in the water. The moon came out from behind a cloud and in the moonlight I watched the older child as he was playing at the water's edge. Little Alcibides, growing restless in his father's arms, tugged at my sleeve begging me to pick him up. I did so and pressed him to my heart because he was now the temple of the Father, the Son and the Holy Spirit whom I serve and adore. I adored Christ present in the pure souls of these Philippians fresh from the waters of baptism and I gave thanks that Christ called me to be an instrument of his grace and truth. I rejoiced that I could live yet another day to give him to more souls. One day I knew my enemies—his enemies would succeed in putting me to death.

We returned to the prison where I spent the rest of the night preaching to the unfortunate people detained there. It is hard, very hard for a Jew who has known the God of Abraham, Isaac, and Jacob all his life to understand the depravity of the Gentiles. Having been reared in Tarsus, I had had a glimpse of the amoral way of life of the Gentiles that a Jew from Jerusalem would never have had. They are a depraved and perverse generation who walk in futility with their understanding clouded in darkness. They are estranged from the life of God through the ignorance that is in them and the blindness of their hearts, because they have yielded to despair and sensuality, doing things, which are shameful even to mention.

Since the beginning of creation of the world, God's invisible attributes are clearly to be seen, because the things he has made reveal his everlasting goodness and power. As the psalmist says, "The heavens speak of God's glory and the firmament shows forth his handiwork."

Although they knew God, the Gentiles did not glorify him or give him thanks, but became arrogant intellectually and their minds have been darkened and while they claim to be wise with their philosophies, they have become fools. They substitute images made like men and beasts for the glory of the living God. They worship money and gold and creatures, rather than the creator. For this reason, God has left them to wallow in the hedonistic desires of their hearts so that they do dishonorable things.

Preaching all night to the prisoners of Philippi, I brought to mind their hidden sins until they were ready to open their hearts to let the poison flow out. The light of dawn was filtering through the bars of the prison when Alexander came to me. Joy sparkled in his eyes and with a smile he informed me, "The magistrates have sent word that you are to be released." He motioned to me to walk out the open door. "Go in peace."

Blessing Alexander with my outstretched hand, I told him, "It isn't going to be as easy as that. Silvanus—Silas, as I call him, and I—we are both citizens of Rome. We were publicly beaten and without a trial, although we are Romans. We were thrown in jail and now they plan to put us out secretly?" I waited while a look of astonishment registered on his face, before continuing. "By no means!" I answered my own question. As I made myself comfortable in a corner of the jail, I told him, "I shall wait for them. Now, Alexander" I commanded, "run and ask them if they will make mockery of our great Roman laws."

I couldn't help but laugh as Alexander ran in confusion to do what I asked. Within half an hour, the head magistrate walked in the jail. He was the fellow who was so impatient to get us out of his way when we appeared before him. I eyed him closely and demanded, "Is this the way you treat Roman citizens?"

Everyone in the jail was delighted to see the magistrate squirm as his face reddened. Stammering he said, "It was a—regrettable—mistake. If you would just let me—"

"If news of this were to reach Rome—" I goaded him.

He interrupted me, "What do you want me to do?" I could see that he was very nervous and was willing to appease me.

" Exonerate me publicly in the forum." I wanted my Christian converts to see their spiritual father victorious in this conflict with the magistrate of their city.

Wringing his hands, the magistrate considered what I asked of him. Finally he said, "I'll do what you ask, if you leave Philippi in peace."

"For the time being, I shall leave. Only for the time being."

Philippi was a triumph that cost me dearly. With my nerves still on edge from the beating I received, Silas and I returned to Lydia's house, thankful to be reunited once more to Timothy and Luke who treated my wounds.

The Lord in his Providence sent me persecution, but he also sent me a doctor to bind up my stripes. Luke was a great blessing to me always knowing how to soothe my agitated spirit as well as my physical distress. A dear companion—gentle friend—to whom I can reveal the anxieties of my soul, Luke gives me encouragement when I need it most. I am especially thankful that of all the men I have known he is the one God chose to share my final imprisonment with me. Even now it is a comfort to me to look across this prison cell, here in Rome, and see him sleeping as I listen to the wind moaning in the night, recalling all these things that happened to us for the sake of Jesus' Name.

Timothy was profoundly grieved when he saw what the lictors had done to me with their lashes.

"Dear Father Paul," he said with deep sincerity, "you should have let me go to the magistrate instead of you. You should have been the one to go with Luke to safety. I am young and can bear it easier than you. I should have been beaten. I am young and can bear it easier than you." His wide brown eyes were troubled.

"It is because of your youth that I had you sent to Lydia's house when I saw trouble afoot." I rumpled his hair roughly with my hands, scowled at him, and said, "I'm not as old as you seem to think."

"I am not a coward." I could see he was perplexed.

"No, my son, you are not a coward. It is not time for you to suffer for the gospel as I do. I am forming Christ in you. When I am killed for preaching the gospel,"—I glanced at him to see the effect of these words on him.

He shook his head. "Never! Never, Father Paul." There was sorrow on his face.

Remembering the reaction of the apostles when Christ spoke to them of his approaching death, I asked him gently, "Would you deprive me of the favor of suffering for Jesus?"

Not knowing how to answer, he kept silent.

"Timothy, you will be a great minister of Christ some day. Maybe sooner than you think. When I see that you are ready, I will lay my hands on you and make you a priest of Jesus Christ. Would you like that?"

"My Father in Christ," Timothy answered, "I was afraid to ask you for that grace. I want to be a priest more than anything else I have ever wanted in my entire life. Perhaps then, I too, shall be worthy to suffer for the name of Jesus as you do." His eyes were shining with faith, hope, and love. How wonderful it is to have a son—a spiritual son like Timothy! With joy in my heart, I asked, "You truly understand that it is a great joy to suffer for him?"

He nodded. My heart was brimful with happiness, because God had given me a son with mind, heart, and a soul like mine. I saw myself in him. He reminded me of myself when I was twenty. Furthermore, I saw in him the making of a great priest of God. The time for me to lay my hands on him was to be sooner than I had anticipated.

We left a healthy church in Philippi and traveled to Thessalonica some seventy miles distant over steep mountainous terrain. For three Sabbaths I preached in the synagogue in Thessalonica, converting a number of Jews and very many Gentiles. Because of our success we brought the wrath of the rulers of the synagogue down upon us, causing them to hire certain loafers of the town and paying them to cause an uproar against us. What they did was this. They accused us before the magistrates of setting up another king against Caesar—King Jesus. We had no choice but to leave.

Next we went to Berea on the banks of the Astraeus where we discovered the first synagogue that did not persecute us. Instead the Jews of this city received the word of God and relished it, making it possible for us to establish a lively community of Christians comprised of both Jews and Gentiles. There wasn't a single dark cloud on our horizon in Berea, but one blew in from Thessalonica when the Jews from that city pursued us to Berea and began causing trouble. Once more we had to move on, but not before a church was well established.

Until this time I had sheltered Timothy. Now I was faced with a grave decision. Having been forced to leave the new founded church in Thessalonica prematurely, I felt that I ran out on them just when they were being born to the faith and needed strengthening. I decided to send them Silas and Timothy. I called Timothy aside.

"Are you ready to have me lay my hands on you and make you a priest forever?" I scrutinized his face looking for an answer.

Without a moment's hesitation he replied, "Yes, Father Paul. In the depths of my soul, I believe, in all truth that I am ready."

He knelt before me. Certain that I was doing God's will, I laid my hands on him. He arose a priest of the living God. Then I explained to him what I had planned.

"Luke and I are going to Athens. You and Silas will go to Thessalonica. Stay away from the synagogue," I cautioned. "I don't want you persecuted. Preach only to our converts and do it quietly. I want you to live to join me in Corinth."

Part of my soul left me when I said farewell to Timothy. I didn't want to go to Athens. Macedonia was the territory I wanted to harvest. The Christians of Berea arranged passage for Luke and me on a vessel sailing for Athens and so reluctantly we were on our way to "the glory of Greece."

With the ship rocking gently in the summer sun, the emerald green waters of the sea blending with the cerulean blue of the mountains were refreshing to my tired spirit. It was good to rest—to retire from the land and all its problems.

Our ship, a freighter, carrying a cargo of silver from Macedonia to Rome, skirted the Macedonian coast, darting in and out of the jagged rocks that jutted from the sea fashioning islands that resembled bastioned fortresses. I gave myself up to the sun and the sea, relaxing on the deck, praying and dreaming of future conquests. We passed Marathon and drew near to Sunium. Before long Luke was directing my gaze across the horizon.

"Soon you will get your first glimpse of Athens," he said with enthusiasm. When we drew nearer, he exclaimed, "See the sun flashing on the golden tip of Athena's spear over the Acropolis." He was excited and so was I.

"That statue of Athena Promachos is seventy feet tall. Although I don't care for the pagan religions, I find their art and architecture superb."

I had to agree with that. We Jews had never developed architecture worthy of the name. When we docked at the Piraeus, Athens was clearly visible five miles away down the straight walled road. Once inside the city, I remarked to Luke that I had never before seen so much marble in my entire life. Nor had I ever seen so many altars to idols in one place before. When I commented on the great number of pagan altars, Luke explained to me that once there had been a plague in Athens and the Athenians erected altars to each and every god to try to propitiate them all to end the plague that was decimating the city. After having erected altars to all their gods and the plague still raged on, they began erecting altars marked "to the unknown god."

I did not like Athens. I was exasperated to see how the city was given to idolatry and the vain philosophies of this world. I met all kinds of philosophers—Epicureans, Stoics, Platonists, Peripatetics. When I mounted the Areopagus and preached to them of the living God and of life, and faith, hope, and love, they just sneered at me displaying unbridled contempt.

Although Luke would have like to stay longer in Athens, I insisted we begin our return to Macedonia, because I could not forget Timothy and my other spiritual children. Even though Luke had many friends in Athens that he had not seen since his school days, he nevertheless agreed at once to what I proposed. Together we headed towards Corinth, where we were supposed to reunite with Timothy and Silas when they accomplished the work I sent them to do in Thessalonica.

CHAPTER 4

Summer was ripening into autumn with the fields of grain turning golden under warm and sunny skies. Everywhere along the Corinth road, vineyards were bending low with sweet purple grapes. If I were going to return to Macedonia, I would have to go before winter. Bad weather would close the treacherous mountain passes on the road that wound over rocky terrain with cliffs that plunged as much as a thousand feet straight down to the sea. In a couple months all shipping would come to a standstill with the great sea vessels putting up in various harbors until spring. On my way north, I decided to visit Corinth, a great trading center—the crossroads of the world, located as it is on the main shipping lanes from East to West and North to South. Situated as it is by the narrow isthmus with a harbor on either side, commerce flourished until Corinth became one of the richest cities of the world. Because, it was also one of the most materialistic and wicked cities, I felt that it would be far easier to preach the gospel in Corinth to sinners than it was to sophisticated philosophers and aesthetes such as I had met in Athens.

When we left Athens, they were preparing for the annual Eleusian mysteries. I knew nothing at all about them. As the road we were traveling northward drew nearer to Eleusis, I began to question Luke.

"I know very little about the Eleusian mysteries. I would never join a religion that is sworn to secrecy, because I could never enter blindly into any society in which I had to make vows to keep secret things that I would later learn. Does that make sense to you?" Luke asked as our caravan wound its way along the seacoast.

The road was hot and dusty. A sea gull was flying over our heads making the peculiar chirping noise that only they can make.

"Yes, by all means," I replied.

"I would never embrace a religion being ignorant of what I was embracing." I blew the dust off my toga that had collected on it as we traveled.

"I do know, however, that it has something to do with the worship of Demeter—the goddess of fertility and marriage—and Persephone, the goddess of the underworld. This very road is the one the candidates for initiation follow on Boedromion the fourteenth every year."

"Where do they go?"

"All the way to Athens—by the light of the full moon with torches. The priests of the Eleusian mysteries carry with them their sacred things—whatever they might be," Luke said with derision. "They take them to the Acropolis. A couple days later the candidates purify themselves by bathing in the sea. Then they sacrifice pigs."

"Pigs? Horrible filthy creatures!"

"They wind up the celebration with a grand parade back to Eleusis."

"What do you think they do in the initiation?" I asked chasing away a fly that kept buzzing around my face.

"It is hard to say," Luke said thoughtfully. No one has ever violated their secrecy, as far as I know. Some people think they lead the candidates though dark subterranean passages and frighten them with symbolic apparitions which they devise and finally bring them back out into the light of day."

"Strange business. What kinds of people are attracted to that sort of religion?" I was curious.

"Plato was one of them. So was Cicero."

I offered up a silent prayer of thanksgiving that I had been born to Jewish parents. The city of Corinth came into view shining white and gleaming across the dazzling turquoise of the gulf where the harbor was filled with ships that one would have thought it impossible to maneuver in and out of the port. As we crossed the isthmus I saw a very strange sight. A ship was hoisted up on the land in the port of Lechaeon on the Gulf of Corinth and was put on rollers and taken across the isthmus to the Cenchreae harbor on the Saronic Gulf.

"Why don't they dig a canal?" I asked Luke who was watching the transfer of the ship from one harbor to the other with great interest.

"They have tried it many times, but for some reason it has always been abandoned."

Since my imprisonment here in Rome I learned that just last year Nero went to Corinth, determined to have a canal put though the isthmus. I hear it was quite a performance he gave. They say he stood on the isthmus, took up his lyre and sang an ode to Neptune and Amphitrite. With a golden spade, I was told, he broke ground for the canal with a musical accompaniment. He then proceeded to make a tedious speech to the laborers—six thousand of whom were Jews captured by Titus Flavius Sabinus Vespasian in Galilee. But already I have been told Nero, too, has given up the project, leaving the abandoned canal dug part way across the narrow isthmus.

Corinth is truly beautiful. There is no other city like her with the Acrocorinth behind her rising up two thousand feet above the sea. However I soon learned that the mountain was not all beauty. On the top there is an iniquitous temple of Venus Aphrodite that boasts of one thousand priestesses dedicated to the goddess of sensual love. What they did on that mountain I did not even care to consider. They were hierodules, temple slaves engaged in ritual prostitution.

Once inside the city we saw the famous fountain of Pirene. As I observed women drawing water from its open marble basin, I thought of the Samaritan woman with five husbands that Jesus encountered at the well. From what I heard Corinth had its share of women like that. Jesus confided to the Samaritan woman at the well that he is the Messiah and thirsted for her soul. I would give the Messiah to Corinth.

In entering Corinth, we passed many pagan temples. These places always make me shudder. We saw the odium, the amphitheater, the basilica of the Roman proconsul, and finally, we located the Jewish synagogue. In the shops that we passed, we noticed an exotic collection of merchandise for sale.

Using the money the Macedonian Christians gave us before our hasty departure, we rented a house in one of the more modest sections of the city. As I paid our rent, I looked at the coins carefully for the first time. They bore the image of Claudius on one side. On the reverse there was a triumphal arch with "De Britt" inscribed on it to commemorate Claudius' jubilant invasion of Britain. When we were still in Antioch, I heard that he had even taken the name Britannicus to commemorate his capture of those far away people. Perhaps someday I would get to Britain.

The following Sabbath I went to the synagogue where I preached the name of Jesus to the Jews, carefully so as not to drive them to fury and expel me before I had a chance to get a good hearing. As providence would have it, a man who was listening to me preach followed me when I left the synagogue. He was a very distinguished looking Jew, cultured, with the language of an educated man.

"Excuse me," he began, "I am also a Christian and I would like to invite you to come to my home and explain certain thing about the faith to me."

"There are Christians in Corinth?" I was astonished. I observed him closely. He was middle aged, graying at the temples, well dressed and his manners were impeccable.

"I have only recently come to Corinth. I don't know too much about it. My name is Aquila. I just came here a short time ago from Rome. Claudius made an ordinance that all Jews had to leave Rome because of the agitation that was being caused in his city by the Jews over a fellow Jew named Jesus." Aquila shrugged his shoulders in resignation.

"That is news! You mean the Christians in Rome have caused so much stir that the Jews have been forced to leave?" We were walking towards his home.

"Exactly. My wife is a Latin speaking Roman of an old noble patrician family of high position. I had a very successful weaving and tent making business in Rome. We had to sell everything and leave." He sighed.

"I know what it is to suffer for Christ," I showed him the scars I bear from being stoned and lashed.

"I have not yet had to shed my blood but if things get any worse in Rome than they are now…"

I interrupted him. "Who is running the church in Rome?" My mind was already guessing.

"Peter, The Apostle Peter…a giant of a man. How the Christians of Rome love him! He came frequently to our home. He is the one that baptized Priscilla and me." Aquila looked at me with increased interest and inquired, "You know him?" He pointed to a house just ahead.

"We are home."

"Yes, I know him." Right then I had a strong desire to board the next ship and head for Rome. If it hadn't been for the work that still remained for me to do where I was, I would have done just that.

In the atrium of Aquila's home, a charming woman whom he introduced to me as his wife greeted us.

"Priscilla," Aquila said with enthusiasm, "God directed us to Corinth. I am certain of it now. We have an apostle here—a friend of the Apostle Peter." Aquila beckoned to her. Although her dress was of very fine linen, she was a picture of Christian modesty and restraint. Welcoming me cordially, she asked if I would celebrate the Holy Sacrifice in their home.

I nodded. It was good to have a flock even if it only consisted of two sheep."

"It is quite a coincidence. My family business in Tarsus was the same as yours. The Cilician goat hair is unsurpassed." It was truly providential that they had come to Corinth.

"We came here, "explained Aquila," because we decided we could make a good business manufacturing sails for the large number of ships that winter in the harbors of Corinth where they outfit themselves annually."

"An excellent idea. Perhaps we could work on it together," I ventured.

The money the Macedonians had given me would run out and I was opposed to taking money from the community in which I currently was living, until I was ready to depart. Then I would permit them to give to me a collection to send me on my way.

"It sounds like a good idea." Aquila quickly agreed. "I don't plan to invest too deeply until I see how the market is and how we like Corinth. I considered Ephesus also. It is an excellent place for someone in my business." I observed his hands that lay open on his lap. They both bore weaver's callouses.

"I know the business inside and out. I can even do the weaving that we hired laborers to do," I offered.

"I, too, can weave a good fabric. I have even taught my wife how to operate the looms. It is always good to know how to support one's self."

Already, I was growing to like Aquila. In time we were to become very good friends.

I had come to Corinth with little confidence, because of the persecution of the Macedonians, combined with the sneering contempt of the Athenians. I had not planned to stay long in Corinth; providence chose otherwise.

Winter came and with it much snow. Because Timothy and Silas had not arrived and the roads were impassable, I had no choice but to stay in Corinth and wait for them to come in the spring.

Luke and I lived that winter in the home of Aquila and Priscilla. I busied myself preaching in the synagogue every Sabbath. On weekdays I wove sailcloth. Luke set up his medical practice. From all our contacts with the Corinthians, we slowly began to establish a Christian community.

The households of Artemis and Apollos were the first fruits of Achaia. I baptized the former with my own hands. Luke baptized Apollos and his entire household. I continued preaching in the synagogue as long as I could. As a result, the head of the synagogue sought me out and I baptized him. When he—his name was Crispus—became a Christian many of his friends followed him into the church, causing a tremendous fury in the synagogue. The last time I entered the synagogue, the incensed unbelievers rose up screaming, blaspheming the name of Jesus. I shook the dust from my feet, left their synagogue and never entered it again.

One of my converts, Zenas, opened the doors of his home to the growing church. Although we stayed away from the synagogue and all unbelieving Jews, I was afraid that they might begin to persecute us at any moment. In the dead of winter, it would have been exceedingly difficult for me to flee. The Lord reassured me. One night as I was praying in my room alone after the house was silent, I was absorbed in the nearness of God. I adored him present within me and his love inundated me like the giant rolling breakers of the sea washing on the coast. I was submerged in his love as he spoke to me in the depths of my spirit, telling me not to be afraid. He told me to speak and not keep silent, that no one would harm me in Corinth and that he had many people in the city. He refreshed my soul, gave peace to my troubled mind. Because of the assurance he gave me, I relaxed and ministered to my growing flock. Later I would face persecution again, but for the time being it was God's will for me to have rest and tranquility and I was thankful for it.

Spring came as it always does and with the spring came Timothy and Silas. I was proud of my son Timothy. Although he was maturing, it amused me to notice that he was imitating my own peculiar mannerisms.

"Father Paul," he radiated enthusiasm, "our converts in Thessalonica are faithful and true to Christ in the face of grave persecution. They speak of you all the time and want you to come back to see them. They especially want you to explain to them about the second coming of Christ."

"Timothy I am certain that what you told them is true and right, but I shall write them a letter and expound this teaching for them, but as for our immediate plans…"I paused and they both looked at me expectantly.

"Yes, Father Paul, what are we going to do? Timothy asked.

Aquila who overheard the conversation from the next room stuck his head in the open door and repeated Timothy's question

"Yes, Father Paul, what are we going to do?"

I knew that Aquila was with me in whatever project I had in mind. I grinned at him

"Ephesus—we are going to Ephesus. I want to go to give the light of Christ to the Ephesians who live in great darkness with their Asiatic goddess." I was confident that Aquila would accompany me to declare war on Diana. I observed him closely to see his reactions.

Quietly he remarked, "Priscilla and I will be of great help in building up the church in Ephesus.

"Glad to have you with us!"

We sailed as soon as we could get things ready. As our ship pulled into the harbor at Ephesus, the first thing I set eyes on was the temple of Diana that was outside the city walls on the banks of the sea. Right then and there I had a vision of it toppling—falling. I saw its marble pillars lying on the ground until they sank into the marshy earth. I could see them covered with water, deep water on which floated lilies. I could hear hundreds of frogs singing a funereal dirge to the fallen dead Diana.

Aquila found a house—a beautiful place—in the best part of Ephesus. Priscilla set herself to the task of making it into a home. The synagogue received me well and I preached with fervor, but I was restless and unable to settle down to the conversion of the Ephesians, because I felt suddenly compelled to go to Palestine. I simply had to go to Jerusalem.

Promising the Ephesians to return to them, I set out for Jerusalem, intending to keep my visit there as unobtrusive as possible. I had no desire to antagonize the high priests and the government authorities for there was still much work left for me to do.

Seventeen years had gone by since the day I set out for Damascus and encountered the Lord on the road to that city. Because I had changed physically in those years as well as spiritually, I was confident no one would recognize me, even if they still remembered me at all. I wanted to see my sister, Rachel, who had married a wealthy merchant and a member of the Sanhedrin. They were rearing their family in the shadow of the temple. It had been twenty years since I had last seen my sister. When I visited Tarsus, she was in Alexandria. Now I was sure she would not recognize me at all.

A young boy about fourteen answered the door of her home when I arrived. He looked very much like my father.

"Your mother—is she at home, David?" I ventured.

"How did you know my name?" the lad answered not paying attention to my question.

"I just guessed. You look like someone I used to know and his name was David."

Suddenly Rachel appeared a doorway at the other end of the room. Because she did not know who I was, to save her embarrassment I said, "My dear sister, you look just like Mother."

"Saul? Saul! It is you!" She came running to me arms outstretched. "I'm speechless—simply speechless," she cried.

"It will be the first time. I used to think you would never stop talking."

Overcoming the surprise at seeing me, she exclaimed. "You are quite a talker yourself from the reports I have heard of you. They say your words are fire. I want you to know right away that I am proud to be the sister of the Apostle Paul. Her smile was sincere and her eyes crinkled at the corners the way mother's used to do.

"You are proud?"

"I also am a Christian. There was a quiet joy reflected in her eyes as she spoke those words.

"It makes me truly happy to hear that. I have wanted to come to see you for a long time. Something always seemed to hinder me. I am glad I came. What about your husband?"

"Jacob is a Christian, too. We have much to be thankful for."

"I thought he was a member of the Sanhedrin." I said registering surprise.

"So was Nicodemus," she said softly.

Jacob was strong, morally strong, and I admired him tremendously right from the start. With men like him in the Sanhedrin, there was hope for Israel. As I looked around Jerusalem upon my arrival that day, I recalled how Christ prophesied that the temple would be destroyed and remain desolate. Realizing during this visit that the heart of the church was not in Jerusalem, but in Rome, I knew I would have to go there where Peter, the big fisherman of souls had taken up residence. Jerusalem was like a dying man in the throes of his final agony,

After I had been with Rachel several days, I finally broached the subject that we had so far refrained from mentioning. I wanted to know about my parents and their deaths.

"I visited Tarsus.," I began, "and I heard that Mother and Father had died of a plague." I glanced inquisitively at Rachel as she busied herself arranging a large bouquet of anemones. She set the flowers down abruptly.

"Yes. That is true…but I was with them a short time before that." There was a touch of sadness in her voice.

I confessed to her my sorrow. "It was a great personal tragedy that I could not convert them to the faith."

Rachel came and sat beside me as I looked out a window from an upper room, watching night descend over the temple.

"You did not know? No one told you?" She leaned forward on her chair. "Mother and Father both died Christian."

"No!" I couldn't believe it.

"Yes!" she insisted. "It is true. I baptized them myself with water in the name of the Father and of the Son and of the Holy Spirit."

"I just can't believe it. Father seemed so set against it."

She smiled at me quietly. "He never persecuted the church the way you, did Saul."

I glanced up at the sky. Stars were beginning to come out and twinkle overhead.

"Thanks be to Jesus for his grace," I exclaimed. I had so much to be grateful for considering that I had, in fact, been a persecutor of Christ and his Church. I waited for her to tell me more about our parents.

"It really happened, Saul, and they were proud of you, too. Father said it was a good joke. Just before he died, he laughed and said that he would get to heaven before you do and he will be right on hand to greet you when you finally get there."

"The joke is on me all right. His little sister outdid the Apostle Paul with his so-called fiery words. Where I failed to convert them you succeeded." I pictured father in heaven with Christ. It is a picture I cherish.

"Little sister, you amaze me!"

"It was you Paul, or rather Christ in you. Mother and Father saw him in you and became believers in the Lord Jesus." She grew thoughtful. Together we sat in silence both remembering things that happened in years long past.

"Oh. Paul," she exclaimed, "I almost forgot—your inheritance. I have been taking care of it for you. I have invested it wisely and have even made you a nice profit."

I reached over and pulled one of her curls.

"I thought you had grown up," she said laughingly.

"I have, but I haven't forgotten how to pull your hair."

"I haven't forgotten how to kick you in the shins, either, so don't tempt me. Now lets call a truce and have some supper. Your nephews will be starved."

Rachel reminded me very much of our mother. Staying with her and her husband and sons those few days was almost like being home again in Tarsus. I did pay my respects to the Jerusalem church while I was there, but I did it quietly, not wanting to cause another furor.

One of the greatest joys of my life was offering the Holy Sacrifice in my sister's home and giving Christ to my family after having given him to so many others. I would have loved to stay longer with Rachel, but I wanted to stop in at Antioch on my return trip to Ephesus. Silas who sailed with me to Caesarea, left me there, going to Antioch when I came to Jerusalem and I was to meet him there.

When I got to Antioch, Silas informed me that he had firmly decided to remain there, leaving me without a companion. Consequently, I chose Titus to labor in the missions with me and I never returned to Antioch again. On the way to Ephesus, we passed though Galatia where I learned that Judaizers were trying to circumcise my spiritual children. I wish they would mutilate themselves and leave my converts alone! I straightened matters out as best I could and promised to write the Galatians a letter giving them further instruction. From Galatia we went to Phrygia and on over to Ephesus.

Priscilla and Aquila were anxiously awaiting my return. They had done much while I was in Jerusalem, making contacts among influential people in the city. They even counted the Asiarchs, the richest men of Asia among their friends.

"Father Paul, we are so happy to have you with us again," Priscilla welcomed me. "The church here is a seed pod, just waiting to burst open and grow."

I glanced at Aquila. "How is business?"

"Couldn't be better. We have all we can handle. I have ten weavers working for us now and I'm hiring more all the time," he announced confidently.

Later that evening, Aquila came to my room and we settled down for a long conversation.

"Have you made any converts in Ephesus?" I inquired hopefully.

He offered me a glass of wine. I no longer drink water, because it was the bad water that caused me so much illness.

"As soon as we came to Ephesus," Aquila explained, "I went to the synagogue and talked privately to many of the men about Christ. You know I can't preach. Well, one day, a Jew from Alexandria came to our synagogue and got up and began to preach about the Lord Jesus. He was very eloquent, but poorly instructed. However, he did arouse the interest of a large number of people in the faith." He sipped his wine and waited for me to take in what he was saying.

"Did he teach them error?" I was truly alarmed.

Aquila's eyes avoided mine, because he knew how much it grieves me when something goes wrong with the church.

"We brought the Alexandrine Jew home with us and he stayed here for awhile. We instructed him more correctly. He had never even been baptized and the only baptism he knew was that of John the Baptizer."

"Very good," I set my wine glass down on the marble top table beside me. "Where is he now?"

"He's gone to Corinth. I told him that there was a church there that needed help."

"Help? What's wrong in Corinth?"

Aquila still avoided looking at me.

"I don't think things are going well in Corinth," he said very softly.

"I hear that some have lapsed into gross immorality. One man even took his father's wife. There are all kinds of quarrels and divisions among the converts. They have even instigated lawsuits against each other. Worst of all…," Aquila paused. I knew he wished to spare me.

"Continue," I insisted with authority.

"Worst of all, when they meet in church it is no longer possible for them to partake of the Eucharist, for each has his own supper first. Some are even drinking and getting drunk." Aquila sighed deeply.

"Corinth is a wicked city. I'm not surprised, but I am grieved, deeply grieved." I pondered the situation in Corinth a few seconds and came up with a solution.

"I will send Timothy and Titus to them. They will straighten things out."

Aquila rubbed his finger pensively up and down the bridge of his large hooked nose and replied., "That is a good plan. But I think you personally should reprove them. Perhaps—perhaps a letter from you would mean something to them."

I valued his advice for he was an astute person. I thought about what he suggested. Already a letter to the Corinthians was taking shape in my mind.

"Perhaps it would be a good idea," he concluded, "if you were to go to Corinth yourself."

"Yes—I shall go to Corinth again. But now I want to start knocking down the pillars of Diana's temple." I detested what I had seen of the religion of the Ephesians. "Timothy and Titus will correct the wrongs at Corinth, I must work here while I have yet time. After I am finished in Ephesus, I am going to Rome." I spoke with determination. "Perhaps on the way to Rome, I could stop in again at Corinth."

"That could be dangerous," Aquila exclaimed, "going to Rome, I mean. Claudius has banished all Jews from Rome. I could see he was alarmed by the prospect of my visiting Rome."

"I am a citizen of Rome," I protested. "To Rome I shall go. Peter is still there. I believe that I can help him—that he will need me."

Aquila shrugged and shook his head. "It is only a matter of time until Christianity will be outlawed in Rome."

"Rome is a city of over a million inhabitants. Once Christ is well established there, no power on earth will be able to outlaw him," I protested. "If Peter can brave the opposition so can I."

"I am convinced of that," Aquila replied.

"When the churches in Asia, Achaia, and Macedonia are secure, then I will sail for Rome." I spoke with determination.

"I am in favor of your going to Rome from the standpoint of the church and its welfare, but I shall hate to say farewell to you, Paul. Perhaps you will even go into Gaul?"

"Spain is where I would like to go, if it is the will of God, perhaps even to Britain. In time we shall gain the whole world for Christ. All the idols will topple in the dust." I remembered the vision I had of Diana at the bottom of a stagnant pond.

"Diana will be a hard one to topple," Aquila told me warming to the conversation. "She is the rallying point of the Ephesians and has many followers from all points in the empire who come for the festival—the Artemisia—in May.

"When they come to the festival next May, they will hear about Christ." I said with resoluteness. "How do you think is the best way to win the Ephesians?"

"They are great lovers of magic. Almost all of them dabble in the black arts, soothsaying, divination, seeking after miraculous cures. Sorcery is in the very air they breathe. It all stems from the cult of Diana, I believe. They say she fell from the heavens."

A door had been opened to me in Ephesus, but I knew I would encounter many powerful adversaries. I was made welcome in the synagogue. I had enemies, but also many friends. For three months I was able to preach in the synagogue, before they began to persecute me and drove me out. I made the most of my opportunity preparing myself, bracing myself, as it were, for the fury that I knew would be unleashed against me. The Holy Spirit warned me that in Ephesus I would suffer greatly. In the months to come I was crushed beyond measure—even beyond my strength. I became weary even of life. I felt that I was already carrying my death sentence. Learning not to trust in myself, I put all my confidence in Christ who rose from the dead. He it is who delivered me and will deliver me from such great perils. I was laid low—stricken by a fever. I believe it was a pestilence arising from the mosquito-infested marshes that surround Ephesus. It sapped my strength.

Without Luke, I would never have lived through it. I had just returned from preaching at the synagogue when the dizziness and the fever overcame me, forcing me to take to my bed. Overcome by weakness and trembling I clung to Christ. In the delirium of the fever, I fought wild beasts in the arena of Ephesus.

From time to time, I would awaken to find Luke standing over me placing cold wet cloths on my brow and reassuring me. I was weary of life. I longed to dissolve and be with Christ, but he wanted me to continue in the body for the sake of the church. So, in time, the fever broke, the wild beasts were slain, and gradually my strength began to return.

Once again I began to discharge my ministry in accordance with the mercy shown me. I did not lose heart. Christ was my treasure. Even though outwardly, I was getting older, inwardly, I was being renewed day by day. My afflictions were preparing me for an eternal glory beyond all measure. I know that if my body is destroyed, I have a dwelling eternal in the heavens. In my illness I groaned—yearning for that heavenly dwelling. Sighing because of the burden of my illness, I prayed that my mortality would be transformed into life eternal. I had great courage knowing that, as an exile here, I walk by faith and not vision. I wanted to leave my body and go home to be with Jesus. I strived to please him in all things, suffering countless afflictions. Although it was difficult, I endured persecution, bearing in my flesh the death of Christ, so that his life might radiate from my mortal body. I felt death at work in my mortal flesh, but I experienced life in Christ. I knew that the one, who raised Jesus from the dead, would raise me up with him. Christ is my life!

When I was well enough to return to the synagogue, I learned that evil forces had used the time of my illness and absence to build up strength against me. When I rose to preach again, I was drowned out by jeering and blaspheming of the holy name of Jesus, the name that should cause every one to kneel in adoration.

I walked out of the Ephesus synagogue as I had out of a good many others in days gone by. Because, as usual the Jews rejected Christ, I grieved over them with great sorrow and sadness in my heart. But I know Israel will yet be saved, because Christ did not leave us in ignorance concerning the mystery of the Jews rejection of him. They are only partially blind and will remain so only until the full complement of the Gentiles that Christ calls will have entered the household of faith. When his house is complete with the Gentiles that he has favored with divine election, then all Israel shall be saved.

Because the house in which we lived was not large enough to accommodate the growing church, I needed to find another building. First I had to straighten out the Corinthian church. I sent Timothy and Titus to Corinth to tell the Corinthians that if I had to come personally to straighten out their abuses that I would not be lenient. This taken care of, I set out to find a place where I could preach in Ephesus, but I was not very successful. Time rushed by.

The tent making business was prospering. Priscilla had many guests to our home and among them the most prominent people of Ephesus. Even the Asiarchs were often at table with us. One of them—a very likeable person—had dinner with us at the time I was pondering my problem of finding housing for the church.

Epaphras, as the Asiarch was called, became a good friend of mine, even though he was unable to suggest a place for me to use as a pulpit. He was the first of the Asiarchs that I met, and I must confess that my eyebrows went up when he told me that he was also a priest.

"You are a priest?" I asked unable to conceal my surprise, as I carefully surveyed the sophisticated Epaphras reclining beside me at table.

Laughing, he explained. "The Emperor Claudius bestowed on me the title of 'high priest,' as he has on the rest of the Asiarchs, because we pay for certain expenses out of our own pockets for the gladiatorial contests. Since Claudius calls these games his cult worship and since we are expected to pay for part of it by virtue of our election by the people to the office of Asiarch, he calls us his 'high priests.' It's farcical—but you know politics." He dismissed the whole thing by waving his hand.

"You are not forced to sacrifice to him or worship him in any way?"

"No. On the contrary, it is rather the other way. Claudius needs us to support his interests in Asia. I do only what is expedient—but as for worshiping the old fellow—well, I know him too well for that." He laughed loud and long and so did we.

"Your physician here." Epaphras inclined his head toward Luke, who was reclining on his other side, "tells me that our climate has not agreed with you—that you have had a fever."

"He is quite recovered now," Luke declared. "We let him out of quarantine a couple weeks ago. He is perfectly safe company now." Luke smiled. "Unless of course, he gets into an argument with you. If he picks a quarrel with you be forewarned—he won't quit. He just won't quit."

"I have no quarrel with Paul," Epaphras replied sincerely to Luke and then turning to me said, "I admire you, I always admire a fighter. I have heard of your fight with the local Jews. I applaud you for your fearlessness. It tells me much of the religion you preach. Perhaps you will even convert an old cynic like me." He smiled at me enigmatically, and I began to thirst for his soul. As I waited for him to continue, all the while I was studying his face which was noble and without any trace of sensuality in his refined features.

"Converting an old cynic is my business—at your service." I bowed my head and returned his smile. "You are not as old as I am."

"He is older than he looks," quipped Aquila with easygoing familiarity

"I'm old in spirit. As for the religions I have seen—I am cynical. Epaphras spread his hands out the table in a gesture of frankness. "This Diana cult—it is a lot of nonsense. What effect does it have in the lives of her devotees? None! None whatsoever, except that they have a frolic and throw prudence to the winds every spring when they hold her festival."

"You are right," I agreed. "Paganism has nothing for the spirit or the mind of man."

"I read the philosophers when I went to school in Athens," related Epaphras meditatively so that I could see that he was doing some honest soul searching. "I thought the philosophers were wise until someone told me that my favorite philosopher had sex with little boys. Then my interest in philosophy died, and I became an embittered old cynic"

Luke spoke up. "There are things of beauty in the thought of the philosophers. Some of them have very high concepts of virtue, but human nature is corrupt and is unable to attain to such ideals without the grace of God."

"Yes, it is the same situation with the Jewish people. We had a beautiful moral code in the Law of Moses, but corrupt human nature is unable to keep the law. The law is spiritual but man is carnal. Man in his natural state is born into sin. He does the evil that he does not wish to do. He does the very evil that he hates." I paused briefly to let them comprehend my words. "The Greek philosophers saw beauty in virtue but being born sinful were unable to attain to it. I know that in me, that is, in my flesh—no good dwells, because I can wish to do good by myself, but I do not find the strength in myself to accomplish the good. Do I make myself clear, Epaphras?"

"I never thought of it that way, Paul. But I see your point." He tapped his finger on the table for emphasis. "Man *is* by nature corrupt. He bears within himself the very seeds of his destruction." His thought went racing on.

"Yes, Epaphras, the wages of sin is death."

"It is very obvious in my work as a physician," Luke added. "I see people continually destroying themselves just by overeating or drinking. Unable to control their gluttony they suffer physical ills until they eventually succumb."

"I have seen men lust for the power of public office," Epaphras commented, "lust for power to such an extent that they murdered other men and eventually fell at the assassin's hand themselves."

Aquila, who so far had kept quiet giving me a chance to get acquainted with the Asiarch, observed, "It happens in commerce, too. I have seen men so greedy for money that they sell defective and inferior goods to make a quick profit and end by losing their clients and their reputation. When they are bankrupt they take their own lives."

"Men destroy themselves by yielding to the pleasures of the flesh," I said. "They fall into all kinds of depravity—they go mad or kill themselves and others." I looked for a responsive chord in the heart of the Asiarch. "Aeschylus, Sophocles, and Euripides, among your Greeks have well portrayed the tragedies of corrupt human nature. You all know the story of Oedipus who killed his father and married his mother. When Jason deserted Medea she killed her own children. Phaedra fell in love with her stepson, Hippolytus, and when he repulsed her advances, she accused him of ravishment and hanged herself."

"Paul. You are right," exclaimed Epaphras. "But all men are not equally corrupt in a state of nature. Some have more control over their passions that others."

I nodded my agreement. I could see that Epaphras had a truly noble spirit.

"Would you believe me if I were to tell you that I am the worst of sinners?" I gazed into his soul. His eyes were fixed on mine.

"The Apostle Paul? The worst of sinners? What are you trying to tell me?" I had piqued Epaphras' curiosity.

"I think I understand." Luke ventured.

"Just this," I said. "It is God's grace that sustains me and Christ who wins the victory over evil in me. If he were to leave my soul, I would fall lower than any one else. He delivers me from death. He is my life and his spirit wars against the flesh. Praise God! It is Christ who gives me victory!"

"You mean" asked Epaphras "that Jesus Christ dwells in you and overcomes death and evil for you?" In wonderment he stared at me.

"Exactly. God sent his son, Jesus Christ in human flesh to condemn sin in the flesh, so that the law of God might be fulfilled is us, making it possible for us to live, not according to the flesh, but according to the Spirit." I could see that my words were illuminating him.

"The holiness of your life, Paul, bears witness to what you say." Epaphras folded his hands on his breast and sat pensively watching the flame of the oil lamp as it danced on the table before us.

" I castigate my body, afraid that I who have preached to others might myself fall. The Christian who lives in the Spirit of Christ has his mind filled with the things of the Spirit. The flesh inclines one toward death, but the Spirit inclines us to life and peace, so that a true Christian is one who has died to sin—one who…"

"To die to sin…" Intrigued by this thought, Epaphras interrupted me. "It is a beautiful ideal—is it truly possible?" Epaphras asked more to himself than to the rest of us gathered at the table.

"If you receive Christian baptism, I promise you that the living God will make your body and soul his temple and sin shall not have power over you. You will die to sin and be alive to Christ Jesus forever." I prayed silently for Epaphras to make the right decision.

"Immortality!"

"By no means! Not immortality of the soul as the philosophers speculate but eternal life. There is a tremendous difference. The wages of sin is death, but the gift of God is life everlasting in Christ Jesus, our Lord. Sin put Christ to death. Because of my sins and yours, Christ Jesus died—but sin did not have power over him. He rose from the dead, glorious and triumphant—nevermore to die." I was preaching and Epaphras was listening.

"Is there proof—real proof—that he actually rose from the dead?" Epaphras demanded.

"Five hundred people saw him in one place at one time."

"Perhaps it was a fraud or an illusion," Epaphras suggested. I could see that he wanted to believe, but he had not yet assented.

"Epaphras," listen, I *know* him. He is nearer to me than breathing. I took a deep breath. "He is closer to me than these hands of mine," I put my hands forth on the table. "I know him. He is within me." The Spirit was himself testifying to Jesus through my feeble voice. "I know that as he rose from the dead, as he promised he would, he will also bring me to life eternal as he also promised. In destroying sin, he destroyed death. Death holds no terrors. He has enveloped it in victory."

Epaphras looked at Aquila and then at Luke. "This you both believe?"

Luke was the one to answer. "This I know. When Paul baptized me in the waters of the Aegean, I experienced a mystical death, dying to sin. I came forth a new creature—no rather I came forth a child of the Living God filled with his life, love and Spirit."

"And you, Aquila?"

"Peter baptized me. He was with Jesus from the beginning. He witnessed the resurrection. Ever since I was baptized, I have walked in newness of life." Aquila professed his faith and I felt that the profession of a merchant meant more to the Asiarch than the profession of faith of an Apostle.

"The cynic in me is dying," Epaphras said practically in a whisper. Is it truly possible to hope for so much? To hope for eternal life and happiness?"

"Christ within you will be your hope of glory, Brother Epaphras," I added with a smile.

Thanking the Lord for the grace given to the Asiarch, we took him that very night down to the sea and baptized him, marveling at the work of grace in his soul. The old cynic died and the new Epaphras was distinguished for his holy simplicity.

I still had found no answer to my own problem as to where I would do my preaching. One morning determined to solve the problem, I set out into the city resolved not to return home until I had found a suitable place.

Because we were now experiencing the hottest days of summer, I strolled down the street through the market place in the early morning where shoppers were busy trying to provide for their needs so that they could return home before the afternoon sun made the city streets unbearably hot. As I usually do, I studied the faces of the Ephesians as they hurried past me in the street. Near the theater, I spotted a blind man sitting with a cup in his hands. I had seen him before, because he sat in the city square everyday begging from the people as they hurried by. Perhaps I mused, I had found a way to attract the attention of the Ephesians who were so fascinated by occult happenings. In imitation of Christ, I approached the blind man and with compassion began talking to him. He was a typical blind beggar such as one sees in all the cities of the world. He felt sorry for himself and bitter towards those who threw a few little coins into his cup. He must have heard me draw near, for he rattled his cup and held it up to me. I began to talk to him.

"Have you always been blind?" I asked with genuine sympathy.

"What is that to you?" he snarled and spat on the street at my feet.

"I thought I might help you, but if you aren't interested I'm sorry I bothered you." I turned to walk away.

"Help me? How? A few coins?" He snapped sarcastically.

"I might help you to see. Do you believe in miracles?"

"Miracles!" He spat again. "Hah! I have prayed to Diana. I have offered many sacrifices—nothing ever came of it."

"Jesus Christ will heal your blindness." I fixed my eyes on him.

"I have not heard of him." He was becoming interested. "Is he some strange foreign god?"

"He is the son of the Living God. I am his priest. Once, I too, was blind. He cured my blindness. Will you believe in Him if He also heals your blindness?" I prodded his soul.

"If he gives sight to these," he pointed to his sunken sockets, "I will worship him and no one but him! You mean he really healed your blindness?"

"In more ways than one!"

"Will you ask him to give me sight?" Faith was budding in his soul.

"I will." I stretched forth my hand and touched the eyelids that seemed to cover vacant spaces in his head. "Be made whole!" I withdrew my hand. He shrieked when the light of day fell on his eyes.

"I can see! Look," he yelled to everyone in the streets of Ephesus, "I can see! Jesus Christ healed me! This man is his priest."

Instantly, a large crowd of Ephesians who were supremely delighted with the miracle surrounded me. I took the opportunity of preaching to them. From that day forward every time I ventured out into the streets, the sick, the deformed, and the demented sought me out pleading for cures.

As I walked away from the blind man who was spreading the good news of the miracle Christ performed for him, I observed a lecture hall across the street. A sign in front of it informed me that one Tyrannus lectured there to his students each morning from eight to eleven on the subject of the "Glories of Greece." Perhaps, I decided I could rent the hall for the afternoons and preach during the time when work came to a standstill during the heat of the day.

When I made my way inside, Tyrannus was explaining the writings of Aristotle to his students. While I was waiting until he finished, I surveyed the hall and found it to be perfect for my purposes, since it was centrally located and large enough to accommodate a fairly big crowd. That very afternoon I preached my first sermon in it to a large gathering of Ephesians who heard of the miracle of the blind man.

As the months went by, Christ worked more than the usual number of miracles by my hands in order to convert the Ephesians. Even handkerchiefs and aprons were brought to me and after I touched them were taken to the sick who were often cured.

When people came to hear the word of God, I always asked them to give up their practices of magic and to leave their magic books and accouterments at the rear of the auditorium as a witness to their faith in Jesus Christ. When the pile of magic paraphernalia became rather large, I burned it publicly outside the city wall within sight of Diana's temple.

With the church in Ephesus flourishing and growing bigger every day, I began to draw up plans to go to Macedonia and Achaia and then return again to Jerusalem. After that I planned to go to the big city on the Tiber—Rome. After Rome there would be new worlds to conquer in Spain and perhaps Britain.

Timothy returned from Corinth where he left Titus. Since I planned to go to Philippi shortly, I sent Timothy and a fellow named Erastus there to wait for me. My success in Ephesus caused me to leave that city sooner than I planned. Although it was my intention to remain in Ephesus for the Artemisia in May, the silversmiths, of all people, were the ones to drive me out of town, creating a near riot in the city protesting that I was ruining their business. Because of my preaching, they were facing bankruptcy since they couldn't make money selling their silver statues of Diana anymore. Joyful to hear this, I set out for Philippi.

Happy to be back in Philippi, I rejoiced to see my converts—my family—Lydia, Alexander, Helen and the poor little one from whom Christ had removed the demon. Although I even hoped to get another look at the magistrate who had me flogged, I could not, because he was no longer there.

Once I saw that my spiritual children in Philippi were walking in the ways of truth, I decided that the time had come for me to go to Corinth and take care of the problems there.

I heard what the Corinthians were saying about me. They said that the letters I wrote them were ponderous and informative, but that my physical appearance is weak and my language is inferior. I did not spare them. They soon learned that I was intrepid, teaching them that they must be subject to the higher authorities for all authority comes from God.

While I wintered in Corinth I wrote a letter to Rome telling the Romans of my intention to visit them. Come what may, I was resolute in my decision to go to Rome, which occupied all my thoughts.

Although I had booked passage on a ship sailing for Syria as soon as the shipping lanes were open again in the Spring, I did not take it, because fortunately I learned of a plot the Jews of Corinth had made against me, before they had a chance to put it into effect. I was shocked to learn that they planned to kill me as soon as I boarded the ship. Thank God I learned of their plans and slipped away from Corinth on the road to Macedonia before they even knew that I was gone.

While I remained in Philippi in the home of my former jailer, Alexander, until after the days of the unleavened bread when I sailed for Troas, I sent Timothy and a number of other teaching disciples to Troas.

Although I stayed in Troas only seven days, during that time one of the most awesome events of my entire life and ministry occurred. Because of all the excitement, I went away and left my cloak in Troas at Carpus' house and with it my parchments and books, including my copy of Matthew's gospel.

Something very wonderful happened in Troas. I hesitate to speak of it even now. It was the first day of the week and all the Christians of Troas were gathered together in Carpus' house to hear me preach and to receive the Body and Blood of Christ from my hands. Since I only had time for a brief visit, I preached longer than usual. When midnight came I was still preaching.

There was a young boy, Eutychus, sitting by the window. I noticed that he was getting drowsy, because his head was nodding and he was having trouble keeping his eyes open. Then the calamity happened. He fell asleep, toppled over and fell out the window. We were on the third floor of the house, making it a fall of twenty-five feet or more to the ground.

Running to the window, I could see him lying crumpled on the flagstones of the garden below.

"Stay where you are everyone," I ordered. "Luke, my physician, and I will attend to the boy."

We hurried down the three flights of step. The boy looked lifeless as Luke examined him, kneeling beside him, listening for a heart beat. After a few moments, Luke looked up at me with sorrow and announced, "Paul, Eutychus is dead."

Kneeling beside Luke and bending over Eutychus, I embraced the boy and whispered to Luke, "Don't be alarmed. There is still life in him."

Luke shook his head. "No," he insisted in quiet tones so that the people upstairs leaning out the windows would not hear.

I stretched myself out over the still body of the boy and prayed. Almost imperceptibly I felt breath stirring in him. Yes! He was breathing. Then his eyelids fluttered. Eutychus opened his eyes, smiled at me, and said, "Father Paul, thank you—thank you, for coming for me."

Eutychus rose to his feet. "I'm perfectly all right, now I must go find my mother." With that he slipped away from us. Luke and I continued kneeling—both of us struck with awe.

Luke looked at me and with much trembling said, "Paul, he was dead until you touched him."

"Sssh!" I commanded. "Don't tell them." I signified the gathering of the church that was observing us from the window.

Overcome with emotion Luke exclaimed, "Blessed be Jesus in His Apostle!"

I quoted to him the words Christ used in raising Lazarus. "I am the resurrection and the life, he who has faith in me, even if dies, he will live, and whoever lives and has faith in me will never die."

When we returned to the congregation, Eutychus' mother was carefully looking him over to be sure he was all right. In amazement she cried out, "There is not a mark on him!"

As I offered the Holy Sacrifice, thanking God with all my soul for the wonders of his grace, Eutychus knelt with the rest of them and received the Body and Blood, Soul and Divinity of Jesus from my hands.

After this event, my greatest need was to be alone. I needed to withdraw to pray and to meditate on what had happened and to give thanks to God for restoring Eutychus to us. I sent my company of fellow travelers on the ship to Assos where I arranged to join them. Because I preferred to go alone by land, I bought a camel and spent the time on the way alone with Christ as I rode the thirty miles to Assos.

The oleanders were in great profusion of boom. Their deep rose flowers with the blue sea and the mountains behind them spoke to me of the love and joy that are in the heart of the Creator. I was conscious of Jesus everywhere and of Paul nowhere. I was Jesus. I was Christ and I was going to Jerusalem. I knew that at last—my hour had come.

Because it was raising Lazaras from the dead that sounded the bell announcing the passion of Christ, I felt that raising Eutychus from the dead was a sign to me that my time to bear witness to Christ with my blood was at hand. When the chief priests and the Pharisees saw Jesus call Lazarus forth from the tomb, they began to plan and scheme to put him to death.

Knowing that I had a baptism in my blood to undergo, I wanted it to be accomplished. It was time for me to go up to Jerusalem as Christ had done that last time. I was firmly convinced that raising Eutychus was the sign I had been waiting for. Christ had lived his public life and ministry in me now he would manifest his passion and agony in me. I was to be the victim and the priest. I was ready to die for the holy name of Jesus—ready to be poured out in sacrifice.

Resolving to hasten to Jerusalem and embrace my cross at once, I boarded the ship at Assos together with Luke and Timothy and sailed to Miletus, where I insisted that they dock. Because I wanted to say farewell, my last farewell to them, I sent for the priests I ordained at Ephesus and had them come at once to Miletus. When they assembled I addressed them plainly.

"You know how I have lived with you ever since I first came into the province of Asia. You are familiar with my trials with the Jews and their plots against me. I have shared everything with you. I have been your teacher both publicly and in your homes, urging everyone to believe in Christ Jesus and repent.

"Now I feel that I must go to Jerusalem. I don't know what will happen there, but I do know that the Holy Spirit counsels me that I will be persecuted and imprisoned. I am not afraid. All I want to do is finish the course and the ministry I received from Christ, which compels me to witness to the gospel.

"This is the last time you will see me in this world. You know I have always given you the entire gospel. Be sure to rule well the Church that Christ bought with his blood. After I leave, some will come to try to destroy your flocks. Some of you even might say things that might lead some sheep astray. Be careful and be vigilant. Remember that for three years I have told you to be on your guard.

"And now I turn you over to God and his grace, for he is able to keep you and sanctify you. Always remember to help the weak that are among you. Imitate me as I imitate Christ. You know I have worked with my hands to provide for my needs and have never coveted any man's silver, gold, or clothing. Always remember that the Lord Jesus says that the one who gives is far more blessed than the one who receives."

Having said this I knelt down and prayed with them. Our reunion was touched with sadness for we both knew that we would never again see each other on this earth. They embraced me, but were grieved because I said they would never see my face again on this earth. Promising to see them all again one day in heaven, we boarded the ship and went to Cos. The next day we were in Rhodes and from there we went to Patara at the mouth of the Xanthus, where we found a ship crossing over to Phoenicia, and boarded it. After sighting Cyprus and leaving it on the port side, we sailed for Syria and landed at Tyre where the ship was due to unload her cargo.

When we stayed in Tyre seven days with the disciples there, they all warned me not to go to Jerusalem. However, I knew that it was God's will for me to go to there and my heart was joyful at the thought of living Christ's passion in my own flesh.

Leaving Tyre, we went to Ptolemais and. spent the day with the Christians there. The next day we went to Caesarea where we stayed at the house Philip the Evangelist, who had four daughters—virgins with the gift of prophecy. They warned me not to go to Jerusalem too.

While we were staying on there for some days, an old friend from Judea—the prophet Agabus—arrived. Although he was more hunched back than ever and had a hard time getting around, with the help of his gnarled homemade staff, he ambled straight to me as soon as he spotted me. Dramatically he took my girdle and bound his own hands and feet with it and said, "The Holy Spirit says the Jews will bind the owner of this girdle in this fashion in Jerusalem and turn him over to the Gentiles."

I froze for an instant until I heard Timothy plead, "Father Paul, let's go to Rome now. Please don't go to Jerusalem."

I patted him comfortingly on the shoulder.

Luke who was observing the whole proceedings agreed with Timothy.

"Paul, I think we should go straight to Rome. What is the purpose of going to Jerusalem? Peter is in Rome."

Some of Philip's daughters began to weep for me. Timothy was struggling to keep his emotions in check. With joy and serenity, I smiled at them all and said, "Why are you so upset?" Some were actually weeping openly. It was heartbreaking for me to see them so sad. "I am ready for be arrested and die for the Lord Jesus."

When Timothy finally realized that God's hand was at work in our lives, he exclaimed, "The Lord's name be praised!"

"Amen," sighed Luke.

The words of the prophet came to my mind about how the Lord Jesus was to be led to the slaughter like a sheep. I was to be the lamb of God.

Jerusalem was doomed and dying, having written its own death sentence because it rejected Christ, not recognizing the time of his visitation. Over twenty years before I had fled from Jerusalem when as a result of my bearing witness to Christ in the temple, certain of the Jews were determined to put me to death, so as to silence my preaching. Now I was returning in the maturity of age to be a witness to Christ—resolute—fearless—before all my enemies. As the road from Caesarea wound up and over the hills outside the city, I caught my first glimpse of Phasael, also known as the tower of David, the great tower of Herod's palace gleaming golden yellow in the sunlight. When he built his palace in Jerusalem, Herod the Great had outdone himself in his passion for luxury and magnificence. I could see the pinnacles of the temple close by the tower in the distance. In his love for building, Herod began the building or rather the rebuilding of the temple. So that there would be no desecration of the holy place during the construction, he had a thousand priests trained as stonemasons and carpenters. To my mind, old Herod the Great, the founder of the Herodian dynasty, seemed to typify Jerusalem. I remembered the Herodian slaying of the apostle James and what I had seen of the Herods with my own eyes. When Jesus was born in Bethlehem, it was Herod the Great who sat on the throne. When he heard that the King of the Jews was born, old dying Herod, his body already bloated and corrupting, ordered the murder of all the male babies in Bethlehem, so there would be no king but Herod. Because someone said that his own sons might become kings before their time, he had them murdered. Their mother, the beautiful Mariamme, died by his command. When Augustus Caesar emerged emperor of the world after his victory at the battle of Actium that caused Anthony and Cleopatra to commit suicide, Herod realized that he would have to go to Augustus and promise him the same loyalty he had given Anthony. Not knowing if he would return home alive, or if Augustus would finish him, Herod gave orders that his lovely Mariamme be put to death, if he did not return. The thought that another man would possess her incensed him to the point of madness. When he returned home as the friend of the new Caesar, his wife had heard of what he had proposed to do with her. Because her enemies told Herod that his wife was planning to kill him, he had her slain. Many of his relatives he killed. Some were stabbed, some strangled, others poisoned. Five days before he died, rotting and stinking—completely diseased and half insane—he had his son Antipater killed. Such was the king who gave Jerusalem her temple.

I reached the city gate—the gate of Benjamin. On the left was the fortress Antonia where the Roman garrison was located. This was my triumphal entrance into Jerusalem. Luke, Timothy, Titus, and I strode boldly through the narrow streets. As we walked along, the temple wall, I recalled that Christ foretold the destruction of the Temple, saying that there wouldn't be one stone left upon another. I felt that the prophecy would soon be fulfilled.

The stench of burning fat and animal flesh emanated from the temple, nauseating me. Many years before, Isaiah wrote that God did not delight in the blood of animals. Still the blood from the slaughter of animals ran in a never-ending stream in the temple and had to be piped into the Kidron below. God wanted mercy and not sacrifice and still the thank offerings, the burnt offerings, and the sin offerings continued with the priests getting rich off the literal fat of the land. Only an animal declared perfect by the Levites could be sacrificed. If a man bought his own animal with him, the chances were that it would be refused. So the custom arose of buying animals for the sacrifices right there at the temple—animals that the Levites had already inspected. Because all money transactions in the temple had to be done in the temple's own coinage, there were money changers in the temple changing Greek and Roman money into shekels and half shekels. Furthermore a temple tribute was levied on all male Jews. No wonder the high priests sought to kill Jesus—he denounced these practices that were making them greedy and rich.

The Jews of the old covenant built their temple on the rock of Mount Moriah. Christ established his church on the rock that is Peter. And Peter was in Rome. As I gazed at the pinnacles of the temple, I though of how Jesus had wept over the city.

I was coming to Jerusalem as Christ did knowing that he was being delivered into the hands of the enemy. I was laying down my life in obedience to God's will as he had done. After a brief stop at my sister Rachel's house, I left to go to the house of the Bishop of Jerusalem, my old friend James. Because the city had changed little, I had no difficulty finding his home. Although James was happy to see me, my presence in Jerusalem caused him a good deal of discomfort and embarrassment. As soon as we were seated, he came right to the point.

"I have heard many things about you, Paul, over the years. I have heard how you have been expelled from almost every synagogue in Asia and Macedonia." His eyes avoided mine. "You have enraged the Jewish communities everywhere you have gone." His eyes were narrow slits as he studied my face.

"I have gained many souls for Christ!" My eyes burned into his. "There are now Christian churches where pagan altars stood."

"You eat with the Gentiles—all kinds of things which are contrary to Jewish law!"

I could see disapproval and mistrust in his eyes. "You even wear the toga," he continued in dismay. "Your Gentile Christians are completely separated from the synagogues. In short Paul—you no longer keep the Law of Moses. I hate to say it—but it is true. You are more Roman than Jew!"

There it was. The same old question that had been with the church in Jerusalem from the beginning. Very patiently I began to try to get him to understand.

"Now there is only Christ. It doesn't matter if one is Greek, Roman, Jew or Gentile. We have all been baptized into one body. We have all received the same Holy Spirit. We are now the body of Christ." I could see at once that I had not touched his soul.

"We do not see things the same as you do," he said flatly. "In Jerusalem we are Jews—yes, Christian Jews. We try to keep peace with the rest of Jewry in the city by upholding the Law of Moses and worshiping in the temple."

Trying to understand the situation of the church in Jerusalem to the best of my ability and to show charity to James, I waited, giving him time to explain himself fully.

"We all keep the law here. I am certain that you do not want to scandalize your Christian brothers, Paul, by not keeping the law while you are here." His eyes pleaded for me to understand. "I am certain you do understand," he said in conclusion.

James had aged a great deal. It had been twenty years since I was a guest in his house. From where I was sitting, I could observe the inner courtyard of his home that was filling up with worshipers. Since it was the first day of the week, they were waiting for their bishop to offer the Holy Sacrifice. Studying the faces of the members of the Jerusalem church, seeing that they were all Jews, I knew I had to phrase my remarks very carefully.

"I don't want to cause anyone to stumble and fall. I try to please everyone so that many people will be saved."

"Good!" James rose from his chair. "Then I am sure you will agree to do what I shall ask of you. I want Jewish Christians to see that you are a good Jew."

"What exactly do you propose for me to do?" I stood up and faced him, deciding that I would accept whatever he asked of me as God's will.

"Tonight a multitude is sure to assemble here, knowing that you are back in Jerusalem. At the present time, we have four men who are under a vow, according to our Jewish customs. Join them. Purify yourself with them and when your vow is fulfilled, you, yourself, will pay the offering to the temple treasury for the five of you."

He was asking me to go into the lion's den. I recalled what the prophet Isaiah had written about being led like a sheep to the slaughter. What James was asking of me would take me right into the public view of my enemies. If I were to comply with his request, I would spend the next seven days praying in the temple—the most public spot in Jerusalem where Jews from all over the empire would see me.

I had enemies in every synagogue in every town that I ever visited on my missionary journeys. Just recently in Corinth the Jews had plotted to destroy me. In Lystra I had been stoned. The synagogue rulers in Thessalonica pursued me to Berea. If any of my enemies spotted me in the temple, they would howl for my blood. In the Greek and Roman cities they had been powerless against me. If I were to spend seven days in the Temple, I would be walking right into their hands. They would have me in their power just like they had Jesus when he came to the temple and taught there on the eve of his last Passover. "Brother James," I said without any trace of emotion, "I will be most happy to do as you ask. "I feel that it is God's will."

Great peace descended upon my soul as I spoke these words. "Thank you, Paul. I knew I could count on you." Surely he did not realize what he was asking.

"Now come," he insisted, "let's go into the assembly of the faithful and tell them what you are going to do." He drew me by the arm.

Together we walked before the assembly of Christ's followers in Jerusalem. With the introduction that I was going to purify myself and offer sacrifice in the temple, James presented me to them. A murmur of approval rose to my ears. Briefly I addressed the assembly telling them of the work Christ was doing among the Gentiles, omitting any mention of my quarrels with the Jews. Because I could see at once that I was out of place in Jerusalem's church, I paid my respects, excused myself, and retired to my sister's home.

Although Rachel was happy to have me with her, she feared for my safety, worrying that the Jews might rise up against me and stone me when I told her of my planned purification and sacrifice in the temple. Her husband Jacob agreed with her in no uncertain terms.

"Look, Paul," he spoke to me like a blood brother. "I am a member of the Sanhedrin. I know how Ananias, the high priest, feels about you. Reports have come in from the synagogues far and near. You are their most hated enemy. Don't—please don't expose yourself to this danger." His eyes were grave as he spoke.

"I *must* go Jacob. I must bear witness to Christ in the temple of his Heavenly Father. He, himself, said that his Father's house is a house of prayer and we have turned it into a den thieves. Look, it is his Father's house as long as it stands." I tried as best I could to explain my actions and myself.

Rachel and Jacob exchanged fearful glances and I felt that I had convinced neither of them.

"I love and serve Christ, too." Jacob protested vociferously and I know that he has foretold the destruction of the temple and all Jerusalem. Must you be destroyed in it? Why don't you leave and go to Rome?"

"It is God's will that I remain here a little longer," I said softly and with an air of finality.

Glancing from the window before us as we sat in the upper room, I pointed to the city. "You are right. Jerusalem will be destroyed and the Gentiles will overrun it. Our Lord told us that the enemies of Jerusalem will throw up a rampart about the city and will surround it and shut it in on every side and will dash it to the ground with her children within it." Just the thought of it was enough to make any Jew tremble.

"When, Paul, when will it be?" Jacob asked as we looked out at the walls that seemed to hold the city in a secure embrace.

"Soon. It will be soon. I have a vision of the Roman Legions surrounding the city and of our proud people refusing to surrender. Rome will build a rampart and encompass the city. The people within will starve. They will throw the dead over the walls to rot." Dropping my head in my hands, I hid my face as I continued my recital of what lay in store for Jerusalem. "When the people become weak from hunger, they will stack the dead bodies in the houses. A stench, an abomination of uncleanness, will hover over the city. When deserters defect and creep out in the night, the Romans will grab them and crucify them in a forest of crucifixes outside our city walls. I can see men murdering each other for a loaf of bread. I can see a woman roasting her own child and eating it. The priests and the Scribes and the Pharisees will call on God to save them and to save their temple and he will not hear them, for they rejected him and crucified him when he came to save them. I can see the Romans entering the burning temple and taking the shewbread and the sacred vessels and carrying them away to Rome. And yet our proud people will not surrender."

Jacob was staring at me in horror and disbelief.

"Are you sure, Paul?"

"There will not be one stone left upon another."

"What shall we do, Paul, Rachel and me and the boys?"

"Do as Jesus said. When you see the armies approaching flee from Judea to the mountains."

"Will we have time to escape?" he asked hanging on my words

"Yes, those that are faithful to Christ and heed his warning and flee to the hills will be saved."

Jacob was filled with awe by my words.

Pondering what I had just told him, he said, "I will do everything in my power as a member of the Sanhedrin to help you."

"Thanks. Take care of Rachel and your sons." Perhaps I had told him too much. It was time to change the subject.

"David looks just like my father." I wanted to reassure Jacob and so I told him, "I'm going to Rome when I am finished in Jerusalem. Perhaps you would like to go with me?" From the window we had an unobstructed view of the Antonia where I noticed that the soldiers were changing guard as we talked.

"Perhaps, we will have to come to Rome when you get finished with Jerusalem!"

Rising early the next morning while it was still dark, I made my way to the temple. As I approached the temple gates one of the priests, mounted on the high pinnacle, was watching for day to break so that he could give the signal for the morning sacrifices to begin.

When the trumpet sounded, the gates of the temple opened before me. I knew that the sacrificial lamb was ready to be offered. The priest was piercing the throat of the lamb with his knife while another priest caught its blood in a golden bowl and began sprinkling the altar with the fresh blood. Soon the entrails of the lamb would be washed and the body quartered in readiness for the most solemn part of the ritual.

I heard the great gong—the Magrephan sounding. As the temple was filling up with the worshiping Jews and the many priests, the smell of incense hung in the air. I joined the other worshipers in falling down before the Lord God of Israel. The burnt offerings were being placed on the altar. The psalm of the day was sung and with the others I prostrated myself as the silver trumpets pierced the morning silence.

When the sacrifice was over, I strolled through the Court of the Gentiles and Solomon's porch. The moneychangers and the market of animals for sale for the sacrifices were there as they had been before Christ drove them out and upturned their money tables on the ground. Going to a moneychanger, I gave him some of my coins bearing the image of Claudius and in exchange received the shekels I would need to pay the temple treasury upon the completion of my seven days of prayer.

The morning watch was changing in the fortress Antonia that overlooked the temple esplanade. On each corner of the fortress, there was a tower and from the top of the southeast tower, which was seventy cubits high, the entire temple could be observed. The fortress housed the Roman garrison that was always on the look out for the least sign of revolt among the Jewish people. They were ready instantly to send out soldiers to quell the smallest riot. Herod the Great had built this fortress and named it in honor of his friend Anthony, before the latter fell from power at the battle of Actium.

As I walked through the temple courts I saw many Hellenist Jews from all parts of the empire, even spotting one of our Christian con-

verts from Ephesus—a man called Trophimus, who had come with
us to Jerusalem. I greeted him briefly, and walked up the steps leading into the Temple proper. No Gentile was allowed to pass beyond
that point upon penalty of instant death. Signs to that effect were
everywhere in evidence. I joined the four men that James had
arranged for me to be with and began the ritual.

Although a number of the Hellenists seemed to be watching me
closely, the days passed without incident. No doubt my enemies were
biding their time, waiting for the right hour to strike—waiting until
they had a large enough mob to make the attack. I could feel their
eyes on me as I passed them in the temple courts as I came and went.

Fearlessly, I continued my prayers. They had no need to hurry for
they knew that I would be there for the specified number of days.
When the seven days were almost up, they assembled one morning,
waiting for me when I entered the Court of the Gentiles. Because
they were all huddled together ready to strike, I braced myself,
knowing they would probably try to throw me over the temple wall
into the Kidron. If that didn't kill me—falling from that
height—they would finish me off with a few well placed stone boul-
ders. Commending my spirit into the hands of the Father, I waited.

Charging at me, the leader of the mob was shouting for everyone
in the temple to hear. "Help, men of Israel!"

From all directions men came running at me. The leader, a tall,
thin, young Jew rushed at me, denouncing me with upraised fists.
Thrusting a wiry finger in my face, he cried, "This man teaches people everywhere things that are contrary to our law and our temple."
He pointed melodramatically in the direction of the Holy of Holies.

I kept calm, quietly praying.

"He brought Gentiles also into our temple, desecrating this holy
place!" Violently he motioned to the band of men who had been
plotting against me all week long. In one body they lunged at me,
beating their fists into my face, and anywhere else they could strike.
Because I did not want Timothy to be involved, I had ordered him to

stay at Rachel's house and I ordered my other friends to stay away from the temple, because I did not want them involved. I was totally alone.

When they began dragging me out on to Solomon's Porch, I knew I was going to meet the same fate that Stephen had met in the Kidron. Just as they were lifting me up, preparing to dash me over the wall, I heard a voice cry out.

"Stop! Stop! I command you in the name of Rome." It was the Roman tribune with his soldiers. I said a prayer of thanksgiving.

"Out of the way!" Claudius Lysias, the tribune in command of the garrison, thundered with commanding authority in his voice. The Jews stopped beating me. The fellow who had been so brave in denouncing me turned on his heels and ran into the mob that thirsted for my blood and was now seething with frustration at having me snatched away from them, just at the moment when they were going to throw me to my death. Furious at the appearance of the Roman tribune they tried to seize me from the Roman soldiers. Grabbing a whip, the tribune cracked it over the heads of the rebels. When this failed to stop them, he cut into them with the lash.

"Stand back!" he roared. The soldiers upon his order drew their swords. The mob became quiet.

"Bind him in chains." The soldiers clapped chains around my hands and feet.

"What has he done?" Claudius Lysias demanded of my attackers.

The Jews took this as a license to riot again, causing so much yelling and screaming that the tribune could not hear any of the accusations that were hurled against me.

"Take him to the barracks. Pick him up and carry him!" They carried me across the temple courts where the priests and the Scribes and the Pharisees had tried to apprehend Christ when he preached here to a riotous bloodthirsty people. How many times he slipped out of the temple away from them without their being able to touch him, because his hour had not yet come. From the time of his birth when Herod plotted to kill him until the time he let them take him, there were many who sought his death. They would never have taken him, if he had not laid down his life, coming willingly and freely to Jerusalem, even as I had done. He humbled himself, following the will of the Father to his death on the cross. For this reason God has exalted him, placing his name above all other names. May every knee bend when his name is spoken!

As Christ delivered himself to the powers of darkness, I also was delivered. As they dragged me through the mob, the chains cut into my flesh. I was being taken to the Antonia where Christ was taken to face Pilate. We walked up the stairs where Christ had trod—blood stained—wearing a crown of thorns and the scourge marks of human cruelty. I had kept silent until now. On the stairs where Christ received the cross, the Holy Spirit within me inspired me to speak. I called to the tribune in Greek.

"May I tell you something?" Surprise shown in his face when he heard my Greek.

"Do you know Greek?" he inquired. He looked at my bald shaved head and said, "I thought you were an Egyptian—the one who recently stirred up four thousand assassins to sedition and led them out into the desert."

"Absolutely not!" I protested. "I am a Jew from Tarsus in Cilicia—a citizen of a very fine city. But I am asking your permission to speak to the people." I pointed to the mob that followed us from the temple to the Antonia.

"If you will explain the cause of this commotion, you may speak. I intend to see to it that justice is done in this miserable outpost of civilization and I intend to see that these detestable people," he flung his hand in the direction of the mob that was still howling for my blood, "are brought to submission."

Christ was near to me when I mounted the steps he himself had mounted. As I stood on those steps made holy by his presence, the Holy Spirit within me prompted me to bear witness to the Lord

Jesus. After calling the mob to silence, I began addressing them in classical Hebrew rather than in Aramaic, the common tongue. When they heard my Hebrew they became very quiet, for it was the language that spoke to them of Yahweh, the law, and the temple.

"Men of Israel—Brothers and Fathers, please listen to what I have to say in my own defense." By now the mob was composed of the ordinary people of Jerusalem as well as those who sought to kill me. "I am a Jew, born in Tarsus in Cilicia, but I was reared in this city as student of Rabban Gamaliel who instructed me according to the strict interpretation of our law. Just as all of you are today, I was faithful to the law. I persecuted followers of the Way that I now follow—even to death, arresting and throwing men and women into prisons. The high priest and the elders can attest to that, because I even got letters from them to go to Damascus and search for Christians there to bring them back to Jerusalem to be punished. However, something very extraordinary happened as I was drawing near to Damascus. Suddenly about noon, I beheld a great light all around me, causing me to fall to the ground. Then I heard a voice calling my name and asking me why I was persecuting him. He said he was Jesus of Nazareth. Overwhelmed, I asked him what he wanted of me. He told me to go to Damascus where I would be told what to do. Because the light blinded me, my fellow travelers had to lead me by the hand into Damascus.

"In Damascus, a man named Ananias, an observer of the law, and well respected, healed my blindness. He simply said, 'Regain your sight,' and instantly I could see again. He then told me that I was to be a witness to Jesus before all men. I was to be baptized, he informed me, and all my sins would be washed away.

"Later when I returned to Jerusalem and was praying here in the temple, I fell into an ecstasy and I saw Jesus. He told me to hurry and leave Jerusalem, because people here would not accept what I had to say about him. He told me to go to the Gentiles, far away, with his message of salvation." When I mentioned the Gentiles, the hated "goy," the mob went wild with the fury of the demons of hell and began screaming.

"Put him to death. He has no right to live!"

"Stone him! He took Gentiles into the temple!"

All the devils in hell were unleashed against me. Insane with rage, they threw dust in the air and rent their clothing.

Claudius Lysias, furious that they had dared test his authority with such an uprising, yelled, "Take him into the barracks and scourge him! Torture him and find out what he has done to cause such rebellion."

The soldiers jerked my chains causing them to bite into my flesh. In the crowd, I spotted Timothy and my eyes met his and locked for a brief instant. I felt the strength of his prayers.

The centurion grabbed my wrists. They pushed me through the door with such force that I fell flat on my face on the flagstones of the inner courtyard of the fortress where I remained, unable to get up, because my feet were chained together. One of the soldiers kicked me in the ribs and yelled, "Get up! We will show you what we do with Jewish pigs."

I clung to Jesus repeating his name over and over in the silence of my soul. Grabbing the chain that bound my hands, they pulled me to my feet. I looked around at the inner court of the Antonia where they had brought me and saw that it was about one hundred and sixty feet square and paved with large blocks of stone.

"Tie him to the whipping post," commanded the centurion.

Tearing off the chain that was by now embedded in my flesh, they led me to the pillar where Christ was scourged. I kissed the cold marble that had pressed against his holy face which I hope to see again soon in heaven.

This was to be no ordinary lashing like the one I had received from the lictors in Philippi. Two soldiers came at me with leather thongs bearing metal barbs on the ends. The metal barbs would tear my flesh from my bones, laying bare every nerve in my body until I writhed in agony. They would beat me until I was senseless. How had Christ kept silent when his nerves screamed with pain? The Holy Spirit in my soul commanded me to speak.

"Is it legal for you to scourge a Roman and without a trial at that?"

The centurion yelled, "Halt!" just as the first lash was just about to dig into my body. Dumbfounded, the centurion asked, "Are you a citizen of Rome?" He was horrified at the violation of Roman law that he was about to commit, well aware of the serious trouble that would befall him if he scourged a Roman.

"I am a citizen," I replied calmly.

Instantly, the centurion bounded across the flagstones and dashed up a flight of stairs disappearing into the inner chambers of the fortress. I noticed a low chair in the courtyard where I pictured Jesus sitting covered with thorns and with a mock scepter in his hand while the soldiers danced around him on these very flagstones, making a parody of worshiping him.

Claudius Lysias wasted no time. Almost instantly he charged down the stairs into the courtyard with the centurion at his heels. Nervously he studied my face, as I was standing there naked and bound to the pillar.

"Are you a Roman?" he asked anxiously.

"I am."

He reached down, picked up my clothing and personal effects from the flagstones and began to search through them. Glancing up he eyed me coldly.

"I obtained Roman citizenship at a great price," he said thinking, I imagined, that I was a wealthy and prominent person. At once his manner changed towards me.

"I am a citizen by birth," I said flatly.

The Tribune Claudius Lysias, alarmed by the enormity of what he had almost done, ordered me unbound. When I was dressed, he said, "I am greatly honored to save a citizen from those dogs out there that were beating you in the temple."

I was then taken to a cell where I was treated as befits a citizen of Rome, but I was not to remain there very long. I was turned over to my accusers the next morning when the centurion came to my cell and ordered me to accompany him. Under a heavy guard of soldiers, he escorted me through the streets of Jerusalem. I was being taken to the palace of the high priest—to the very spot where Caiaphas had judged Jesus deserving of death. Just as he was taken before the Sanhedrin they took me. With my hands bound behind my back, I was led into the chamber and made to stand before the council of elders who were sitting in a semicircle belligerently watching every movement I made. I knew that the one who presided would be seated in the middle of the semi circle and that there would be a secretary on either end of the group of elders. One would take down the testimony of the defense, the other the testimony of the prosecution. I figured that they might even go so far as to bring in false witnesses against me as they had done against Jesus.

Slowly I surveyed the faces of the men who were to judge me. These were the very men of Israel who should have been the first to recognize Christ and to proclaim his gospel. Instead because of the perversity of their hearts they denied him—most vociferously of all—and demanded his death.

I was determined to bear witness to Christ before the high-ranking authorities of our religion. They would have the gospel preached to them. I would not even give them a chance to bring forth lying witnesses against me. My eyes rested briefly on the face of my sister's husband Jacob, seated among the judges on the bench. We exchanged glances and I knew I could count on his support as I began to speak.

"Brothers, my conscience is clear." I spoke with confidence and with the authority I received from Christ. One of the judges, a man of some years, ordered all those standing near me to strike me for my boldness. As I reeled under the blows, I could feel my eyes beginning to swell shut. Smoldering with fire in my breast, I glared at the man who ordered me struck and thundered at him.

"The Lord is going to strike you!" I then called him a whitewashed wall, referring to the way tombs are whitewashed to make them look clean and hide the corruption they contain. "Are you going to sit there and try me by the law and at the same time violate that law by ordering me to be struck?" I demanded of him.

I remembered how Ananias condoned the action of the soldier who struck Jesus as he stood before him. Recalling his restraint and obedience, his meekness and his humility, I resolved to exercise greater control over my fiery nature. The entire Sanhedrin was aghast at what I had just said. Even Jacob had horror written on his face.

Someone addressed me, "You are insulting God's High Priest?"

So it had been the high priest Ananias who had in violation of the Law ordered me struck. The irony of it all occurred to me. It was rather they who were insulting God's High Priest—Jesus Christ—in my person. Nevertheless, I imitated Christ's obedience and humility.

"I did not know, brothers, that he is the High Priest, the law says one must not speak evil of a ruler of the people."

Because Ananias had me struck in defiance of the Law—and I knew his kind—I would not spare him, but would exercise the authority of the One High Priest and turn the trial against them. Ananias was a Sadducee—a professional priest—who believed in little else beside himself. Although he was the power behind Jewry, he desired to be on good terms with Rome. In this very room, his predecessor Caiaphas, declared Jesus to be deserving of death. Thereupon the elders of Israel fell to the level of beasts. Leaving their judges' seats they came forth and struck Jesus in the face, spitting on him while he stood patiently and permitted them to spend their ungodly fury upon his sacred person. His silence enraged them all the more.

Now—once more—Christ was standing before the Sanhedrin in my person. As I studied Ananias and the rest of the elders, the Holy Spirit within me pleaded for me to speak out. They did not want the light and truth of Christ, but preferred to remain in darkness for their deeds were evil. Before me I saw other Sadducees—the priests; Jacob and the rest were Pharisees. I decided to throw a hot coal into their midst. As a Sadducee, Ananias and the other Sadducees did not believe in life after death. On the other hand, the Pharisees proclaimed their belief in the resurrection of the body. I decided to take advantage of the quarrel that existed between the two factions to turn the trial to my purposes and my advantage. The Pharisees detest the way the Sadducees try to curry favor with Rome. Being a strong nationalistic group, the Pharisees have always refused to make oaths of allegiance to the Roman emperors. Furthermore the Pharisees are proud that they keep the Law—every jot and tittle—as the Scribes give it to them. I leapt to the attack.

"My brothers, I am a Pharisee. My father was a Pharisee, and before him his father, as far back as we can remember, we have been Pharisees." Since we have always been a self-righteous and close-knit minority, I observed the Pharisees who were on the judges bench sit a little taller in their seats when I said this.

"I am on trial because of belief in the resurrection of the dead."

"Resurrection from the dead! Hah!" sneered Ananias. He had fallen into the snare I had laid for him. Jacob shot a glance at me. I could read in his eyes that he had understood what I was doing when he sprang to his feet and said, "Honored elders of Israel, the belief in the resurrection of the dead is without question true, just, and well-founded. Life after death is real. We shall all one day rise!"

A Sadducee, a fat little fellow with a big red nose, shouted, "Nonsense! Listen to your priests. Death is the end of personal existence."

Ananias banged his fist on the table, "Silence!" He tugged nervously at his long white beard. The Pharisees were not about to be silenced.

Jacob took the floor. "We find no evil in this man" he announced. "What if a spirit has really spoken to him or an angel?" With this remark, Jacob pulled a good punch at the High Priest, because Sadducees don't believe in angels either. At the mention of the word "angel" the Sadducees and the Pharisees were at each other's throats.

I walked to the center of the long judgment table where the elders had been sitting. I say had been sitting, for now they were all up milling around and ready to break into violence.

I banged my fist on the table. The time had come. I was going to release the pent up denunciation of the Jews that had been smoldering in my spirit for twenty years or more. The Holy Spirit in my soul took command of the assembly. With fire I began to denounce them using Christ's words.

"Woe to you both, Scribes and Pharisees. You are snakes full of venom, sons of those who stoned the prophets, a perverse bunch of people. Jerusalem will know judgment. Your city will be destroyed, and you within it."

Frozen in their tracks, they stood and listened. When they recovered from the initial shock, they were ready to dismember me on the spot. Quickly I escaped them, calling to the soldiers who brought me to the Sanhedrin. When they saw the danger to which I was exposed they spirited me out of the palace of the High Priest and took me back to the Fortress Antonia.

That night, as I stood in my cell looking out over the temple, with the fire of the altar glowing in the night, my heart was lost in prayer. The presence of Christ enveloped me, giving me to drink of his living waters of love, joy, and rapture. As he refreshed my weary body, mind, and soul, he spoke in the depths of my spirit, telling me that I would bear witness to him in Rome, just as I had in Jerusalem. The Jews would not have me–to Rome I would go.

Now that I was certain that it was God's will for me to go to Rome, I had only to appeal my case to Caesar, whenever I so chose. The local Roman authorities would have no choice but to send me to

Rome since I had the wealth at my disposal to make the appeal. For the time being, however, I decided to play along with the tribune and see what would happen.

When I heard the bolt of the cell door rattle, the centurion threw open the door, announcing, "You have a visitor."

It was David, my nephew! Rachel's oldest child.

"What are you doing here, son? You shouldn't have come." I scolded as I ran my hand through his thick and curly black hair.

"Mother sent me." He was out of breath. "She said I should be willing to risk my life to save you, the apostle of Christ."

I waited while he caught his breath.

"What is wrong, boy?" I knew Rachel wouldn't have sent him to me unless it was really a matter of life and death.

"My father heard a plot in the Sanhedrin to kill you," David's youthful voice trembled as he spoke. "Some of them have sworn under a curse not to eat or drink until they kill you."

"So. How do they plan to do this?" I was amazed at the evil to which they would stoop.

"There are more than forty of them. They have conspired with the chief priests, asking the Sanhedrin to have you brought up for trial again tomorrow. On the way to the High Priest's, they plan to ambush you and kill you on the spot." I marveled at the boy's bravery in face of danger. I pressed his hand in mine and then went to the door of the cell.

"Centurion!" I called. He came at once. "This boy has something to tell Tribune Lysias." I handed the centurion a fistful of coins. "Take the boy to Claudius Lysias at once." He smiled at the coins in his hand and hurried away with David.

I waited alone in the cell, and as I waited I looked out over the doomed city. The smell of animal flesh and fat burning in the temple filled the air with an unbearable stench making me nauseous. I would be glad to leave Jerusalem.

An hour passed. When the centurion returned, he was excited. I could see that something was going to happen at once.

"Hurry," he directed. "We are going to Caesarea immediately to the Roman Governor Felix."

Pondering what he proposed, I said, "They will kill me on the way."

"With two hundred soldiers—seventy cavalry and two hundred men with spears? Hah!" he snorted. "Rome will not turn a citizen over to those greasy Jews. What would they think of us in Rome if we allowed a mob to seize you and kill you right from under our noses?"

I nodded. He was correct in his reasoning. I was going to go to stand before Governor Felix—the successor of Pontius Pilate. The residence of the former governor of Jerusalem and Judea was in Caesarea in the palace built by Herod the Great. Pontius Pilate and his wife Claudia Procula had lived there, but Pilate had passed sentence on Christ in Jerusalem because he came to the city for the Passover to ensure law and order.

I was beginning to look forward to my encounter with the Roman governor. There were a number of things I wanted to tell him.

CHAPTER 5

Without incident, we left Jerusalem at night, riding at a fast gallop to Antipatris and then on the next morning to Caesarea, a magnificent city built by Herod the Great on the seacoast in honor of Augustus Caesar for the purpose of ingratiating himself with the new emperor. For a crowning touch to his city, Herod built a temple to Augustus high overlooking the sea. It bore within it an heroic statue of the emperor. For himself Herod built a splendid palace with a wide spreading view of the Great Sea that has a harbor equal to the Athenian Piraeus. Upon Herod's death, the Roman Governor took occupancy of the palace.

We entered the palace gates and right away I seemed to sense the ghosts of its former occupants—Herod and his family, Pontius Pilate and his beautiful Claudia, the granddaughter of Emperor Augustus. Now it was the residence of Antonius Felix, Procurator of Jerusalem and his stolen wife the Princess Drusilla, the youngest daughter of Herod Agrippa I. Originally she was destined to marry Epiphanes, the son of the king of Commagene, but the marriage never took place, because Epiphanes refused to be circumcised. Her brother Agrippa II gave her in marriage to Azizus, the king of Emesa. When she was only fifteen or sixteen years old, Felix, previously married to the granddaughter of Mark Anthony and Cleopatra, persuaded her to leave her husband and marry him.

Marcus Antonius Felix, born a slave, owed his position to the wealth and influence of his brother, Pallas, who also born in slavery had managed to rise to the status of a prominent freeman. The princess Drusilla was the daughter of King Herod Agrippa, whom I had seen in Jerusalem. Since it is difficult to keep the various Herods and Agrippas separate, I mention that he was the one who flung the severed head of the Apostle James into the city street. Such was the father of Drusilla. Her aunt was Herodias—the woman who demanded and got the head of John the Baptist on a silver platter.

Incestuous and adulterous marriages were common among the Herodians. Herodias, the aunt of Drusilla and the sister of Herod Agrippa married her own uncle, Herod Phillip. She gave him a daughter, Salome. With the violent blood of Herod the Great coursing through her veins, Herodias found life with Herod Phillip insipid in their sumptuous Roman villa. When Herod Antipas, her husband's brother, came to Rome to visit them in their plush estate, she decided that she preferred him and the excitement that he could offer her. She left Rome and went to live with her husband's brother in the great palace of Herod the Great overlooking the Dead Sea.

When John the Baptist denounced them for their immorality, Herodias demanded his head. When Christ appeared before Herod Antipas the night before his crucifixion, Herod, having brought his court to Jerusalem for the Passover, was still fresh with the blood of the Baptist on his hands. Without doubt Herodias and her daughter Salome watched as Christ refused to answer his questions.

Now I was about to meet another one of the Herodians. I sat in the long entrance corridor that stretched from the main gate of the palace into the inner court. Somewhere beyond I could hear foot steps in the distance shuffling along the marble floor. One of the Governor's soldiers ushered me into a council room where I was told to remain standing before a dais that bore a throne with two slaves, with ostrich plumes in their hands, standing on either side, waiting for the governor to appear. Another slave stood at the far door of the chamber with a silver trumpet placed to his lips. Two shrill blasts rang out and echoed through the marble room.

"His Excellency, Marcus Antonius Felix, Roman Governor of Judea!"

Great pomp heralded the arrival of the governor. I watched with interest as I saw the man, who had been born a slave and had risen to the position of governor, prance into the room with all the airs of a prince. His toga was made of silk and edged not in red, as is the custom, but in gold. Felix, handsome like one of the statues I had seen in Achaia, had a taste for the royal life. He was also arrogant.

The centurion who had been in charge of our hasty trip from Jerusalem to Caesarea stepped forward—his tunic crisp and his armor gleaming—and handed him the letter that Claudius Lysias had written to Felix.

"A letter from Claudius Lysias to Your Excellency," he reported extending the letter to Felix.

Disdainfully Felix sneered at the centurion. With a flick of the hand, he signaled for one of his soldiers to take the letter and read it to him. As the soldier read the letter Felix assumed a bored look while he meticulously pondered his manicure. Loudly the soldier read:

"Claudius Lysias to His Excellency Felix, the Governor Greeting! Whereas this man was seized by the Jews and was on the point of being killed by them, I came upon them with troops and rescued him, having learned that he was a Roman."

I listened carefully to that last statement. Who was he trying to fool? He rescued me, he said, having learned that I was Roman! The soldier continued reading the letter.

"And wishing to know what charge they had preferred against him, I took him into their Sanhedrin. I found him accused of violations of their law, but not of any crime deserving of death or imprisonment. And when I was told of an ambush that they had prepared for him, I sent him to you, directing his accusers also to state their case before you. Farewell!"

Felix studied me with interest and asked from what province I came.

"Cilicia," I answered tersely.

Felix yawned. "I will hear you when your accusers come." Signaling to two soldiers who were in attendance, he commanded officiously, "Take him to the prison."

I was led through a subterranean passageway under the palace and up on the other side of the building into a tower from which I could observe the sea and the sky in one direction, and the rolling hills of Samaria in the other. Some twenty-five miles to the north lay Galilee, the land Christ loved.

The cell was quite adequate with a writing table, supplied with a lamp and a chair. Weary from the trials and the wild ride through the night and morning, I sank down into the sack of hay provided for a bed. As the sun was sinking into the sea and the blue of the heavens was turning to brilliant red, gold, and mauve, a jailer, a friendly young man from Puteoli just south of Rome, I learned, brought me supper. As he put my supper on the table by the open window—there were no bars for we were high up in the tower—he asked politely, "Why are you here?"

As I explained to him as best I could the events that had brought me to his jail, he listened attentively and commented: "It is hard to understand those Jews. In Rome, one god more or less makes no difference. As for me, I believe only in what I can see and touch with my hands." He held up his hands and opened and closed his broad sturdy fingers.

"What's your name?" I asked seeing in him a prospective convert.

"Julius." His friendly and open way of looking at me made me determined to win him to Christ during my stay in Caesarea. I liked the way his honest blue eyes looked directly into mine when he spoke to me.

After he had left me alone again, I reflected that it didn't really matter where I am, for God is everywhere and in every place I can work and pray for the spread of Christ's kingdom. No man can measure the height or the breadth or the depth of his love. If I were to journey to the farthest star he would be there when I arrived. If I were to spend my days in this jail—as I was to do for the next two years—he would be with me. Even here I would bear witness to him, completing the sufferings of Christ in my own flesh. Paul the Apostle in chains for the gospel would live in his prison cell the life of Christ the priest, the mediator between man and God.

I glanced at my supper tray. There was a portion of fish, a vegetable—some bread and wine. I left the food untouched, carefully preserving the bread and wine. Later that night when the stars came out and the moon rode high over the sea and when I could hear the rolling breakers in the stillness of the night dashing themselves on the shore, I took the bread and broke it and the cup of wine and blessed it, offering up the holy sacrifice for the sins of the world and for my own sins. I was in prison and Christ visited me. I was hungry and he fed me, thirsty and he gave me to drink of his Spirit, his love and his life. I rejoiced that he found me worthy to suffer something for his sake. Prostrate on the flagstones of my cell, I lay awake the rest of the night adoring the Father, the Son, and the Holy Spirit. When the morning sun filtered into my window, it found me still lost in the wonders of God's love.

At noon Julius informed me that I had visitors. Following me from Jerusalem, Luke and Timothy brought with them my personal effects that I left at my sister's house. I was really glad to see them. Luke was the first to speak.

"Well quite a sumptuous jail," he joked. "It is a lot more worthy of you than the jail when you and Silas were the guests of the Philippians" His gentle eyes grew sad and solicitous. "Now tell me honestly are you all right?"

"Are you really all right, Father Paul?" Timothy dropped a bundle of my parchments on the table.

Rubbing my side, I replied, "All except for a bruise here where a soldier kicked me."

Already Luke was tugging at my robe and laying bare my aching side. With his fingers he skillfully probed my ribs.

"Nothing broken" he diagnosed. "Subcutaneous bleeding. We will put some hot compresses on it and have it better in a few days." He looked at my wrists and throwing back my sleeves, saw what I had been hiding from everyone. My wrists were swollen and some of the sores made by the chains were suppurating.

"Let me clean those purulent wounds." Luke was giving the orders now and I had to obey. He did not spare me. I held my breath and grimaced as he prodded, cleaned, and scraped. He finished by pouring wine into the gaping holes in my flesh.

"Where is your mercy, man!" I whispered between clenched teeth as the fire of the wine mingled with my blood.

Luke chuckled and replied, "Here all the time I was under the impression that the Apostle Paul was made of stone and bronze. So resolute was he in the face of the wolves in Jerusalem."

"Who is weak, and I am not weak?" I replied without shame. "I am no stoic."

Because Timothy, I could see, was very much worried and distressed by my imprisonment, I wanted to cheer him up. "I am going to Rome," I informed him in high spirits.

"Rome, Father Paul?" He seemed quite anxious.

Luke dropped his bandage and asked. "Really? Are they going to set you free?"

"I didn't say that. Just believe me. We shall see Rome." I wanted to reassure Luke and Timothy with the comfort with which Christ comforted me. I explained that they would have to let me stand trial before Caesar.

Five days later Ananias, the High Priest, arrived in a cloud of dust. From my tower cell I watched as he rode up to the gates of the palace, bringing with him a number of the elders. In a body, they stormed into the palace.

A short time after they arrived, Julius came to inform me that the governor was waiting for me in the council chambers. I followed Julius down the circular stair of the tower into the dungeon. We crossed through the subterranean passage way and then up into the corridor just outside the council chamber.

When we were inside the council room, I was given a chair. Face to face across from me, Ananias was sending forth venomous looks in my direction as we waited for Governor Felix to arrive.

When the silver trumpets of the soldiers at the door announced the arrival of Antonius Felix, he appeared with his customary pomp with his golden slippers gliding quickly over the highly polished marble floor. With great, assumed dignity, he mounted the dais and motioned for the slaves with the ostrich plumes to begin fanning him. Impatiently Felix waved his hands towards the prosecutor, one Tertullus that Ananias brought with him.

Rising to his feet, Tertullus began their case against me. I could hear Ananias conferring with the elders from Jerusalem with the sibilant sounds of their voices echoing through the hall like the hissing of adders. As Tertullus was unrolling his parchment containing his brief of the case, I observed a woman, wearing costly jewels and robes, slipping silently into the rear of the council chamber and taking a seat in the shadows. I figured that the daughter of the Herods was overcome by her curiosity and came to see the apostle of Christ.

Clearing his throat impressively, Tertullus launched his attack.

"Whereas we live in much peace under your administration," he bowed obsequiously before the Governor, "and whereas many reforms are in now in progress because of your vision," he bowed again, "we always and everywhere receive them, most excellent Felix, with much gratitude."

As Tertullus continued his fulsome address, Felix gave him a nauseating smile.

"But not to detain you too long, I entreat you to be kind enough to grant us a brief hearing." He hesitated a moment. "We have found this man to be a pest" he spat out the word pest, "and an agitator of riots among Jews throughout the entire world." He pointed a finger at me, "He is the head of the Nazarene sect." He waited for his accusations to penetrate, "He even tried to defile our temple, but we caught him. We wanted to judge him under our law. However, Claudius Lysias, the tribune, came upon us with great force, taking him out of our hands, ordering his accusers to appear before you. By examining him yourself, you will discover all these things with which we charge him." Tertullus bowed deeply and took a seat, resting his complaint.

Heaving a sigh of relief that Tertullus was finished speaking, Felix called me to speak in my defense. Welcoming the opportunity, I confidently arose and placed myself at the foot of his throne and began by appealing to his sense of Roman justice.

"Because I know that for many years you have been a judge for this nation, I shall be glad to explain my case to you." Felix yawned and waved his hand for me to proceed. "You can easily verify what I am going to tell you. About twelve days ago, not more than that, I went to Jerusalem and to the temple to worship. I did not dispute with anyone or cause any disturbance in the temple, nor in the synagogue, nor anywhere in the city. The charges that are brought against me cannot be proven." Before continuing I paused, looked at my accusers calmly, and I surveyed the governor with self-assurance and confidence. "But I admit that I am a follower of the Way and in it I serve the Lord of my fathers, believing what is written in the law and the prophets. I believe and hope that there will be a resurrection of the just and the unjust," I glanced at the Pharisees among the elders, "as do many of my adversaries. I always strive to have a clear conscience before God and man.

"After having been away from Jerusalem for several years, I returned to bring alms and to offer sacrifice and fulfill vows. I was in the temple doing this when they found me. I was alone and not disturbing anyone. However, there were some Jews from Asia in the temple at the time of the disturbance, but they are not present here to accuse me of anything. These men who *are* here, let them state what I did wrong, when I appeared before the Sanhedrin. Perhaps it was because I shouted out that they were judging me because of my belief in the resurrection of the dead." I looked steadily at Ananias who was fulminating with rage, murmuring, and eager to speak out against me.

"Silence" thundered Felix. "I am aware of the Christian sect. It has been the policy of Rome throughout the empire to leave the Christian sect alone. It is not—at the present time—a crime to be a follower of the Way. When Lysias the tribune comes to Caesarea, I will decide this case." He dismissed Ananias and his retinue with a flick of the finger. Turning to me he said, "The prisoner is to remain here with the privilege of seeing his friends as often as he wishes."

Luke and Timothy, who were sitting near the Princess Drusilla, came forward and accompanied me as I returned with Julius to my cell. It was time we begin drawing up plans for the future.

A few days later something very interesting took place. I was busy with my parchments when Julius informed me that the governor wanted to see me at once. Laying aside my quill and ink, I immediately followed Julius through the winding corridors of the palace to an elegant room festooned with red curtains where Felix was reclining on a plush red cushion eating a cluster of grapes. Beside him was the woman I had seen in the council chamber.

"Ah!" he remarked jauntily. "Come in, my fellow Roman. The Princess Drusilla wants to meet you."

So that's why I was summoned. I nodded curtly and replied: "Greetings to the governor and to the Princess Drusilla."

Completely lacking in the modesty that should have characterized a Hebrew princess, she was dressed in Roman attire. Her arms were bare and wrapped around one of them was a golden bracelet fashioned like a snake in the Egyptian style, probably a trinket from his former wife, the granddaughter of Cleopatra. Her face was beautiful with a sensuous beauty that reflected the lust of Antonius Felix. Fussing with her elaborate hairstyle and smiling at me with an uncertain, self-conscious smile, she motioned for me to sit on a cushion across from her. "I was at your trial." she began uncertainly. "I saw you. You are interested in law and justice?" I doubted that.

"As the daughter of King Herod Agrippa and sister of King Agrippa, I am concerned with all Jewish affairs." She exchanged glances with Felix and continued, "I could never understand all the nonsense of the high priests and the elders and all their law. I hear you are proclaiming a new religion for us all, Jews and Romans. I should be interested in hearing about it. The old was too difficult to keep. Why just consider the marriage laws..." she fell silent.

Did I detect a trace of remorse in her conscience?

"There is no way to escape the justice of God." She seemed to squirm when I said that. "A man will be rewarded for his good deeds and punished for his evil ones. Each of us will have to stand before the judgment seat of the living God." I probed her soul. She squirmed under my gaze. Turning to Felix I continued, "I am certain that as a judge of the people, Your Excellency, you have a strong sense of justice and the desire to punish evil." As he watched me intently, his face was cruel and arrogant.

"Why even the idol worshipers I have met among the Greeks in Macedonia have a natural born feeling that to be unchaste and adulterous is wrong. Romans used to have a high regard for the sanctity of the home," I added remembering Felix' origins.

"Enough, enough of your silly religious prattle! Tell me about it some other day!" snapped the governor.

Lowering her eyes, and biting her lower lip, Drusilla cringed with shame. I waited in silence for Felix to resume the conversation or else dismiss me. Nervously he stood up and paced over to the window. Drusilla picking up a bunch of grapes from the silver tray nibbled the fruit while trying to ignore me.

"Come, let's get to the point of this interview," Felix blurted out impatiently. It was obvious that he was emotionally agitated.

Calmly I surveyed him, as he paced from the window to the center of the room and back again.

"Look, old fellow," he began, "I can get you out of this prison—free—completely acquitted—out," he hesitated before making the plunge, "—but it would cost you—a sizeable amount of that fortune of yours." He toyed with the gold ring that he wore on his right hand.

Bribery! He wanted me to pay him for my freedom. It was fantastic! His audacity appalled me. He thought that I would stoop to paying him a bribe!

"Your Excellency," I was treading my way carefully, "you are mistaken. I will have to wait in your prison until the wheels of Roman justice set me free. I stood up. "And now if you will allow me return to my cell, I shall take leave of you."

Showing great annoyance, he sent a slave to fetch my jailer.

Several times during the next two years Antonius Felix tried to extort money from me in exchange for my freedom. Each times I shrugged my shoulders and dismissed the subject, content to remain where I was until God was ready to take me to Rome in the working out of his providence. As it turned out, I stayed in Caesarea longer than Felix. When riots broke out in his territory, Rome recalled him.

The new Governor Porcius Festus had the reputation of being a man of integrity. I hoped that he would investigate my case that Felix had postponed for two years in the hope of extorting money from me. After he had been in Caesarea only three days, Festus went up to

Jerusalem to take a look around the city, because it was famous for its rebellious spirit and he had to make an account of it to Caesar.

When he returned from Jerusalem, I was not surprised to see that a large number of Jews came with him, demanding that he release me to them. If he did that, I was as good as dead.

On trial once more, this time before Festus, I was accused of many serious charges that they could not prove. When I was finally given a chance to speak in my defense, I denied all their accusations. "I have committed no offence against the Jewish law, nor against the temple, not against Caesar." I was getting impatient to have my freedom.

I could see that the new governor was trying to curry the favor of his people for without doubt he was wishing to please them when he asked me: "Are you willing to go up to Jerusalem and be tried there before me on these charges?"

I'd had enough! I did not wish to be returned to the prison cell there in Caesarea for another two years, nor did I wish to be returned to the bloodthirsty Jews of Jerusalem, even if the Roman Governor would go up with me and try my case. I remembered only too well the justice of Pilate when he sentenced Jesus to death, all the while proclaiming him to be innocent. Fixing my eyes intently on the governor, I took matters into my own hands.

"I am standing at the tribunal of Caesar and that is where I should be tried. I have done nothing wrong to the Jews, as you know very well. If I had done any wrong or committed any capital crime, I would not refuse to die. However, since their charges against me are completely unfounded, I refuse to be turned over to them." I paused to make my next statement ring in their ears by preceding it with a moment of silence.

"I appeal to Caesar!" I even repeated in Latin to be sure there was no doubt about what I was saying. "Caesarem appello!"

Gleefully I surveyed my enemies. They had lost, for Festus now had no choice but to send me to Rome to let Nero decide my case. What Nero did with me did not matter. All that was important was that I would have a glorious chance to give witness to the Lord Jesus in Rome!

Before I sailed for Rome, I had the opportunity to meet more members of the Herodian family when King Agrippa and his sister Bernice came to pay their respects to the new Roman Governor. Festus, unsure of himself and wanting to make friends with as many elements in Jewish life as possible, decided to flatter Agrippa by dragging me before him and having me relate my case to him. I did not mind because it gave me one more chance to give witness to the Lord to the rulers of the Jewish people.

Staging a magnificent performance for King Agrippa, Festus constructed an elaborate throne for the King in the council chamber. All the prominent men of Caesarea were summoned to be present for my audience when Festus entered the audience chamber with all the pomp and ceremony he could arrange—silver trumpets—foot soldiers—even purple carpet—giving Agrippa and Bernice a grand royal welcome. With six slaves to attend him, Agrippa climbed up the stairs to his throne and with grand solemnity seated himself with great dignity.

I was called to stand before Agrippa who was easily recognized as the brother of Princess Drusilla, because the resemblance was evident in his charming and handsome face that had not yet developed the sensual avaricious look about him that his father had, the day I saw him order the slaying of the Apostle James. He was still young. Time would change him.

When Festus arose to address the audience filled with curiosity seekers, I surveyed those present and saw another chance to preach the gospel. Festus began to speak "King Agrippa and all here present, I examined this man," he pointed at me," and found that he has done nothing deserving the death penalty, although a large number of Jews have begged me, both here and in Jerusalem, to have him put to death. Since he has now appealed to Caesar, I have no choice but to send him to Rome, but I still having nothing to write to Caesar about him. So I have brought him before you, hoping that after you examine him, I might have something to put in writing for the emperor. It doesn't seem right to send a prisoner all the way to Rome without stating the charges made against him."

With that Festus seated himself with a flourish of his scarlet cloak on his gubernatorial throne and turned the proceedings over to Agrippa who, with all the dignity of his thirty-five years, looked down at me and condescendingly said, "You are free to speak for yourself."

I rose to my feet and began to preach Christ, and him crucified, to the men of Caesarea—to the Roman Governor and to the Herodian royalty.

"I consider myself fortunate, King Agrippa, to be able to defend myself today before you against all the accusations the Jews have made about me, because I know you are well acquainted with Jewish customs and controversies. Please listen to me patiently." I knew that he had been educated in Rome and was even in Rome when his father had the Apostle James slain, but I still felt sure that he was schooled in Jewish ways.

"Everyone knows about my early life, how I was born in Tarsus, and went to study with Rabban Gamaliel in Jerusalem, becoming a doctor of the Jewish law. Many can attest to the fact that I have lived as a Pharisee in strict observance of the law. Because of my hope and belief in the promises made by God to our fathers, I am standing trial—I am talking about belief in the resurrection of the dead. All twelve of the tribes of Israel have believed in the resurrection of the dead. It is because of this hope that I am accused by the Jews.

"At one time, I felt it was my duty to persecute the followers of Jesus. This I did in Jerusalem. Having received authority from the high priests, I arrested many of them and had them thrown into prison. When they were tried facing the death penalty, I voted against them. I dragged them out of the synagogues to punish them, trying to force them to blaspheme the name of the Lord Jesus. In my extreme wrath and fury against them, I even tracked them down in foreign cities."

I was pleased to note that the men of Caesarea were listening attentively to my recital. So also were Agrippa and Festus.

"But one day when I was on the way to Damascus with authority and permission from the chief priests to arrest followers of Christ there, I saw a bright light all around me and my companions—it was brighter than the sunshine. We all fell to the ground. I heard a voice asking me in Aramaic, why I was persecuting him. I asked him who he was. The voice told me that he was Jesus whom I was persecuting. He then told me that I was to stand up, that he was appointing me to be a witness to what I had just seen and heard and to future visions he would send me. He said I was to open people's eyes that they may turn from darkness to the light, that their sins might be forgiven and that they might find a place in his kingdom, going from the dominion of Satan to the kingdom of God."

I looked up at Agrippa who was shaking his head in disbelief and sneering contemptuously as he exchanged glances with his sister. He then looked over at Governor Festus, and raising a finger to his head made a gesture to the effect that I was demented.

Ignoring them, I continued for I was determined that they would hear the gospel of Christ.

"Therefore, King Agrippa, I obeyed the vision, going first to Damascus and Jerusalem and then to all Judea and finally to the Gentiles, declaring that they too should repent and turn to God. This is the reason the Jews seized me in the temple and tried to kill me. But with the help of God, I stand here to testify, saying only what the prophets and Moses said would come to pass—that Messiah would suffer and by his resurrection from the dead would proclaim light to our people and to the Gentiles." I paused to catch my breath

"Paul, you are mad," yelled Festus. "Your great learning is driving you crazy." He laughed uproariously.

"I am not mad, your Excellency," I replied remembering that the same accusation had been hurled at Christ to discredit him. "I speak truth. The King knows about these things and I am addressing him, without hesitation, because I am sure he is aware of what has been happening." I was smoldering with rage. Walking closer to the king, I asked, "Do you believe in the prophets, King Agrippa?"

He did not answer.

"I know you do." I answered for him.

"Hah!" he sneered, "you think in a short time you can make a Christian of me!"

"I wish not only you, in a short time or longer, would believe as I do and be as I am, except for these chains." I held up my wrists for all to see.

Adjourning to another room Agrippa, Bernice, Festus, and their companions pondered my fate, deciding that I had done nothing to deserve death.

In conclusion Agrippa proclaimed: "If he had not appealed to Caesar, he could go free."

Since I had appealed to Caesar to Caesar I would go. I saw God's will being made evident in the events that transpired. It would be good to sail the seas once more—to have wind at my back and the stars plotting my course—a straight course to Rome.

The wind whistles. The shutter on my cell window rattles and shakes as if being struck by a giant's fist. Night has fallen and I can no longer watch the distant bend of the Via Laurentia for Timothy. O Lord, hasten Timothy to me! Let me look once more into the face of my dearest son before I come to you. He can come undetected to the window here at night and talk to me. I will impart to him my spirit, your Spirit and strengthen him for the building up of the churches. Luke is sleeping at the other end of the cell. He is ready—even eager to spill his blood with mine for the glory of your holy name.

The guard is sleeping outside the cell. At any moment the order can come for me to face the executioner's sword. If it comes tonight—then at dawn I—I will be with you. Perhaps Timothy will arrive too late.

My death and the deaths of Peter and Luke will satisfy Nero and the terror of the persecution will run its course with the deaths of the shepherds of Christ's flock. When the Emperor rode his chariot into the circus and the populace screamed out with one voice against him blaming him for the fire which destroyed half of Rome, he lashed out at your followers blaming the blaze on us and inaugurating a blood purge such as the city has never before witnessed. With the deaths of the apostles the populace will be satisfied. Peace will once more return to the flock of God and you will raise up new shepherds who will be willing to die for the sheep

I recall when I first set sail to come to Rome. Festus was making arrangements for my journey while at the same time I was drawing up my own plans. I wrote to Titus who was still in Jerusalem, inviting him to join Luke and Timothy in accompanying me to the imperial city. Festus released me in the custody of my jailer Julius—he had served both in the Augustan cohort and in the Praetorian Guard—who was to return to Rome after a rather long tour of duty in Caesarea.

With my arm chained to his, we left the prison in Herod's tower, boarding a ship of Adramyttium that was bound for ports in the Province of Asia. Since it was late in summer, sailing would soon become hazardous. Already the winds were beginning to blow and there was a chop on the sea, but I was not eager to spend another winter in prison in Caesarea. When Festus arranged for me to go to Rome with Julius, I jumped at the opportunity.

The captain gave the order for the anchor to be drawn up over the side. The mainsail was unfurled to the wind and we were underway as I stood on deck with Julius and watched Caesarea recede on the

horizon. Once out to sea, the ship steered northward and began following the coastline.

"There is no need for us to be chained together any longer," Julius
said as he unlocked the chains that bound me to him. Picking up our
belongings from the deck, together we went below to the large dormitory that all the passengers were to share with a separate dormitory provided for the crew. I noticed a number of other prisoners in
the dormitory in the company of some Roman soldiers. Luke, Timothy, and Titus took bunks near mine. Once we were settled in, we
returned to the deck where the air was fresher.

Julius was in a talkative mood. We had grown to know each other
quite well. As we strolled around the deck he said, "I admire you, sir."

We paused at the stern and watched the wake of the ship while the
sea gulls circled above, hoping that some scraps of food might be
thrown into the water for them. For a few moments, I stood looking
at Julius' well chiseled face that reflected his military training in its
disciplined appearance with his strong jaw and his steady unwaver-
ing eyes. His hands were strong and muscular. Very erect in his tunic
and military gear, he was in the prime of life. The sun glistened on
his helmet and I could see myself reflected in it.

"I admire you also, Julius. I admire your self discipline—your
strength, your forthrightness, and honesty." I leaned against the
ship's railing and gazing into his serious brown eyes said, "The first
day I met you, you said you only believe in what you can see with
your eyes and touch with your hands. Do you still feel that way?"

Thoughtfully he studied a passing ship as it glided along the horizon. Then he replied, "Over the months I have seen something in
you, sir, something which I did not see when I first met you. I have
felt something in your presence that I can not put my finger on." His
face was pensive—serious. I kept silent waiting for him to continue.
"I was at your trials—both of them—before Felix and Festus. I also
heard what you told the Jewish King Agrippa. You saw someone—Jesus—who chose you to be his minister. You are appointed to

give spiritual vision to men who live in darkness as regards the soul—sight to people who see only with the eyes of their bodies." The sunshine flickered in his eyes. He raised his hand to shield them. "I would like to see with the eyes of my spirit—the way you do. The things of the spirit are all important to you. You are not afraid of death—or of Festus—or even of Nero. You are strong like a commander of an entire army. I was with Vespasian on one campaign. Your strength surpasses his. You know I was a palace guard when Claudius was emperor. Pallas sent me to Felix on a special mission. I know Rome."

I was anxious to find out all I could about the imperial city. Soon I would be there and would witness to Christ before the entire world. I had to learn as much as possible about the Roman soul—the Roman mind—if I were to convert them.

"You knew Claudius?" I asked drawing him out. In the distance I could just make out the coast—hazy and gray. With the ship rolling gently, the peace of the quiet waters was conducive to conversation.

"Yes, I knew him. I even knew Caligula. My father was a palace guard for Caligula. I was eleven years old when Caligula became Emperor. He was on the throne for only four years. My father took me at times into the palace."

"Caligula—that was a nickname was it not—Little Boots an odd name for an emperor," I commented, drawing in a deep breath of the salt air.

"It was the name the soldiers gave him. My father said that Caligua or Gaius—his real name—used to wear a soldier's suit and boots when he was a small boy—so they nicknamed him Boots."

"It was the soldiers that stabbed him wasn't it?"

"Yes. One of them could no longer endure the obscenities he used for passwords in the palace. He was crazy you know. He tried to make everyone think he was a god. He called Jupiter his 'other self.' He even sat in the temple of Castor and Pollux and demanded that the people worship him, making the senators kiss his feet and thank him for the privilege. Frequently he went screaming through the palace yelling, 'I am a god!' I remember once when I was a child he made me bow down before him and worship him as I was strolling on the Palatine." Julius smiled and shrugged his shoulders. "I never have had any religion but I could see that Boots wasn't worthy of adoration. Some of the emperors have tried to get the people to worship them as representing the state. I cannot worship the state either." He threw up his hands. "Did the state give me my life?"

I shook my head in agreement as his thoughts went racing on.

"Do you know," he asked soberly" that Caligula sent out the army to conquer the ocean? My father told me that when the soldiers came to the sea, Caligula called a halt and commanded the men to gather sea shells as trophies of victory."

"He was insane," I agreed. "There is no doubt of it. I heard that his uncle Claudius was hiding behind the curtains in the palace the night the soldiers killed Caligula. I heard that either our Jewish Prince Herod Agrippa or the Praetorian Guard found him there and nominated him—poor mentally unbalanced Claudius—for emperor."

"Yes, Claudius was the butt of all the court jests. The soldiers had no respect for him. You, sir, are nobler, more regal than any of these I have seen wear the purple. If you were a commander in battle I would give you my entire allegiance. You are a leader of men and I respect you for that." Julius spoke with warmth and sincerity.

"I am a priest of Jesus Christ!" I exclaimed immediately. "An apostle—he is my strength—the master of men that you admire in me." I was praying for the conversion of his soul. Julius continued telling me about Rome and his experiences there.

"Claudius couldn't even run his own household. A former slave, Pallas, became his steward. Another freedman, Narcissus, was his secretary. They ran everything. Pallas made his brother Felix the Governor of Judea and then sent me out there where you found me.

I was glad to leave Rome. Very happy to get out of Claudius' palace." Julius sighed deeply as if remembering something.

"Why?" I probed

"Messalina! The Empress—Claudius' wife was a bitch. I mean, sir, she was a nymphomaniac. Her lust was insatiable—reckless. They say she even disguised herself and went to the brothels and even kept the fees that the patrons gave her there." He grimaced with a deep furrow ploughing his brow. "The palace was no place for me. It was dangerous to be there. Men who spurned and repulsed her advances sometimes lost their lives."

What kind of trial would I get when such people were in control of the empire? I thought I had seen depravity in Corinth, but I was beginning to discover that Rome was unbelievably degenerate. I remembered what Christ said that the healthy have no need of a physician. The people to whom I was being sent were sick—with a morbid fatal illness. I possessed the cure. They were filled with a deadly poison and I rejoiced that I had the antidote.

"Messalina died—Claudius took another wife didn't he?"

"Died!" exclaimed Julius "That is a polite way of expressing it. She was murdered." I kept silent and waited for him to explain.

"While Claudius was in Ostia on one occasion, Messalina formally married a young man—Gaius Silius, I believe his name was. She married him with all the customary marriage ceremonies and pomp. Narcissus told the emperor that she was involved in a plot to kill him. She was slain. Then Claudius married Nero's mother. She was Caligula's sister, Agrippina." Julius puckered up his mouth as if he had tasted something sour.

"You mean, Nero's mother was the sister of the insane Caligula?" It looked as though I were to stand trial before a mad man. Nero was the product of adultery, incest, brutality, and murder.

"Yes. She was thirty and Claudius was fifty-seven. She persuaded Claudius to adopt her son Nero. She had plans for Nero right from the start. Next she managed to marry Nero to Claudius' daughter, because she wanted Nero to be made emperor instead of Claudius son, Britannicus."

Julius paused and watched a few gulls that were circling overhead.. They made a breathtaking picture against the deep blue cloudless sky. It always amazes me how these birds just seem to hang in the air barely moving.

"Agrippina was Claudius niece? He married his niece?"

"Exactly, Agrippina proceeded to take over the running of the Empire, sitting beside Claudius on the imperial dais! She even recalled Seneca from exile where Claudius had sent him as a punishment after Claudius had accused the philosopher of improper relations with Julia, the daughter of Germanicus.

"Seneca? He is the famous stoic philosopher that was Nero's tutor? Is that right?" It seemed as if I had heard that somewhere. I could see nothing, admirable in the philosophy that produced Nero.

"Seneca tutored Nero, all right, but I don't think it did much good. Oh, there were a few humane things Nero did, like making a law that the gladiators were not to fight to the death in the arena. That was done to placate Seneca. Seneca writes Nero's speeches for him. He preaches a beautiful philosophy, but he condones the worst of Nero's crimes." Julius showed contempt for the philosopher who did not live what he preached by shaking his head.

"What does he preach?" I asked with interest.

"He believes that there is a living God who is a Spirit dwelling within a man's spirit. He teaches that virtue is its own reward, but does not believe in life after death. According to him, a man has the right to control his dying and may freely take his own life when he no longer chooses to live. They say he lives ascetically—never drinks wine, eats very little and sleeps on a hard bed. And he is fabulously wealthy." Julius sat down on the bench on the starboard side and invited me to join him.

"Tell me more about Nero and his court?" The better I knew Nero, the better I could stand before him giving witness to the truth.

"Well, let's see. Agrippina had another friend of hers, Burrus, appointed prefect of the Praetorian Guard. Then she really held the power. Claudius hardly realized what was happening because she did it all so smoothly. It was only after five years of marriage that Claudius learned what Agrippina was trying to do. He named his son, Britannicus, his heir."

"What did Agrippina do then?" I was amazed by the Roman way of life.

"She fed old Claudius poisonous mushrooms. He died after twelve hours of horrible agony. Nero and Claudius' daughter whom he married, her name is Octavia, rose to the purple. Then to crown the whole affair, the Senate deified Claudius."

"They proclaimed that Claudius was divine? That he was a god?" It was incredible

Julius laughed, a brittle hollow laugh.

"Yes, Nero remarked that mushrooms must be the food of the gods since Claudius became divine by eating them."

"Is Agrippina the real power or is Nero?" I wondered just who I had appealed to for justice.

"Neither one. From what I hear it resides between Seneca and Poppaea Sabina."

"Poppaea?"

"Nero's new lady. He stole her from her husband Salvius Otho just recently—everyone knows about that." He was surprised that I was ignorant of all this.

"I have never concerned myself with imperial affairs before—never had any need to until I appealed to Caesar," I explained.

"Nero wants to put away Octavia, the wife his mother gave him. Agrippina was furious. She also knew Nero's lust. She and Seneca allowed Nero—he's only twenty-two now—to indulge himself without restraints. Nero disguises himself and goes to brothels. He even practices all kinds of lewdness with young men he finds in the streets of Rome. Nero even accosted one of the Senators. The man was put to death because he defended himself against Nero's lust."

Such was the world Christ came to save. Such were the Romans to whom I was to bear witness to the truth. Julius had still more to say.

"Just before we set sail from Caesarea, I heard from some friends of mine in Rome who are in the Praetorian Guard. They said that Nero's mother offered her body to Nero to satisfy his lust if he would not divorce Octavia."

Julius did not seem to feel the horror of what he was relating to me. It was enough to make me sick at my stomach.

"They told me that Nero tried to murder his mother with poison many times, but she regularly takes the antidotes."

"This is about all I can stomach of this conversation, Julius. It seems that I will have very little chance of converting Nero and his household." I stood up not wanting to hear any more.

"Don't give up all hope," Julius said restraining my arm with his hand. "They say that Poppaea Sabina is a devotee of Judaism."

"A devotee of Judaism!" That I found impossible to believe.

"They say she sends money to the temple of the Jews in Jerusalem and that she surrounds herself with high ranking members of the synagogue in Rome—that she goes to them for advice."

I realized at once the import of what he was saying. The Jews want to put me to death and they hold influence over Nero's Poppaea!" One word from her would be all that it would take.

Abruptly Julius pulled me back down to the bench. Looking me in the eye, he said bluntly without preamble, "Sir, you might not convert Nero, but—you have converted me. Will you receive me into your faith?"

I was not surprised, for Julius had been the object of many prayers the past couple years. "As soon as I have instructed you in the faith," I replied with a warm smile.

It was time for the evening meal. Together we went below into the ship's refectory where Luke, Timothy and Titus were waiting for us.

The next day we reached Sidon where Julius gave me complete freedom, even permitting me to go ashore to visit the Christians there. I did not stay long—only a few hours.

We put to sea again sailing northward from Sidon, passing under the lee of Cyprus. Because the winds were against us and there was a slight chop on the sea, the ship began to pitch and roll as she trudged her way through the waters off Cilicia. We were close enough to the Cilician coast to see the mountains—purple and gray against the cloudless sky. There was no rain in sight. We put in at Myra in Lycia and went ashore, because we had to find another ship—one that would carry us from there to Rome. The ship we boarded was an Alexandrine freighter carrying a cargo of wheat to Italy. We made slow progress, reaching Cnidus with difficulty because the wind was against us. Then we sailed under the lee of Crete—off Salome—and with difficulty came to a place called Fair Havens, near the town of Lasea in Crete where the captain decided to lay over in the harbor, putting in a fresh supply of water and comestibles.

Hoping to put our time on Crete to good use, Julius agreed to what I proposed with the proviso that he accompany me ashore. After Titus and I scrambled down the gangplank with Julius leading the way, we made our way to the market place where we inquired in the various shops if there were any Christians on the island. We were directed to the home of a Jewish couple, Jonathan and Rebecca who welcomed us with open arms and hearts.

"Yes," Jonathan told us, "there are many Christians on Crete. Unfortunately, though we have no priest. We have been praying for God to send us one. Your visit here is truly providential." Right then a plan began to formulate in my mind.

"We would be truly blessed," said his wife "if you would offer the Holy Sacrifice for us here in our home."

I quickly agreed to what she had suggested. Jonathan sent a slave to invite the other Christians of the region to come to the breaking of bread. While we waited for them to assemble Jonathan tried to persuade me to remain in Crete.

"Stay with us he pleaded. We need you. There is no one to minister to the church here."

From the window of his house I could see the ship in the harbor. "Perhaps we could arrange to stay for the winter." I replied looking hopefully at Julius.

"It might be more sensible," agreed Julius "for the ship to winter here in Fair Havens. It is very late in the year for sailing. The waters could prove dangerous." I could tell by the expression in Julius eyes that he knew how much it mattered to me for the church to be born on Crete.

"We could talk to the captain and suggest that he lay up here for the next several months," Julius conceded.

Titus added, "I would like to stay and get the church really established." His enthusiasm pleased me.

"Our home is at your disposal," offered the charming Rebecca.

A child entered the room carrying a strange four-footed creature such as I had never seen anywhere before. It seemed gentle enough. However it looked like a miniature lion or tiger. As the child stroked the animal's head it began to purr. My curiosity was aroused.

"What do you have there, little man?" I patted the lad on the top of his head.

"It's my cat, Bobo. Here you can hold him." The child thrust the creature into my hands. It squirmed, jumped, and ran away. I looked at Titus and we all laughed.

In a short time the house began to fill with worshipers. No doubt it was the first time many of them were to be present at the Holy Mysteries. Julius watched with great interest as I gave your body and blood to the nascent church. I addressed a few remarks to the little flock. However, we did not linger, because I wanted to try to persuade the captain to winter in Fair Havens.

Just before we returned to the ship, and as we walked along the shore, Julius stopped me dead in my tracks by saying, "Baptize me, sir—right now. The sea is still warm. We could do it now—immediately, before we board the ship." His eyes pleaded with mine.

How could I refuse! "Yes, my son." It only took a few minutes. How happy it made me to be doing Christ's work once again.

When we boarded the ship, the crew was almost ready to pull up anchor. I hurried to the captain who was busy on the prow with his chief mates.

"Men," I said addressing them all," I believe this voyage is threatening to bring disaster and heavy loss to us—not only to the cargo and ship, but to our lives."

"Nonsense" snorted the captain. "I've been plowing these waters for forty years. I know what I am doing. We shall proceed within the hour to sail. We will winter at a far better place, not far from here." I could see he was determined to push on to this other Cretan port. I studied his face. It was wrinkled and leathery from the years he had spent exposed to the sun, sea and wind. Even though he had been a sailor for many years, I still doubted the wisdom of his decision. Nevertheless, I had business to take care of and so I directed Titus to follow me to the stern where we could be alone. He was curious as to what I had in mind. Because there was no time to waste, I came to the point immediately.

"A bishop must be above reproach, acting as God's steward. He must not be arrogant, or ill tempered, nor a drinker, or brawler, or someone greedy to fleece his pockets."

Titus was puzzled; I knew his soul as well as I know my own. He is one of my oldest spiritual children having been with me to Jerusalem to the council right after my first journey to Galatia when the Apostle James and the others at the council had wanted to circumcise him. I refused, insisting that it was not necessary for my Gentile converts to become Jews. Gradually, all the rest at the council saw things my way. Years before, I had laid my hands on Titus and raised him to the priesthood. Now it was time for me to consecrate him a bishop.

Looking at me, he said, "The Apostle Paul is beyond reproach."

"A bishop," I continued, "must be hospitable—compassionate, circumspect, honorable, righteous, temperate—upholding the word of God so that he will be able to teach sound doctrine and reprove those in error." I directed him to kneel at my feet. Looking down at him I said, "Always speak and teach and rebuke with all authority in the Church." I stretched my hands forth to lay them on his bowed head.

"Father Paul, I am not worthy."

"No man is."

My well beloved son Titus rose to his feet—a bishop of the Church of God. Time was fleeting. The ship was going to sail soon.

"Hurry, my son," I continued. "Go get your things and run to your church! Crete will welcome you as their father in God."

I embraced him one final time. Part of my heart went with him as he sped away. The sea was ominous as we made our way from the harbor. It was choppy and there was a slight swell on it. Before long the wind came up. High in the sky, I saw a few wisps of clouds of the kind that foretell violent storms. When the sun set into the sea that night and I noticed that the sky had a copper green tinge to it, I knew we were headed for trouble.

When I awoke the next morning, the ship was groaning—creaking and pitching heavily. As I made my way up onto the deck, I had to hold onto something so that I would not fall, so violently was the ship heaving. Out on deck, I surveyed the sea, noting that the swell was now rolling and heaving so that it would rock even the largest of the ships, because the waters were churning angrily for many fathoms down. Clutching the railing, I groped my way to the prow where the waves were slamming over the deck. The ship rose up high to meet each oncoming wave. As the wave passed, the ship fell in its trough with a violence that made all the ship's timbers tremble.

The captain told me that he had been at his post all night long. I glanced at the sky. It was severely overcast. The wind was so strong that we could no longer face it. Reluctantly the Captain ordered the ship to turn around, which is a very dangerous maneuver, but we had no choice, believing it would be better to try to retrace our way, rather that to continue being battered by the sea and the gale force winds.

Because the sea was gray and white with swirling billows of foam, and the sun did not show its face all day long, I knew we were caught in a storm beyond the ordinary. We were facing hurricane force winds of the Euroclydon—the most treacherous storm of all on those waters. With no hope of the wind's subsiding, we ran under the lee of a little island which offered us small protection. Timothy, green with seasickness, could not raise his head from the bunk. Since I have a good pair of sea legs, I decided to stay up on deck on the lee-ward side, as long as I could, until the waves washing over the deck would drive me to cover. I preferred the fresh air of the storm to the closed quarters below with seasick passengers. With my weak stomach, one look at Timothy was enough to make me squeamish. Calculating that we could ride out the storm, we managed to secure the ship at Cauda with the crew rushing to carry out the captain's orders. "Lower the mainsail," he commanded. He was soaked and his clothes clung to his lank frame as he balanced himself on the forecastle. When I asked one of the sailors the reason for this move, he explained that we were very near the Syrtis quicksands.

The storm drove the ship along haphazardly with each wave that broke over us seeming larger than the last. The ships timbers moaned as if in agony as the giant hulk groaned and shuddered. Relentlessly the wind slapped the waters through the air. I began helping the crew as they were throwing the cargo overboard in a last desperate effort to make the ship buoyant under the massive wall of water that was cascading over our decks.

The storm was still raging the next day. We began throwing the ship's gear into the violent churning sea. Rain began falling from the bleak, completely overcast sky with the wind whipping it in torrents so that it was impossible to tell what was rain, sea, or sky. About noon the captain announced to us the utter hopelessness of our situation.

"We are doomed without any hope of being saved," he said with a look of black despair. Since it was impossible to stand up, I sank down on my bunk and prayed. Julius was violently sick in the bunk next to mine. The psalms were my refuge and my inspiration, as always, in times of trouble and danger. With the psalmist I declared that we would not be afraid even if the earth shook and the mountains plunged into the sea, even though the surging of the sea be so great as to as to make the mountains quake. With the psalmist, I recalled that the Lord of Hosts was with us.

When I finished the psalm, I fell into an ecstasy in which I was aware of an angel present to my soul, although I did not see him with my bodily eyes, but rather with my spirit. The message that he gave me was that I was not to be afraid, because I had to stand before Caesar and because of that the Lord of Glory was granting safety to all who were on the ship with me. Reassured I fell into a deep sleep, not waking until the gray of morning.

I bounced joyfully from my bed, but Julius was unable to rise. Up on deck, I told the captain and the crew that I had received a revelation that we all would be saved, transmitting some of my confidence to them so that they rallied and continued fighting the sea.

The fourteenth night out we were sailing in the Adriatic when, about midnight, certain members of the crew began to suspect that we were drawing near to land. On taking soundings they found twenty fathoms, a little later, fifteen.

"Rocks!" screamed the captain with terror ringing in his voice "Drop anchor," he yelled. Immediately four anchors were dropped from the stern. Luke and I walked the deck together, studying the crew, some of whom were beginning to panic. When we caught some of them trying to lower a life boat into the sea to make a get away deserting us, I went to inform Julius who thankfully was feeling a bit better.

"Unless those men remain in the ship, we cannot be saved, because we need them for navigation," I informed him.

At once, Julius rounded up the rest of the Roman soldiers on board; they put a stop to the escape, but, nevertheless we lost the life-boat, because when the men were discovered in the act of trying to desert, they cut the boat loose. We really could not afford to lose it, but there was absolutely nothing we could do to retrieve it, as it floated quickly away on the dismal, churning sea.

Morning came—bleak and somber. I scanned the horizon—no land in sight. The wind howled and shrieked like a madman. I went to the crew and told them again that all would be saved, insisting that they take some food for their refreshment.

"I beg of you to take some food. Not a single hair on your heads shall perish." I took bread and broke it and gave thanks to God. As I began to eat, I encouraged them to do the same. They all became more cheerful and partook of a little nourishment. There were two hundred and seventy six souls on board.

Because the sea hammered the ship mercilessly, causing us to fear it would break in pieces, we threw the rest of the cargo overboard. When it was broad daylight, we could discern a sandbar and a bay where the captain told us he planned to run the ship aground. We slipped anchor and were committed to the furious sea, unleashing the fastenings of the rudders and hoisting the foresail to the wind. Rapidly we drew near the beach. A loud crash of splitting timbers and we were aground with the prow stuck fast in the sand and the stern beginning to break under the frenzied pounding of the sea.

The Roman soldier, second in command after Julius, came shouting—"Kill all the prisoners before they escape!"

"No!" Julius countermanded. "Swim to safety everyone!"

Luke, Timothy, Julius, and I ran for the rail. It was a long jump to the water.

"I'll go first," Julius volunteered. "I am a strong swimmer; I will help the rest of you."

Timothy jumped right after Julius. Luke followed. I climbed up on the rail, stood poised in mid air for a few instants and then taking a deep breath made the plunge. I sank far, far, down into the churning waters. Just as my lungs were about to burst, I surfaced and began swimming towards the shore. A strong undertow held me in its death like grip. With all my strength I pulled to free myself. The short distance to land seemed like miles. Thanks to you, Lord Jesus Christ and to your loving providence, no one perished.

Malta was where we had beached. This we learned from the natives who came curiously to greet us and help us build a fire. While the others were drying out before the fire, I went to gather some firewood to lay on the blaze. Just as I drew near the fire and was bending over to lay the sticks on it, I saw one of them move. I had picked up a viper by mistake! The reptile writhed in my hands. Before I could drop it into the fire, it turned and sank its fangs into my hand. I jerked my hand, trying to free myself, but the snake held me fast with its undulating body hanging suspended from the fangs which were deeply embedded in my flesh.

Luke saw what had happened. Instantly he was beside me, snatching the sinister creature loose and hurling it into the fire that now blazed from the sticks I had just put on it.

The natives formed a ring around me with one of them acting as their spokesman, shrieking at the top of his lungs: "You must be a murderer, even though you escaped from the sea, justice will demand your life."

With open mouths they all gaped at me with a murmur of agreement coming from the crowd of natives. I ignored them for the moment.

Luke, examining my hand, was greatly alarmed.

"A nasty thing—the bite of a viper!" he said repressing a shudder. "Let me suck the poison out with my mouth."

"By no means! You might have a cut in your mouth and the poison would enter it. I don't want you to swell up from it and drop dead." I jerked my hand free from his grip.

"I will be perfectly all right," I insisted. "No harm will come to me, because I have to stand before Caesar." The angel was very clear on this point.

I felt no effects from the snake bite, except for a little pain around the wound. Luke looked at me with doubt in his eyes, but he had been with me too long, however, to doubt me very much. When I nodded to reassure him, his doubts gave way to faith.

Although the natives waited for me to swell and die, I had other plans. I had an audience and I intended to preach to them. The people of Malta heard the gospel. When they finally decided that I was not going to die, they thought I was some kind of god.

"No! Friends," I cried, "it is the Living God, the Father of our Lord Jesus Christ, who has delivered me from the evil of the serpent and from the watery grave of the sea. He will deliver you from death—the death of sin—and the death of the body—if you believe in him and are baptized." Christ made many converts that night.

The headman of the island—his name was Publius—put us up in his home for three days. Since my host's father was very ill with fever and dysentery, out of gratitude to Publius, I laid my hands on him and prayed for his healing. By the grace of our Lord Jesus Christ the man was made completely well.

Within a very short time—minutes practically—news of this miracle spread all over Malta, causing the sick to come asking for cures for all kinds of afflictions, and by the grace of God they were made whole. From this small beginning, in the three months we remained in Malta, the church grew large and flourished.

When an Alexandrine ship, the Castor and Pollux, put in at Malta, sailing from Alexandria to Italy, we joined it. On calm seas we sailed for Syracuse and on to Rhegium. At length we arrive at Puteoli on the Italian coast.

For the first time, I set my eyes on Italy, a glorious sight! The mountains perched right on the edge of the sea, forming the most beautiful bay I have ever seen. Rich foliage came into view as soon as we were close enough to discern the vegetation. When I scrambled off the ship, I received one of the biggest surprises of my life. A welcoming committee of Christians was waiting for me to disembark. With open hearts they greeted us. Having heard that I was on board, they came out to meet me. In all honesty, I can say they were overjoyed to see me, inviting us to stay with them, letting us know that we were among friends..

I had always pictured Rome and the rest of the peninsula as an alien land filled with evil men. In my first glimpse of Italy, I saw Christ present in the souls of the people. I had still to see the dark side of the land.

After a week in Puteoli, we set out for Rome—Julius, Luke, Timothy and I. We were drawing near our destination—Rome—the goal I had been reaching for these many years.

The road struck right up over the mountainside. On the crest, where we had a tremendous view of the bay, we paused to drink in the beauty of the vista—to gaze down at the sea that was shimmering like an emerald in the sun.

When we started on our way again, Julius approached me

"I have a bit of news for you, Father Paul" he said.

I was happy to note that he no longer called me "sir," but was now using the form of address that Timothy uses when speaking to me.

"What is it, Julius?" I asked wondering what he had learned when he met with his friends and relatives in his native Puteoli.

"Nero has killed his mother," Julius said bluntly.

"Matricide ! How base can the man be?"

"Right below in the bay there, Nero arranged a shipwreck for his mother in which she was supposed to drown, but she was too strong, vigorous and filled with the will to live to be destroyed in such a manner. When the ship went down, she simply dove over the railing and swam like an Olympic athlete to shore." Julius raised his hand and pointed. "If you look over there on that promontory you can see a villa—her villa. Well, she swam to her villa. Nero's soldiers raced after her to run her through with their swords. She didn't stand a chance against them. When the soldiers seized her, she bared her body to them and very calmly told them, 'Plunge your swords into my womb.' It took quite a few blows to take her life, but Nero destroyed the womb that bore him. All of this just happened recently. The people here witnessed it. Worst of all—Nero came and viewed his mother's uncovered corpse. Without emotion he remarked, 'I didn't know I had so beautiful a mother.'"

I could say nothing. Never had I heard of such depravity. What would I say when I met Nero face to face?

"Wait—You haven't heard it all. The philosopher Seneca wrote the letter on Nero's behalf in which Nero explained to the Senate how his mother Agrippina had plotted against him and, when he learned of it, killed herself. The Senate accepted what he told them. When he returned from here to Rome, they came out in a body and greeted him, offering thanks to the gods for having kept Nero safe from his wicked mother." Julius looked at me expectantly, waiting for me to make some comment, but I had nothing to say to such evil. We rode in silence.

When we reached Appius, a band of faithful Christians from the city of Rome were there to meet us, because Peter, their beloved apostle, when news reached him of our arrival, sent them out to bring us home with them to Rome. It was a victory march! Christ was triumphing over the wickedness and the evil of a perverse generation. Surrounded by the children of God—the spiritual progeny of Peter—I rode erect, confident hopeful, jubilant.

When we came closer to Rome, at place called the Three Taverns, another large gathering of Christians was waiting for us. As soon as they spotted us on the road, they cheered, waved their arms, and tried to kiss my hands. Touched by the poignancy of the moment, I felt tears streaming from my eyes, for I was reliving Christ's triumphal, palm strewn entrance into the Holy City. I raised my hands in blessing. With hymns of praise and thanksgiving they ushered me to Rome.

Peter, I was told, would come to see me as soon as I got to Rome. Because he did not wish to divert the love of the people away from the newly arrived apostle to himself, he did not appear with the large number who came to meet me, wanting me to have the joy of triumph alone. It seems that in Rome, I was well known for my missionary work in the provinces. I never dreamed that the acclaim I received would taste so sweet. I referred all the glory to Christ. I was just the bandy legged old man that he had chosen to be his servant

On and on we rode. We passed the sumptuous tomb of Cecelia Matella, entering the city of Rome through the Porta Capena. Because it was covered with green moss, I glanced upward and saw that there was a leaking aqueduct right above it. I took a deep breath; I was ready for Caesar. The Lord had strengthened me by the demonstration of his presence by sending me his followers to bring me into the city.

It was a short distance—once we were inside the walls—to the Palatine. Julius took me at once to the headquarters of the Praetorian Guard where I was given permission to live privately in a house of my choosing—with Julius to guard me—until Nero would get around to hearing my appeal.

I did not get to see much of Rome, when I left the Praetorian headquarters on the Palatine. I did manage to behold a magnificent panorama of the city with the Circus of Maxentius and the Forum. Across the way, I caught a glimpse of the Capitoline where Julius told me Caesar's market place is located. Some of the Christians, who escorted us into the city, were very eager and happy to provide us with a house. It was a pleasant dwelling on the street that runs between the Esquiline and the Caelian Hills—not far from the Palatine. They had chosen to have me live here because it was near to the church where Peter was preaching and giving communion to the faithful.

Since I was to be confined to the house, I was pleased to be right in the heart of Rome. Fortunately the house was blessed with a sun porch on the roof from which I could look out on the passing scene. It was a large house—built in the Roman style around an inner courtyard and peristyle. There was even a bath with hot and cold running water. The water, I soon learned, was heated in the lower regions of the house.

Selecting the room he preferred, Luke unpacked his medical supplies and surgical instruments, anxious to start practicing medicine again. Timothy was eager to see Rome, so when Julius went to the food markets to get some supplies, leaving me in the custody of another soldier, Timothy went with him.

The new soldier, Silvius, ensconced himself comfortably near the street entrance. When we had only been in the house about an hour, I heard someone talking to Silvius at the door. Then a familiar voice resounded through the house.

"Paul, where are you?"

It was Peter!

"Cephas," I called to him with emotion.

He strode into the room with his head almost scraping the doorway arch. He had become heavier, putting on quite a bit of weight. He was a giant! Jumping from my chair, I ran to clasp his hands.

"Paul," he exclaimed pressing my hands in his, "We are so happy to have you with us. Our only wish is that you were free to work with us in the Lord's vineyards of Rome. We have heard of the churches that have sprung up everywhere you have gone in the empire." His person betokened tremendous holiness and every gesture, great charity.

"I am under house arrest—in bonds—a prisoner of Jesus Christ." I nodded toward the soldier.

"No matter, Paul. Rome will come here to see you." He brushed his silver, almost white hair from his forehead.

We sat down in the graceful wooden chairs that were in the sitting room

"What do you think Nero will do with me?" I asked curious to hear his opinion.

"Absolutely nothing! I have never had any trouble from the government here in Rome. Nero is not interested in the laws and the quarrels of the Jewish people. He has no reason to do anything, except to release you." He folded his hands and rested his chin on them.

"That is just how I see it, too. What I am afraid of is that he will not get around to hearing my case for a long time—perhaps a year or two. That would mean that I would be a prisoner here unable to work for the spread of the gospel in the missionary lands. I have a great desire to go to Spain and maybe even Britain. And I hope to return to my converts in Asia again."

Julius and Timothy returned with a supply of food, large enough for an army, and were busying themselves putting it away.

"Don' t worry about your trial, Paul," the big fisherman advised me. "I shall see to it that you have the best advocate we can get. It is just a matter of having him place the matter before Nero. He will handle the entire process for us. There are laws and regulations to deal with these matters. You are a citizen of Rome. You have certain rights and privileges."

"The greatest privilege I have ever enjoyed was seeing so many Christians come out to meet me when I was on my way to the city here. About how many Christians are there in Rome"

I couldn't refrain from staring at the impressive person Cephas had become.

"There are several thousand of us in Rome. Perhaps eight thousand."

I thought I detected a touch of paternal pride in him as he spoke. I opened my eyes in surprise and smoothed down the few strands of hair that still remain on my head. I must have been very unsightly in Peter's eyes. Age and time had contributed to making an heroic looking man of him, but I was scarred from the stonings and the scourgings. To top it off, I was practically bald and people kept saying that I had bandy legs.

"You've been busy, Cephas!" I sighed in amazement.

"Yes, thanks to the Lord Jesus. We are getting old, Paul–you and I. I can't help thinking that it won't be long before I see him again." His voice trailed off into a whisper. The same desire glowed in Peter's heart that burned in mine.

"Nero might hasten my departure. I hear his new woman friend is pro-Jewish."

"Yes, I have heard about her. They say she consults with the local synagogue rulers often." He grew pensive.

"They will do all in their power to have Nero condemn me, if they have heard about my quarrel with the High Priest in Jerusalem." I confided.

Peter laughed a loud, hearty laugh. "I have heard of your exploits with the temple and the synagogues and even the Sanhedrin. I, myself, have stayed clear of the synagogue here in Rome ever since they kicked me out almost twenty years ago for preaching Christ to them. Many have left the synagogue and have come into the church. We also have some Christians and friends in high places. We will try to use our influence to reach Seneca. He has been practically ruling in Nero's stead these past years. But now that Nero has slain his mother, perhaps he will also throw out his philosopher premier and run his own affairs or let that woman, Poppaea, run them for him." Peter tugged thoughtfully at his long white beard. I said nothing, waiting for him to continue talking.

"It is hard to tell what Nero may do now," he continued. "With his background, things don't look too hopeful for Rome. You know his mother was Caligula's sister, but she always seemed sane enough—if you can call marrying her uncle and then feeding him poisonous mushrooms sane. Rome is an evil city." He looked at me in silence for a moment and then continued. "The greatest joy in working with these people of Rome is seeing how they change and are made new after they are baptized and receive the Body and Blood of Christ. The impure become pure. The gluttonous become abstemious. Hatred gives way to love. However we do have to be on constant watch lest they should begin to revert to their pagan ways. I preach on that subject frequently. Our Christians must separate themselves from the society in which they live. As our Lord says they must be in the world but not of the world."

"Yes," I agreed. "Our Lord found it easier to convert sinners than self- righteous men who felt justified in their conduct."

"All the same, at times, I feel that all the devils of hell have been unleashed against us in this city—that they are roaming through the streets of Rome trying to find a way to devour us," he spoke slowly, carefully weighing each word.

"The church thrives on persecution," I remarked, recalling my own experiences on my missionary travels.

"Exactly, but—you see—here in Rome we have had very little if any real persecution—as yet. This is a blood thirsty city where they have even condemned men to fight each other to the death in the circus just so that an audience of bored Romans can have the thrill of watching one man kill another. Also they pit one kind of wild beast against another and sit back and enjoy, really enjoy, watching them slaughter each other, bringing in all kinds of exotic animals—alligators—wild boars—even hippopotami. Abruptly he rose and said, "I must hurry away, but I shall return often." Making no noise as his sandals glided across the marble floor, Peter disappeared into the street in front of our house.

Urgently needing to know if the members of the local synagogue had heard about my difficulties with the high priest in the temple, I decided to invite the rulers of the local synagogue here in Rome to our house so I could converse with them. Immediately writing to them, I informed them that I had recently arrived in Rome from Palestine and would be happy to receive them to discuss Jewish affairs with them. Knowing that they would come to meet a student of the famous and erudite Rabban Gamaliel, I added that I was one of his students.

Three days later, bright and early, they were at my door. It is, I learned, the social custom in Rome to make one's calls in the early morning hours before the heat of the day arrives. After Julius let them in, I met them in the atrium. Although there were two of them, Samuel and Jeremiah, the latter did most of the talking. Because they quickly noticed I was a prisoner, I had to explain the cause for my imprisonment.

Since I was at prayer when they arrived, I was wearing my prayer shawl. I told them that although I did nothing against our people or our customs, I was turned over the to Romans who after investigation were ready to free me, because I had done nothing deserving of death. However, because the Jews objected to their freeing me, I was forced to appeal to Caesar.

"This is the reason why I asked to see you and to speak with you, for it is because of the hope of Israel that I am in chains." When Julius was not actively guarding me, I had to wear chains on my wrists binding them together. I held up my hands so they could see my bondage.

Anxiously hurrying to the reason I invited them to see me, I inquired bluntly "Have you heard anything from Jerusalem regarding my appeal?"

The older of the two, Samuel, answered in slow deliberate unaccented tones. "No, we have not received any information about you from Judea and no one has reported or spoken any evil against you."

I relaxed, trying not to let them see my relief at this news.

"But," He continued, "we want to hear from you what your opinions are about the sect that has arisen in Jerusalem." Although he looked at me very seriously, he seemed to have no animosity toward me. "I believe," he continued, "their followers are called Christians." From what we have heard here in Rome, the sect is being condemned by Jewish leaders everywhere."

They had heard nothing about me, that much was certain. They weren't even aware that I was Christian, for I had not told them. I folded my prayer shawl and placed it on the table beside me.

"What do you hear from Jerusalem?" I inquired looking at Jeremiah, the younger of the two, who was sitting beside Samuel and trying to be inconspicuous. Now that I addressed him, he entered into the conversation.

"We hear of rumors of rebellion among our people. It seems there is a spirit of rebelliousness that I fear will one day lead to open violence against Roman rule." Jeremiah was deeply concerned that the Romans would destroy Jerusalem if our people rebelled.

"What exactly are you referring too?" I asked, studying the face of Samuel whose features were honest but severe. "Ever since Rome took over our lands, the Jews have been rebellious—that is nothing new. They have managed so far to keep our people in subjection," I said, offering my guests some refreshment and water to purify their hands. With marked courtesy they accepted my hospitality. Samuel responded to my question.

"There is a tendency among the young Jews of today to rebel against Rome no matter what the cost might be. It is, I feel, suicidal and will make our situation and that of the entire Jewish population here in Rome and everywhere else in the empire, for that matter, unbearable." Before continuing, he took a sip of the local wine that Luke bought when we arrived in Rome. "We want to coexist peacefully with Rome, but these zealots will end up by having us all exterminated, if they persist."

Signifying his agreement with Samuel, Jeremiah shook his head.

"The relations between Rome and Israel have been like a festering sore ever since Anthony made the half-Jewish Herod, with his detested Idumean blood, King of Judea. Jews have always hated the blood of Edom. As if that weren't enough, they rubbed salt in our wounds when, to celebrate his hegemony, Herod went with Anthony to the temple of Jupiter here in Rome and offered sacrifice to the idol. Right then the Jews became intractable." Jeremiah clicked his tongue against his teeth in a gesture of despair.

"Yes," agreed Samuel shifting in his chair," and if that wasn't enough Caligula demanded that we put an image of him in our temple in Jerusalem! They have absolutely, no conception of the Jewish spirit. If Caligula hadn't died before that statue was placed in our temple, I hate to think what might have happened, for we shall all die for Yahweh before we sacrifice to any idol, be he emperor or myth."

Jeremiah warmed to the conversation, remarking vehemently, "It was almost too much when Pilate took our temple monies and built his accursed aqueduct for Jerusalem with them. I am always furious every time I just look at it. Those detested water works of his have always been a bone of contention among our people."

Because I was determined to make friends of these men, I agreed with them amicably and added my own list of grievances to theirs. "It makes me shudder each time I see that graven imperial eagle when I go in and out of the temple." I was speaking of the Roman symbol we had been forced to put on our temple building.

They both agreed wholeheartedly. Jeremiah, relaxed from the wine and cheese, was speaking freely. "There are an ever growing number of zealots springing up in Galilee."

This was news to me. I listened carefully as he proceeded to explain. "Blatantly several of these zealots have cried out publicly, 'No God but Yahweh, no tax but to the Temple, no friend but the zealot.'"

This *was* news. "What did Festus do about it?"

"He crucified them," said Samuel. "But five more came to take the place of each one crucified." I could tell he was really disturbed by this uprising. He stared at me with great intensity and added, "Rome won't stand for it!"

I nodded. Our stiff-necked people were going to bring destruction upon themselves. The Jewish temperament was such as to be suicidal in the face of Roman oppression.

"I hear that Nero's Poppaea is a proselyte," I ventured, fishing for information.

"Bah! Indeed!" snorted Samuel, slamming the palm of his hand on his knee. "Even in the circus, when Nero appears, the people are screaming for revenge for the death of Agrippina. Poppaea is no friend of ours!"

I lifted my eyebrows in surprise.

"It is an old Roman custom The people feel free to express their real views in the circus by public demonstrations. And as for being a proselyte—a convert to Judaism…" He threw up his hands and did not finish his sentence. "To be completely honest with you," he began again, "we have courted her favor to protect our interests. In view of all the rebellion in Palestine, we wanted to protect ourselves—but as for receiving her as one of us—hah! You know that is impossible. She gives money to the temple and to the synagogue, but that is the extent of it. She only gives lip service to believing in our faith." The Spring sun was filtering into the courtyard and stealing across the marble floor of the atrium. As I noticed a fly buzzing around my foot, I looked up at Samuel and asked, "What about Nero? What is his religion?"

Jeremiah and Samuel both shrugged.

"Nero is an atheist. He imbibed enough philosophy from Seneca to have contempt for the Roman gods and for the Oriental religions. Nero despises all cults. Once he went so far as to take a leak on an image of Cybele and he always claimed to respect her most of all their gods. There is, you know, or maybe you don't since you just arrived in Rome, a temple to Cybele right on the Palatine."

I was learning a lot of things that might one day prove useful in winning Roman to Christ.

"What is the cult of Cybele?" I inquired. "I know nothing at all about it."

Samuel was quick to explain, "It is the cult of the Magna Mater. Her priests are self-emasculated." He shot me a derisive glance and continued. "A new member is placed naked in a pit. Over the top of the pit, a bull is slain with the bull's blood running down over the candidate, supposedly purifying him, and giving him eternal life. The genitals of the bull are then placed in a consecrated vessel and dedicated to Cybele."

Jeremiah looked as if he would burst, so eager was he to speak. He waited for Samuel to finish then blurted, "I just remembered that Nero at one time was contemplating joining the Eleusian religion. You know, Cicero was one of them and so was Plato. Well, when Nero found out that confession of his personal sins was a require-ment for initiation, he quickly changed his mind."

"That's easy to understand." Samuel sneered. "I have heard that in the Eleusian religion they even drink the blood of bulls." He gri-maced with aversion.

Jeremiah could not resist the obvious, "Nero doesn't need to drink the blood of a bull. He has all the characteristics of one already." Every Jew believed that to drink a creature's blood was to become like the creature whose blood it was.

"Are there many devotees of these Oriental religions in Rome?" I needed to be well informed on Roman affairs. I looked at Samuel waiting for him to answer.

"Quite a few of the cult of Isis. The sorrowful mother is very much celebrated here, after having once been outlawed. All the sects—the Zoroastrian Mithras, Cybele, Persephone of the Eleusians, and Isis—all offer the people religions that speak of resurrection from the dead, which the Pharisees have always held to be true. The universal cry of the human soul is for eternal life and happiness. As a Pharisee, I believe in the resurrection of the dead."

"I too believe in the resurrection of the dead," I told them confidently. "But these cults you mention are so much mythology and fantasy. They have no historical truth in them. There never was a living person known as Isis—the sorrowful mother."

"Of course. You are right. It is all myth, but soon," said Jeremiah emphatically, "the streets of Rome will be crowded with the Spring festival of Cybele when her devotees will mourn the death of her son Attis. Her priests will cut their own arms and drink their own blood—a revolting thought! A solemn procession will bear young, dead Attis to his grave. The next day the people will run madly through the streets shouting that Attis is risen from the dead. An image of Cybele, the Magna Mater, will be carried through the streets with the crowds cheering her as 'Nostra Domina.'"

"There was no historic person named Attis." I replied with certainty.

"Of course not. Everyone knows that." Jeremiah sighed deeply. "It is merely the symbolism representing the faith, hope, and religious fervor of these people. There wasn't any one named Osiris either," he added to give weight to his explanation, "but still the devotees of the goddess Isis proclaim Osiris to be her spouse and say that he is risen from the dead. They call Isis the 'Queen of Heaven' and 'the star of the sea' and 'the mother of god.' There are statues of her holding her divine child Horus in her arms. Of course, these people have just dreamed up these ideas.

Samuel reinforced what Jeremiah had been telling me by saying, "These ideas are common to all the pagans. Persephone—another mythological person—is said to have risen from the dead. It is an idea that seems to be born with the human soul—the idea of a god dying and rising from the dead and thus giving eternal life to his people."

It was my turn to speak. "Brothers, it is more than a dream. It is the hope of all mankind. It is truly prophetic that all these pagans have had this idea born, as you say, in their souls. Even in Judaism we have that concept. I studied with Gamaliel. I am sure you know the scriptures—the law and the prophets. Our prophets have foretold us that the Messiah would come, born of a virgin, and suffer and die and rise again, opening his kingdom to all who believe in him."

"I have read those prophecies," acknowledged Samuel. "However, the average Jew thinks that Messiah will be a temporal king who will give us a land of milk and money. Isaiah speaks of a suffering—dying, Messiah. It is hard to understand." The confusion was registered on his classic Hebrew face.

"These prophecies have come to pass." I spoke with conviction. "A real person, Jesus, born in Bethlehem of the house of David as was foretold, was despised, rejected, a man of great sorrow." I looked anxiously from one to the other to see how they were taking my words.

Samuel was the first to speak, "I have heard of Jesus, but I have never taken him seriously." He squirmed nervously under my gaze.

"He rose from the dead. There are historical witnesses to prove it." I rested my case.

"Have you, yourself," asked Jeremiah "ever met anyone who can attest to that?"

I was surprised. Both men were listening to me with open minds.

"Five hundred people saw him at one time. Right here in Rome there is man called Cephas or Simon Peter, who is a witness to the crucifixion and to the resurrection. Many have died to seal their witness to his resurrection with their own blood."

They both listened in silence while I prayed fervently that the Holy Spirit would touch their souls so that they would believe.

"The hope of Israel!" whispered Samuel. "Oh! If it were only true!"

"I saw him myself. Believe me, my brother Pharisee. I would die the most agonizing death rather than deny him."

They looked at each other. Samuel rose nervously. "It is time for us to leave. We will hear more about this some other day. We will think about what you have said and return with some of our friends." Then turning to Jeremiah, he said, "Come, we really must be going!"

They departed swiftly. Perhaps they were afraid that I would baptize them on the spot and they wanted time to consider. I had learned one thing from them. The Jews in Rome were anxious not to make trouble with Nero. Furthermore, they knew nothing of my difficulties. It began to look as if I would be released once Nero got around to hearing my case.

CHAPTER 6

One day followed another. Even though I was confined to the house, I was learning much about Rome and the Roman way of life. Luke told me a great deal about the people, because he came to know them intimately from his medical practice. One day he returned home quite furious. Because it was most unlike the gentle physician to be so enraged, I immediately tried to find what was causing his anger, knowing that he would lose his temper only if it were justifiable to do so. I was shocked at what he told me.

"What is it? Tell me," I insisted, "I don't want you to betray a patient's confidence, but surely you can tell me in general terms what it is that is troubling you."

He blurted it out. "A woman asked me to do an abortion on her daughter. Murder! I called her a murderer and stormed from her house." His face was red with anger as he continued. "She stood there and calmly and coolly asked me to murder her grandchild. These Romans make me sick. They use all the mechanical and chemical means that they can to prevent conception and if they fail to do that, they resort to abortion. Abortion is very common in Rome today," I am told.

The horror of it struck me. I must tell this to Peter so that he can preach against this evil. I thought it was contrary to Roman law to take the life of the unborn. I wanted to walk out from my prison and preach to the inhabitants of Rome. Because, I was so enraged, if I had been free to leave the house, I would probably have denounced the Romans so emphatically that I would have lost my head that very day.

"It *is* contrary to Roman law—but it is accepted in Roman practice. I'm sure Peter is aware of the evils of this city. Chastity and marital fidelity are flagrantly despised by rich and poor alike. Why, prostitution is practiced even in the cellas and between the altars of the Roman temples. There are many in Rome today who are even suffering from what they call the sickness of Venus or venereal disease. It is a result of their immoral sexual conduct. It even causes insanity." Luke was giving me the facts; I was learning why only Christ's death would suffice to give salvation to mankind.

I was certain that in all the annals of history down to the end of time no human being could become more depraved than these Romans. They once had natural virtues—the virtues that are proper to men and women in their natural state. They loved their homes and their children. The famous Lucretia killed herself because she was raped and had, she felt, lost her natural virtue.

Christ would save Rome, restoring to the Romans their natural virtues and infusing them with supernatural ones, such as the human race has never seen or dreamed possible. I remembered the pure, chaste Thecla who wanted to consecrate her virginity to Christ. His Spirit would come and cleanse these Romans of their defilement.

"Jesus is rich in mercy for sinners, Luke. We will make saints of these Romans."

"Something will have to be done about their gluttony," Luke advised. "They have gout—suffer from obesity and have all kinds of ills—resulting from their overindulgence in food. Liver trouble is common from too much wine. They even have a law, I hear, that everyone at a banquet is required—mind that—actually required to drink the same amount of wine. Although the law was passed to curb the over drinking of some, in actuality, it has forced many to drink more—far more—than they want and can handle, because the quota established by law is overly generous.

"If I ever get out of this prison, I will not spare them."

Because I could not conduct my active ministry, I resorted to writing letters. Since I could not fulfill the longing of my soul to revisit my spiritual children in Macedonia and in Asia, I did the next best thing—I wrote to them. In the midst of a depraved and perverse generation, my very dear spiritual children shine like stars. They hold fast the word of life waiting for Christ to come again in glory. My work has not been in vain. Even if I am sacrificed in death for the building up of their faith, I will be joyful and rejoice in my spiritual children. They are my joy and crown, pure and chaste, while those around them wallow in mire, generous and kind, while their neighbors are greedy and crude, walking in love in a world filled with hatred.

I was quite delighted to hear from my children in Philippi who with loving dedication sent me gifts of money to support my work for Christ and even a servant to minister to my needs. Epaphroditus took over the marketing, the preparation of meals and other household chores for us. However, it was unfortunate the way things turned out for him.

The lawyer that Peter secured for me assured me that I had nothing to worry about, saying that I would go free as soon as he could get Nero to hear my case.

Among all my other letters, I wrote a letter to my sister and invited her, no rather I should say, advised her to come to Rome with her family. Bloodshed between Romans and Jews could break out any hour now in Jerusalem.

Jeremiah and Samuel returned to talk more as they had promised, bringing with them some friends, some of whom believed at once in Christ while others disbelieved. In typical Jewish style they ended up quarreling among themselves and left enraged. Later, however, Samuel was received into the church.

Since I was curious about the famous philosopher Seneca, I wrote him a letter and invited him to come to my home, telling him, that I too, am a lover of wisdom—a philosopher of sorts—and would enjoy a conversation with him. He sent my messenger, Tychius, back to me saying he would be happy to pay me a visit and discuss truth and wisdom with me the very next day.

The next morning a curtained litter, carried by four slaves—no vehicular traffic was allowed in the city during the daytime hours—stopped at my door. When a distinguished looking man emerged, I noticed from my rooftop garden that he was not wearing a toga, but only a tunic. Although it was becoming customary to wear the toga only for very formal occasions, I was wearing one just in case he would arrive in one. Throwing it off, I went to receive the famous Seneca into my home. Up close he looked to me to be about sixty-five. His face had an ascetic look with a gray pallor that did not betoken good health. I noticed that his fingernails had a bluish tinge.

Welcoming him as fellow lover of wisdom, I offered him the large comfortable Cyprus chair that we reserve for special guests. To began the conversation, I said, "You have written many treatises on virtue, I am told. I, too, preach virtue to anyone who give me an ear."

He coughed—a long body-racking cough, and said, "I preach virtue but I, myself, am very imperfect. I don't praise the life I lead, but rather the one I ought to lead. And as for my writing, there are times when I wish I had never learned to hold a pen in my hand."

"Why is that?" I inquired.

"There are some things that I wish I had never written."

"I, too, am imperfect," I told him honestly. "I strive for the goal of perfection, castigating my flesh, so that after preaching to others, I might not fall."

"I, too, practice austerity of life, although that is not incompatible with wealth. I have often felt that I would have been a better philosopher, if I had stayed clear of politics and lived in Cordova instead of

Rome." His brow was deeply creased as he confided, "The Palatine is a prison for me." He was experiencing great difficulty in breathing.

"It is difficult for a philosopher to be a politician," I agreed. "Politics is seldom wise."

"Well put. I am convinced that we cannot be wise about everything, but if we practice wisdom each day, examine our conscience daily and be harsh with our faults, and lenient to the faults of others, and by associating with wise and virtuous men, we can acquire a small amount of wisdom." He coughed again appearing to be suffering from chronic respiratory disease. "Asthma," he said. "It is always at its worst in the mornings."

"What do you think," I asked him to fathom his personality, "of the widespread corruption of morals that is everywhere here apparent in Roman life?"

"Well," began Seneca and then paused to catch his breath, "our ancestors complained of the evil in our society. We complain of it. Our children will do likewise, saying that evil is increasing and humanity is falling to unheard of depths of depravity. I feel, however, that if we Romans don't conquer our softness and acquire more natural virtues—such as fortitude, long suffering, patience, thrift, and so forth, the barbarians will overrun us. It is as simple as that. Ever since the dawn of history, barbarians have risen up and overrun every civilization that has preceded us. It will happen to us also, if we don't have strong moral fiber. Here in Rome today men are curling their hair. Nero wears a blonde wig." As an afterthought he said, "Have you heard the latest news? It just broke last night. Nero killed his wife—Octavia."

As I said nothing, he continued speaking, while toying with a small knife he had on his person. "Yes, it is true. She was only twenty-two. She was already living in exile—not bothering him in the slightest. When he sent his soldiers to kill her, poor child, she pleaded for her life, saying that she was content to be just a sister to him." He shrugged. "They killed her. Last night they brought her head to Poppaea."

Nothing I could hear about these Romans would be able to shock me any more. I could not resist asking the obvious question.

"And what about you, philosopher-premier of Nero? Will Poppaea get your head, too? She turned Nero against his mother Agrippina who escaped being poisoned many times, only to succumb to the soldiers' blades. And now Octavia. I hear Nero also did away with Claudius' son Britannicus, Octavia's brother. What will he do with you, now that he is taking control of affairs on the Palatine?"

Soberly Seneca confided, "I have been dismissed from my post because I criticized his conduct. I am leaving for my villa in the country soon. Oh, I used to have some control over him, but what enraged him the most was I told him his poetry reeks. The Senate is furious about the displays of his poetry, music, and athletic skill that he makes them witness. Because he has been forcing senators to take part in his acting and athletic displays, many refuse to attend the Senate when Nero comes to address it, regarding it beneath the dignity of a Roman senator. What it all boils down to is this—Nero has run out of money and there are plots to depose him. The horror of it all is that he has revived the law 'maietas' and is making accusations against men whose opposition or wealth make their deaths politically or financially profitable to him, because he simply confiscates their wealth and property." Seneca went into a spasm of coughing with his face drained of all color.

After pondering for a few moments what Seneca had just told me, I asked, "You might be next—is that it?" No doubt Seneca had a sizeable fortune.

"Exactly! I can't drink anything except running water, nor eat anything except fresh country apples from my own villa and which I guard very carefully." He choked and gasped for breath.

"I don't understand."

"Poison! my dear fellow. I fear a pinch of poison in my food. You can't even imagine the horrible agony that Claudius suffered! I have no illusions about what Nero is like. I would not speak so openly except I know you are an outsider and you also have to stand before Nero's judgment seat."

As he sat crumpled and gasping for breath, I observed the pathetic figure of the great premier who was daubing nervously at the sweat on his brow. I wanted to save his soul—to give him grace and help him attain to the virtue that he professed to love.

"Do you believe in God?" I asked softly.

"Yes, I am a monotheist. I believe in a personal God that loves men. At least sometimes I believe that. At other times—I am not too sure. Sometimes I feel that God was only a first cause and that he simply observes the farce of human life–coldly and from a distance."

At least Seneca was honest with me. That was a good beginning.

"Monotheism is the main dogma of Judaism. We express it this way, 'Hear, O Israel, the Lord your God is One.' Do you believe in life after death?"

"Sometimes I do. I can't seem to be consistent in my beliefs. There is too much of the politician in my make-up. I take on the views of those who I am with."

"I will be glad to give you mine," I proffered with a smile.

"And I would be glad to hear what they are," he replied also with a smile between gasps for breath.

I told him about the Lord Jesus Christ, preaching to him with some of the old fire that converted Sergius Paulus, whom I heard was back in Rome.

"That is the most beautiful religion I have ever heard of. It is your morality that speaks the most to me. You seem to be able to lay hold of solid virtue—to be holy." He paused and looked a long time into my eyes. Then he said, "You are a holy man, Paul. I can feel it. I can also feel the weight of my sins—all the times I condoned Nero's evils on the pretest that if I played along with him I could bring a little good to our people as his premier! The speeches I wrote for him!" A look of disgust played across his face. "Paul, I wrote a letter telling the Senate that Agrippina took her own life. I should have cut off my hand before I did that!" Shame was in his eyes. "I don't have much time to live. Perhaps you don't either, Apostle Paul, so let's be honest. I see in you the lover of wisdom I have always wanted to become. You are holy. Your virtue makes me want to humble myself before you—to pour out the poison that's in my soul to you—or rather to the Living God who dwells so abundantly in your spirit." A cough racked his body, interrupting him and forcing him to sink back into his chair and rest.

"It is Jesus Christ you behold in me, philosopher." I spoke to him openly, warmly and with empathy.

"Jesus Christ," he mused. "He was crucified for truth. I condoned evil. I am too much enmeshed in my way of life to change now. I will probably die at my own hand. You couldn't countenance that, could you?" His voice was almost inaudible.

"Absolutely not! It is murder," I protested vociferously.

"But—it is what I will have to do. My philosophy tells me that I have that right. One of these days," he said in whispers, "one of these days—Nero will send me word to drop dead, Seneca, kill yourself. And I will do it. I'll do it the easiest way I can find," he added as he toyed with his small knife. "I am too much of a coward to refuse Nero and let his soldiers run me through. No, Paul, I cannot embrace a God who is crucified. I'll kill myself. The old stoic will die. I wish I could be like you." He was trembling. "Do not worry, Apostle Paul—you will convert Rome. The young will flock to you. Someday all Rome shall be such as you—a follower of Christ—noble, virtuous, and holy. In that, day no Roman will even remember my tomb."

He was a figure of despair with trace of a tear in his eyes. A tragic man, he rose without another word and left as quickly as he had come.

A little over two years later, it happened, just as he said it would. His wife, Paulina—loyal and devoted and wishing to join him in death cut his veins at the same time he cut hers. Weak from his illness, the old man did not inflict upon her a mortal blow. Although she continued to live, she began starving herself. When Nero ordered her father to die, she joined him in death. This happened about the same time that John Mark came to visit me.

Mark had come to Rome with Peter from whom he learned the first-hand events of Christ's life. I learned that he had written a gospel to bear witness to the Savior down through the ages. Our differences of the past completely forgotten, I received him with my most heartfelt charity and he responded by leaving me a copy of his gospel. It was a joy for me to read it during my imprisonment. When he read it, Luke decided to write an account of the life of Jesus also, because when we were in Jerusalem he learned many things from John the son of Zebedee, especially about the nativity of the Lord. It is especially significant that Luke, a physician, wanted to write a gospel which told of the virgin birth. Every moment he was not with his patients, he spent working on writing his gospel. When that was finished, he began a narrative about the early beginnings of the Church and our missionary journeys.

Something very unfortunate occurred about that time. Epaphroditus fell ill and almost died, despite everything Luke could do for him. As soon as he was well enough to travel, I returned him to the church in Philippi that had sent him to me. Fortunately we found some local Christians to replace his services.

One day as I sat on my roof garden–such gardens are common in Rome, I am told, I saw a procession of four hundred slaves being led through the streets with soldiers beating then with whips to keep them moving. I sent Timothy out to find what was happening. A large angry mob of Romans was demonstrating—protesting loudly that these men, women and even little children were being so mistreated. Timothy returned to tell me that they were the slaves of

Pedanus Secundus who were all being taken to a mass execution—crucifixion I suppose, since that is the execution given to
slaves. The thought of four hundred men, women, and little children
being nailed to the cross, pierced my soul to the depths. According to
Roman law if a slave kills his master, all the slaves of the master must
be put to death—even though the guilty one be known. This was a
measure destined to keep slaves in subjection. So now three hundred
and ninety-nine innocent people were to be cruelly and savagely
murdered to avenge the death of one. The law would be enforced.

The condition of the slaves in the empire was generally fair
because most masters treated their slaves kindly. Of course, there
were exceptions. Even then Nero was busy posing for a statue of himself that was to be one hundred twenty feet tall. When the statue was
completed it was to provide amnesty to slaves who were to be
allowed to run to the statue of Nero to obtain refuge and protection
from a cruel master. What a statue! It was an ill-conceived idea. The
famous Zenodatus did his best, but not even he could make fat
paunchy Nero look like Apollo!

Run away slaves, if caught, could be branded on their foreheads or
even crucified. The reason I mention this is because of Onesimus, a
runaway slave who came to me while I was in prison, because he
knew his master was a Christian and a friend of mine. The poor fellow—this Onesimus—was in great fear and trembling as to what
would happen, if he were caught. I suppose the affair of the murder
of the four hundred slaves of Pubius Secundus threw a scare into
him. In any event, he came to me for refuge. I baptized him and sent
him back to his master with a letter written in my own hand, asking
Philemon to receive him as he would me—as a brother in Christ.
Everything worked out well for Onesimus. Thank God.

Finally my advocate, Quintan, he was called, came to me and
announced that our case would be heard the following week. When
the day of the trial came, Julius was optimistic for my release, saying
that Nero would be kindly disposed towards me because his three-

week-old daughter by Poppaea, the joy of his life, was healthy and thriving and Nero was in high spirits.

When we arrived on the Palatine, we were directed to a small basilica where Nero—he was living at that time in the palace of Caligua—was hearing appeals. The basilica was typical of the Roman courts of law, with one exception, it had a marble dais on which there were two thrones instead of the customary one. My lawyer informed me that Poppaea would join Nero in court.

As we proceeded to our places, I looked around the court, but I did not see a single one of my friends present, all of them having excused themselves. Busy with other affairs they all declined to come, perhaps because they believed that I would certainly be released. Quintin and I were to face Nero alone.

After about an hour of waiting, a fanfare of trumpets announced Nero's arrival as he came waddling into the basilica with Poppaea in attendance. When he walked past me, I was able get a good look at the infamous Nero. At twenty-five and designated a "god," he was already showing the ravages of his debauchery. It was hard to believe that one of the consuls-elect had already proposed that a temple be constructed to the deified emperor. Nero was degenerate—his belly bloated, his face covered with red blotches. In contrast to his body, his arms and legs were puny and thin. He was truly grotesque in appearance, with his yellow curled hair and his watery gray crab-like eyes.

With a lot of fanfare and ceremony, Nero placed his corpulent frame on the purple cushion on his marble throne. With arrogance visible in her every movement, Poppaea sat beside him. Julius had told me that she spent her days preening herself with all kinds of cosmetics such as purple eye shadow. It was well known that she made a mask of dough and donkey's milk and slept in it, believing it would improve her complexion. When she traveled she took a whole herd of donkeys with her and bathed in their milk. Poppaea! She had been the cause of Nero's killing his mother and his wife. Did she think that she would get any better treatment from Nero when he tired of her?

An attorney for the Empire rose and stood before Nero. Stridently he proclaimed, "An appeal to Caesar has been made by the prisoner, Paul or Saul of Tarsus. Some of his own people, the Jews, wanted to put him to death because they charged him with violations of their religious codes. When the procurator examined him, he could find him guilty of no crime, but because he appealed to Caesar, it was necessary, according to our laws, that he appear before you, most august Nero." The attorney bowed obsequiously.

Nero waved him to silence.

"Where are your accusers?" Nero demanded sternly.

The attorney for the empire looked at the court and said, "There are none, most excellent Caesar." Again he bowed.

Nero yawned I braced myself. When Poppaea leaned over and whispered something in his ear, Nero looked at me for a few moments and said, "The Empress is a devotee of Judaism. She does not like your sect. She says you all are a bunch of agitators and troublemakers. What do you have to say about that?"

Ready to tell Nero a few things, I rose to my feet, but before I could open my mouth, my advocate pulled me back down to my seat. When he rose to speak in my stead, I yielded to his legal expertise.

"Mt client," he began, ""has broken no law. It has always been the policy of our august Emperor to see that justice is done in his courts. It is not unlawful for a man to be a Christian any more than it is unlawful for him to be a devotee of Isis—or Cybele or Mithras. For some time Rome has had an apostle of this sect present in the city—a man by the name of Simon Peter who has been in Rome for twenty years and never have you had any complaints against him."

Waving the lawyer to silence, Nero looked straight at me and bellowed furiously, "Why are you wasting my time? I have better things to do than to listen to such idle matters! Get out!" He pointed a fat jeweled finger at the exit. "Dismissed." Turning to Poppeae he smiled and said, "Come, my pet, let's return to more entertaining things." With that he sauntered from the basilica with Poppaea trailing at his heels.

Quintan patted me on the shoulder and said, "You are a free man. Go freely." Feeling twenty years younger, I paid him his fee and strode out of the court. After almost five years imprisonment, I was finally free. Never had the bright Roman sunshine felt so good as I rushed home.

"Luke," I yelled out, once inside the door. "I am going to Asia!"

I did in fact make a journey into Asia and Macedonia. I even wrote Titus and asked him to join me in Necopolis. Most unfortunately my journey was brought to a sudden halt. Something dreadful—horrible happened in Rome, making it imperative that I return there at once. A fire, which had broken out in the Circus Maximus burned for nine days, leveling two thirds of the city to the ground. Nero, away from Rome when the fire started, returned just in time to see his palaces burned to the ground. The Forum and the capitol escaped destruction, as did the region west of the Tiber. Most of the more than one million inhabitants were homeless with their apartment houses destroyed in the blaze. People were wandering aimlessly through the streets of the city viewing the desolation.

Rumors began to circulate that Nero had started the fire. They said that Nero had devised a mad scheme to destroy Rome and rebuild it so that he would live in history as the builder of Rome. It was said that Nero kept relighting the blaze when it seemed to die out. What was worse, he was supposed to be watching the spectacle of the burning city from his tower of Maecenas, singing his poetry about the sack of Troy and playing on his lyre. Whether Nero was guilty or innocent of the fire, no one will ever know for certain, but he did provide relief to the people by opening all public building to the destitute. Tents covered the Campus Martius where many were housed.

Because the infuriated populace blamed Nero for the fire, Nero was looking for a scapegoat to blame for the destruction and desolation of the city. He found one, the Church of Christ! He induced some wretched people into confessing that the Christians were responsible for burning Rome.

Just as I was boarding the ship to sail back to Italy, I heard that Nero had arrested a number of our people and put them to death in the most cruel ways that his mad and fiendish mind could devise. He had some of our people dressed in the skins of wild animals and gave them to savage dogs to devour. Some were crucified. Others were burned alive. He even had the temerity to use some as human torches to light up his nighttime chariot racing.

Because I was needed in Rome to strengthen the Church and bear witness to Christ in my blood, if necessary, Luke and I sailed from Dalmatia. Arriving on the Italian peninsula, we made our way swiftly, renting fresh horses at every ten mile stop on the road, not resting until we reached the imperial city. Under cover of night we entered Rome. Nero had declared a fight to the death, and I was taking up the challenge. The Porta Capena was well patrolled with soldiers crawling all over it. Because we had to pass them without arousing their suspicions, we boldly drew near the city gate. I had heard that if a man were now suspected of being one of Christ's followers he was immediately arrested. We presented ourselves to the sentries as citizens of Rome, stating our professions as tent maker and physician. After probing into Luke's medical and surgical equipment, satisfied that we were what we said we were, the soldiers grunted and nodded for us to pass. Almost as an afterthought one of them asked, "Coming into the city to see the Christians die tonight in Nero's circus? They had quite a show last night. Over a hundred of them eaten by tigers! Blood all over the place!"

I stared at the guard without registering any emotion or surprise. Then I asked, "We can see it tonight, ourselves?"

"Yes, just go to Nero's circus. It's all free. There is even free wine and food, thanks to Nero."

I was not prepared for the dismal sight that lay before us once we were inside the Porta Capena. All the houses were reduced to ash heaps. We saw a young woman sitting in a pile of rubble that had once been her home. A dirty child, with her face tear stained, stood sobbing beside her mother who was also weeping. It was we soon learned a typical scene. Although Nero provided tents for the homeless, some preferred to stay in the ruins of their former homes.

The church where Peter preached was also destroyed. The house of my imprisonment was gone with absolutely nothing remaining of it, except the marble floor and the marble columns of the peristyle.

We had no way of finding Peter or the Church that was in hiding because of Nero's demanding the death of all Christians. We decided that the best course for us to follow was to go to Nero's circus as the soldier had advised. There were sure to be Christians there. Perhaps we would have a chance to talk to some of them and learn the whereabouts of Cephas.

We walked passed the Circus Maximus where the fire started. Then we proceeded across the Tiber making our way to the Vaticanum and Nero's Circus. At the entrance of the arena, there were several large cages with bars on them. Luke and I reckoned that they contained the wild animals for the evening performance. Many people were pressing around the cages. We were trying to pass unobtrusively in the crowd and so we mingled with them. When we were close enough to see inside the cages, we were disturbed to see that they contained not animals, but men, women, and children and even little babies. Many of out Christian people were Greek slaves and had no status at all in Rome, making it easier for Nero to persecute them..

"God forbid!" Luke whispered at my ear. "They are our brothers and sisters in Christ"

The excited crowd taunted and jeered at the caged Christians who remained silent, answering nothing to the accusations that they were responsible for the fire. In the center of one cage, I saw a tall, stately man praying with uplifted arms while his fellow prisoners surrounded him joining in his prayer. Even though his back was turned to me, I thought I recognized him. Obviously the inspiration and guiding light for those who were with him, he began addressing them.

"My brothers and sisters in the Lord, consider it great joy that you are worthy to suffer for the Lord Jesus. Death will come quickly—heaven will open to you. You will behold the beautiful face of the Savior in an eternity of endless bliss. How sweet it is to suffer for Jesus!"

He turned slightly. I was able to see his face. It was Samuel—the elder from the synagogue who came to my home and to whom I preached Christ crucified! I knew then for the first time what was going on. All those with him were similarly clad in animal skins. I had an idea of what Nero had in mind. The people in the cage were almost all Jews! Nero had probably demanded lists of those who had separated themselves from the synagogues and arrested them first. One of the women in the cage was nursing her baby at the breast. A little girl of about five years was standing at her knee asking her mother repeatedly "Mama, why are we going to die?"

"We shall not die little one. We shall live and see Jesus," the mother kept repeating. The child became quiet. Samuel turned just then and was standing right before me, face to face, showing no sign of recognizing me. To do so would have occasioned my immediate arrest. Something whizzed by my ear and struck Samuel in the face. It was a rotten vegetable. Samuel stooped to the floor, picked it up from where it had fallen and kissed it.

Lingering in the shadows for fear someone might recognize us, we hoped to get a chance to talk to Samuel before the slaughter began. I had to learn from him where Peter was. if he was still alive.

The circus was filling up with people. When there remained only a few around the cages, because most of the people had gone into the arena to get seats while there were still some left, I called to Samuel in Hebrew very softly. He came as near to me as the bars would permit

"I am praying for you and for all those with you," I whispered.

"May the Lord bless you," he answered, "I am not afraid—Jesus is with me." He laid his ascetic looking hands on his breast prayerfully. His face was radiant.

"Where can I find Cephas?" I asked so softly no one else could hear.

"In the Christian cemetery," he answered moving away from me for fear someone would become suspicious. In Hebrew, he told his little flock in the cage with him that the Apostle Paul was there to comfort them and pray for them at the hour of their deaths. They looked at me, eyes filled with faith and hope.

I raised my hand in blessing and disappeared into the crowd that was entering the circus where the stalls were packed with the homeless who had nowhere else to go. Demanding that the entertainment begin, they stamped their feet and whistled. The central arena was in darkness as we made our way to seats in the front row where the martyrs could see us and at the same time have our backs turned to the bloodthirsty mob. Also we would be sitting near the exit just in ease we had to make a hasty departure. There was a lamppost in front of us. I observed it for a few moments and turning to Luke who was beside me said, "How odd. There is a man chained to the post."

Together we watched the man on the lamppost who was held fast by a chain around his neck. I then remembered what I had heard of Nero's human torches. A soldier walked in front of us with a torch in his hands. Right before our eyes, he reached up and ignited the garments of the man who smelled of pitch. At once the man was enveloped in flames—a human torch, lighting up the arena. I heard a moan escape from his lips and the prayer, "Lord Jesus, receive my spirit."

I prayed as his screams died out. The people sitting around me found it funny. They were laughing uproariously. Another human torch was lighted. More screams pierced the arena and the name of Jesus came from the holocaust. Shortly the entire circus was lit up with burnt human offerings of Christians who were making the total sacrifice of themselves. The smell of burning flesh was odious and abominable. The people in the stalls were stamping their feet and yelling rhythmically, "Nero! Nero! Nero! Nero!"

After a few minutes of that, the Emperor appeared in his box directly across the circus from where Luke and I were seated. Poppaea was with him.

"The Empress appears to be with child," my physician remarked as she walked to the center of the box. When Nero waved his hands and the crowd yelled louder, he signaled for silence. He was even more repulsive now, wearing the garb of a charioteer, than he was when I saw him at my trial.

"Romans," Nero addressed the populace. Because another round of cheering and whistling began making it impossible for him to continue, he waited until the noise subsided.

"Ten weeks have gone by since the Christians set fire to our beloved Rome Already many of them have given their lives to pay for the dastardly thing they have done to us all." Nero paused and called for his Poppaea to stand up beside him. Holding her hand in his he continued.

"My good wife and I also lost our home in the fire. I promise you, my good people that you will see every Christian in the city die in a way befitting such infamous criminals. On the ruins that surround us we shall build a new Rome—a glorious city such as the world has never known. Rome will rise from these ashes. Already I am making plans to build for my family a new and bigger home. You will do likewise." He paused for them to cheer again. Tonight there is food and wine for everyone at Nero's expense."

The arena went wild with cheering and Nero sat down beside Poppaea and gave the signal for the show to start.

Horrified we saw a beautiful young girl, wearing a leopard skin, being led to the center of the arenas. When I saw a pack of wild hungry dogs being turned loose in the arena with her, I shut my eyes unable to watch any longer. I begged the Lord Jesus to aid her and accept her sacrifice. I ventured another glance at the girl who with beauty and grace was extending her arms in the form of the cross. Peacefully and calmly she stood and waited for the dogs to attack her. I covered my eyes with my hands. I could hear the yelping and the growling of the dogs as they fought over her as she repaid Christ love for love.

"Its all over," Luke whispered.

"I looked up. All that remained of the beautiful girl was a few bones. One of the dogs, still hungry, was gnawing on them.

Luke kept mumbling, "O my God, my God!"

The people were already stamping their feet, demanding more excitement. A mother and her baby and little daughter were brought out next. At the other end of the arena, the soldiers were burning red-hot irons into the flanks of a bull to enrage it before releasing it on the helpless woman and her children. I prayed as she knelt with the baby in her arms and her small daughter beside her.

The bellowing of the bull chilled my blood as the furious animal was charging across the circus with his head low to the ground. The child in terror cried, "Jesus! Jesus!" The bull gored her first, tossing her limp body like a rag doll into the air over his head. She fell dead behind the snorting animal. Turning, the bull crushed her lifeless body under its raging feet.

The mother traced the sign of the cross over her body and that of her infant. The bull charged, his one horn speared her leg; her garments of animal skins were ripped and torn open exposing her slim body. Modestly she reached down and covered herself with the torn fragments. Preparing to attack her again, the bull all the while was pacing the earth. She stood waiting for him, holding her baby in one hand, while with the other hand she tried to hold the skins around her body to preserve her modesty. She, too, died with the name of Jesus on her lips.

Samuel was next. They stretched him out on the ground in the center of the arena. A group of soldiers stood near him, holding axes in their hands. One of then walked over to Samuel and lifting his axe over his head swung and hacked off Samuel's left foot to a loud fanfare of trumpets.

"Jesus!" Samuel screamed in agony.

A second soldier with another flourish of trumpets bounded over to the prostrate Samuel as he lay tied to the ground and chopped off his other foot. A third soldier chopped off Samuel's left hand. Then his right hand was hewn from his body with blood spurting everywhere from his bleeding stumps. Bit by bit his limbs were cut off. Each time the axe bit into his flesh Samuel merely cried out for everyone to hear the holy name of Jesus.

Within ten minutes there was nothing left of him except his trunk and his head. They chopped off his head. When wild boars were turned into the arena to clean up the pieces, the crowd went wild with enthusiasm for this latest way of killing a man. I could stomach no more. Luke and I slipped quietly away from the circus.

We decided to set out at once to find the Christian cemetery where Samuel had told us Peter was living. In the catacombs that run for miles under the city, Christians were safe. Luke learned from caring for the sick and the dying of Rome during the time of my imprisonment that the catacombs had an entrance through one of the places of Christian worship that was located in the shadow of the Claudian aqueduct. With the death screams of those we had seen die in the arena still echoing in our ears, we wasted no time crossing the rubble that everywhere filled the streets We did not speak but continued in silent prayer begging the Lord's mercy upon those who were yet to die that night.

With great difficulty we located the place where the Christian church had been, because all the buildings and familiar landmarks had been destroyed. Eventually we came to a house that Luke insisted was the right one. He probed around in the ruins looking for the entrance to the subterranean burial chambers. We had in fact come to the right place for a large slab of marble swung up before us. An old man rose up out of the ground and peered up at us from a flight of stairs that led into the earth.

"What do you want?" he demanded.

"We are going down there," I said pointing down the flight of stairs that were dimly lit by a torch burning at the bottom on the lower level.

"That is a burial ground" the old man said shaking his finger at me. "If you don't know your way around, you will get lost and never see the light of day again." He glared at us suspiciously. Noisily he sucked at his jagged teeth.

"That is a chance we will have to take." We walked right towards him. He jumped aside and let us enters the stairs. At the bottom of the flight of stairs we found ourselves in a passageway that was very narrow, just wide enough to admit one person. The dead were buried in the shelves that lined the walls on either side. Although the graves were sealed with mortar, the Pharisee in me recoiled at the nearness of the dead. Scratched in the mortar I could read various inscriptions

"Sophia lives!" "Our dear brother—asleep in the Lord." "Rest in peace." "Jesus lives!" These were some of the inscriptions.

When the tunnel turned around a corner, we were almost in total darkness. Groping our way along, we came to a large chamber where there was an altar. Three corridors led from this chamber. We decided on the middle one and began following it. We were soon plunged into pitch-black darkness. We felt our way slowly through the tunnel that branched again. I had a strange feeling that we were in fact lost. Having lost all sense of direction, we were completely turned around. Another passageway—equally dark—intersected the tunnel we were following. Satisfied to follow wherever I led, Luke was stumbling behind me. I stopped and said, "I don't know which way to turn. We don't seem to be getting anywhere."

"Why don't you try calling Cephas," he suggested. "He will recognize your voice and come for us."

I began calling out in Aramaic, "Cephas! Peter! Where are you?"

A voice answered in the darkness. It startled me for it seemed to becoming from someone almost at my elbow. We were at another crossroads in the network of tunnels. "Who are you" the voice asked. "Give the secret word."

"I have no secret words, except the name of Jesus. My name is Paul. This is my physician Luke."

The voice replied, "Wait, I will announce your arrival. If you are welcome, someone will come for you. Otherwise…" He was gone.

A half hour passed. We waited longer still. It was very stuffy under the ground—the air was oppressive, making it hard to breather.

"Let us walk a bit farther," I suggested.

We made our way down the tunnel, coming to another flight of stairs. I almost fell headlong down them. From the bottom of the stairs, I could see a light, a pinpoint, in the darkness. As it grew larger, I could hear footsteps approaching.

"Paul! Is it really you?" It was Cephas! I would know that voice anywhere.

"Yes. Cephas. Here we are." I started walking towards the voice.

The face of the "Rock of Christ" appeared—lit up by the flickering of the torch he bore in his hands. Holding the light to my face, he exclaimed, with profound emotion, "Paul! Luke! Thank God, You've come!" His sonorous voice echoed down the corridors. He clasped my hand.

"I thought you might be able to use us. When we heard of the trouble Nero was giving you, we gave up our journey. We came at once."

He led us through a maze of corridors until we came to his living quarters—couple of rooms off to one side of one of the corridors where the air seemed cleaner and lighter. We sat down on the straw mattresses on the floor—the only furnishings the room provided.

"We just came from the circus," I volunteered.

"How could you bear it?" Peter asked. "Day after day my children are being slaughtered. I am helpless, totally helpless to prevent it. We remain hidden here in the catacombs trying to help those that are still with us. Sometimes we have to venture to the surface to get food and water. We have quite a large community here underground to feed. Many were arrested before they had a chance to come here. The prisons are full to overflowing with Christians." He dropped his head into his hands. "Every day Nero invents new and more horrible ways to kill them. He puts out their eyes—he cooks their flesh with hot irons or roasts them alive on spits over open fires. He throws them into boiling oil. He pulls them apart until they burst open in the middle. He chops them into bits. He takes our pure young virgins and tries to make them sin. They die clinging to their virtue and to the name of Jesus."

Peter had suddenly aged. His hair was now totally white, his face deeply creased with wrinkles.

"We just came from seeing it all," Luke told him.

"I was just preparing to offer the Holy Sacrifice when you arrived. I want you to preach to them, Paul. You have faced many years of persecution. Encourage them. Some of them will surely die in the circus within a few days."

With that he rang a bell. From one end of the catacomb to the other bells began to ring and resound. We followed Peter as he made his way into a chamber just off his living quarters where a number of people were already assembled around the altar that stood in the center of the room.

"Where do they all come from?" Luke asked in amazement, as we saw the multitudes that were gathering for the Sacrifice.

"They live here, just as I do," Peter explained. Here they are safe. Roman law protects cemeteries from desecration. They are safe here."

When the people of God were at last all present around the altar and jammed into the corridors as far as I could see, Peter rose and said, "My very dear children in Christ, God has sent to us the Apostle Paul to help us in our time of persecution. He has suffered much for Christ who appeared to him in a vision on the road to Damascus. He has been in chains for the gospel, beaten by rods, suffered shipwreck, and many other things for the name of Jesus. He will speak to you now."

I poured out my soul to them.

"Brothers and Sisters in Christ, I am ready to die for the name of Jesus. The sufferings we experience now cannot compare with the joy we will know when we behold him, face to face. We are not alone in our time of trial. The Spirit compensates for our weakness, pleading for us before the throne of the Father. I have learned that everything that happens to us serves a good purpose when we follow his will. We are called to be saints—to be holy as he is holy. He has foreordained that we are to become conformed to the image of Jesus Christ." I paused a few moments surveying the faces before me.

"What shall we say when these persecutions happen to us? We know that when God is for us, no one can prevail against us. We also believe that God has a right to ask us to lay down our lives to witness to his truth, because he delivered his son up to death on the cross for us all. He who has not spared even his own Son, but has delivered him up far us, has he not the right to ask us to lay down our lives to be a witness to his truth?" Eagerly the people were receiving every word I spoke to them.

"Did you ever consider that athletes run a race, but only one of them wins and receives the prize? You, too, are running in a race, not to receive a crown that perishes, but an eternal crown. Run to obtain the prize, your crown of glory! Just as athletes discipline themselves to run better, you too must be disciplined. God will not let you be tried beyond your strength—he is faithful and true. What are you afraid of? You have nothing to fear. Yes, Nero can kill your body, just as the Roman soldiers crucified Jesus and put him to death. But you know that the Holy Spirit who raised Jesus from the dead is within you. He will also raise you up to an eternal life of joy and glory. Christ is risen from the dead the first fruits of us all.

"But some of you want to know how the dead will rise and what their bodies will be like. Think of how the farmer sows seed in the earth—a dry little seed which seems to die, but is resurrected a beautiful plant with an abundant harvest. But the seed has to die to itself, before the green shoots of life spring into being. That is the way it is with the resurrection of our bodies. We are the wheat of God. Sown in corruption, we shall rise incorrupt. That which is sown in dishonor will rise in glory. What is sown in weakness will rise in power. So also with the resurrection of the dead. A natural body will arise as a spiritual body. Christ's victory totally devours death!

"Therefore, my beloved brothers and sisters in Christ, stand firm, be faithful, a great reward is being laid up for you in glory! You are the sweet fragrance of God! Thank him that he has called you out of darkness into his glorious light and that he counts you worthy to suffer for him.

"The time is now! The day of salvation is here! Let us go forth enduring all things for him who loved us unto death. We will go forth in patience, in trials, in persecutions, in love, in truth, in the power of God. Dying we enter into life eternal!

"If we are faithful, Nero cannot harm us. You have been given the grace, not only to believe in Christ, but also to suffer for him. Imitate me, little ones, as I imitate Christ. For love of him, I have lost everything that I might be found in him.

"I do not consider that I have already attained the pearl of great price. Rather I forget the things I have already done for Christ, and push forward toward our heavenly calling, for our true citizenship is in heaven. Do not fear him who can kill the body, for Jesus will reform our bodies making them like his glorious body. So, my brothers and sisters, hold fast to the faith, for you have already died and your lives are hidden with Christ in God and you will appear with him in glory.

"Rejoice! The Lord Jesus is with us. Rejoice! Have no anxiety whatsoever. May God's peace, which is beyond the comprehension of men, keep you in Christ Jesus." I raised my hand and blessed them.

As Peter offered the Holy Sacrifice, I knelt before the altar waiting for Christ to be present once again. The bread and wine was consecrated. Jesus was in our midst. Every soul that was there that night was overpowered by the sense of his nearness. After the Sacrifice Peter knelt before the altar and led us all in a litany of prayer.

"Lord Jesus, we believe in you," Peter's voice was loud and strong.

"We are ready to die for you," the people of God responded with confidence.

"Lord Jesus, we hope to obtain all you have promised," continued the bishop of Rome.

"We are ready to die for you," thundered the response.

"Lord Jesus, we love you," Peter said with the fire of devotion glowing in his face.

"We are ready to die for you!" I responded with all the rest.

I was pleased to spot the face of my former jailer, Julius in the crowd. When the prayers were finished, he came up to me. We talked together for a few minutes. He was living a precarious existence for he was still employed in the Pretorian Guard. Loyally he kept Peter informed of all the news that stirred in Nero's palace.

"Aren't you afraid Nero will learn that you are a Christian, Julius, my son?"

"I am ready to die for Christ, Father Paul," he answered without hesitation. "Whenever he wishes, I am ready to lay down my life. He is my commander, I strive to carry out his orders."

I was proud of Julius, "Well said, my son, well said!"

I learned to adjust to living in the catacombs where one day was much like another. Together, Peter and I sustained the suffering and bereaved community of Christians that every day contributed more martyrs for the faith. It was impossible for them to remain all the time in the catacombs. It was necessary to go above ground for supplies. Whenever they ventured out some were invariably caught. As the weeks went by, we learned from Julius that Nero had no intention of slackening the blood purge of Christians. From Julius I also received reports of the breach that was growing wider between the Jews and Romans in Palestine where many Zealots were being crucified in Galilee. The Roman governor was ruling with barbaric severity and even high-ranking Jewish leaders were being nailed to crosses. The Roman soldiers had leveled a number of villages to the ground. Yet the Jews were rebellious.

The Roman Procurator, Florus, seized seventeen talents from the temple treasury. To retaliate some Jewish rebels went through the streets begging coins, they said for their poor, impoverished governor, making Florus furious with the insult. Swiftly sacking the city, he killed six hundred Jews in the area around the Antonia. Rebellion broke forth—rebellion of the entire Jewish people. I hoped and prayed that my sister Rachel and her family could read the signs of the times and flee from Jerusalem. I could see the handwriting on the wall, from what Julius told me. God had numbered the days of Jerusalem. The Jews had been weighed in the balance and found wanting. The little that was left to them was being destroyed. Soon Jerusalem would be desolate and wailing.

The Church in Rome was growing strong from the persecution that was meant to kill it. We were able frequently to secure the relics of the martyrs and bring them down into the catacomb and enshrine them in our altars where many priests were now offering the Sacrifice daily. I found great joy in offering up the Holy Sacrifice on the relics of a pure virgin who had died defending her virtue—confessing her faith in the Three in One.

I was very happy that I had left Timothy at Ephesus with the Apostle John, the last time we were there. John had gone to Ephesus and built upon the foundation I laid there. I knew that he had taken Mary there with him, because Christ had given her to him, since she had no other children beside Jesus to care for her. How much I would love to have seen her once more before she fell asleep. Unfortunately, as she foretold, I did not get to Ephesus while she was still there. Nevertheless I am of good cheer for I know that she watches over me with her prayers and that she will be praying for me when my hour to depart this world comes. She promised me that. I knew that soon I would behold her beauty once more.

John has done great work for Christ at Smyrna, Sardis, and Pergamum where strong Christian communities are flourishing. I knew Timothy would be safe in Ephesus. Now, however, he is determined to come to Rome and be with the Church here in her magnificent and awesome hour.

One night Julius came to me in my cubicle in the catacombs where he frequently visited me. This night, however, he had something unusual to tell me.

"What is it, my son?" The light from the lamp that was hanging suspended from the ceiling behind him formed a halo of light around his head.

"Father Paul," he dropped down on the pile of hay that served as a chair. "It has happened as you said it would."

"Go ahead." I urged him to speak freely. He was strong with a virtue that was supernatural. Fortitude had always been his characteristic natural virtue. Since his baptism the virtue had been perfected by grace and made resplendent by the gifts and the fruits of the Holy Spirit.

"Poppaea died today," he said softly.

"How did it happen?" I felt certain that Nero had something to do with it.

"Poppaea," he explained simply "was in the advanced stages of pregnancy. Nero has been going to the circus without her recently. Last night he stayed out rather late. When he came home, she complained of the lateness of the hour." Julius paused and then said bluntly, "Nero kicked her in the belly. She hemorrhaged to death today. Tonight Nero was at the circus as usual demanding more Christian blood."

"Nero is digging his own grave," I said not surprised at anything that he might do.

"Father Paul," Julius spoke slowly considering well what he was saying, "I have heard of a plot to kill Nero. They plan to put Calpurnus Piso on the throne."

"The plot will fail," I predicted with certainty. "But still Nero has not long to live. He will die at his own hand. When the Senate proclaims someone else as emperor, he will try to drown himself in the Tiber, but cowardice will cause him to run and hide in the cell of a former slave. And when the Senate proclaims him to be a public enemy of the state, he will try to sink a dagger into his own throat. When he falters a slave will do the task for him." Already I had said too much.

Julius overwhelmed me with his questions.

"How do you know? Father Paul" he kept insisting.

Without paying heed to his questions I said, "Be very careful, my son, I don't want Nero and his cohorts to learn that you are a Christian. It is very helpful to have one of us in his Praetorian Guard."

It truly was a great help to be able to anticipate Nero's movements from the information Julius was giving us. That information combined with what I learned from the Holy Spirit in prayer gave me the confident belief, that if we remained steadfast a short time longer, the Church in Rome would outlast Nero. We braced ourselves for the struggle. I knew that Nero would meet the fate of his predecessors who had outraged the Senators and the Praetorian Guard to the point where they would no longer tolerate his miscreant behavior.

Nero grieved ever the death of Poppaea. He had her body embalmed with costly spices and gave her a colossal and very pompous funeral with him delivering an eulogy over her corpse himself, but he did not mourn her very long. Julius related to me what Nero did to compensate for the loss he experienced. It was the most abominable of his deeds to date.

"Father Paul," Julius said with his eyes downcast, "the latest thing Nero has done is horrible beyond belief. He found a young man by the name of Sporus who looks quite a bit like Poppaea. Nero had Sporus castrated and he has married him in a formal ceremony."

"And what do the Senators and the people of Rome have to say about it?"

"They say that Julius Caesar did likewise and so did Anthony. Cicero taunted Julius Caesar with having lost his virtue to King Nicomedes, the ruler of Bythnia. Later Curio said that Julius Caesar was the husband of every man and the wife of every soldier in his army. Such was his reputation. These things are not new to Rome. Anthony kept a harem of both sexes in Rome. I heard someone say it was unfortunate that Nero's father did not have that kind of wife."

"And what do you have to say about it Julius?" I asked him gently.

"I am glad and thankful that you baptized me, Father Paul. I am happy that Christ lives in me and gives me the victory over my flesh so that I can live a chaste and holy life," he replied without hesitation.

"Amen to that, my son. The wrath of God is turned against all ungodly and evil behavior. I hear the Romans even have a goddess of the sewers, Cloacina, and a god of the manure heaps, Stercutius."

Perceiving that Julius had something else on his mind, I grew silent, waiting for him to speak.

"Father Paul," he said with deliberation, "I would like to consecrate my chastity to Christ. I would like to make a vow of total and perpetual chastity to him—that I might be a living sacrifice to atone for the unchaste behavior of Rome."

Upon hearing these words from my son Julius—a Roman soldier, I rejoiced and gave thanks.

"What you propose is very praiseworthy. You have my consent. First make the vow for one year. At the end of that period of time—if you still feel the same way you can make it forever."

There was hope for Rome. A new Rome, a Christian Rome would rise over the grave of the pagan city. As for Nero—he finally heard of the plot to replace him on the throne with Piso. When he did, he seized and tortured some of the plotters. From them, he learned the names of the other conspirators. Seneca and his nephew Lucan, the poet, were among those named. Eventually, Nero succeeded in laying bare the whole plot. In a rage he set out to avenge himself with such ferocity, that it was rumored he had made a vow to wipe out all the Senators and destroy the Senate.

Seneca, poor old Seneca—just as he had foretold—received the order to kill himself. He argued awhile before submitting. His nephew Lucan—also ordered to die—died reciting his poetry. Petronius died by Nero's command. Thrasea Paetus, the leading stoic in the Senate was condemned to death—not for any complicity in the Piso plot—but on the grounds that he was deficient in enthusiasm for the emperor and for not liking Nero's singing and also for composing a laudatory biography of Cato. Helvidius Priscus, his son-in-law was banished. Musenius Rufus and Cassius Longinus were commanded to take their own lives. Seneca's brothers were also ordered to die. I learned that one of them was Gallio, who set me free in Corinth when the Jews tried to have me arrested.

After the horrific blood purge, Nero, satisfied that all threat to his person was ended, settled down to the task of building a house for himself. Slowly on the Palatine arose Nero's domus aurea—his Golden House. The mile square villa that he laid out for himself flowed over the Palatine and encroached on the neighboring hills of Rome. For his amusement, he had gardens, aquariums, game preserves, aviaries, vineyards, rivulets, fountains, waterfalls, lakes, pleasure houses, summer houses, and greenhouses. Some of his porticoes were three thousand feet long.

Inside the palace, marble, bronze, mother of pearl, and gold covered the walls. Having looted Greece of her art treasures, his home was one vast art collection. He prided himself on possessing the Laocoön. On the ceiling of his banquet hall, he had ivory flowers that dispensed a spray mist of perfume at the inclination of his head. In his own dining room, he had a spherical ceiling made of ivory, resembling the sky, having stars that were in constant rotation by means of hidden machinery. As for baths—he had hot ones—cold ones, warm ones, salt baths, and sulphur baths. No matter how many baths Nero had, he could not wash away the filth that encrusted his soul.

His furniture was made of the most expensive woods and inlaid with tortoise shells, bronze, and precious stones. He had tables made of silver. The mattress on his wooden bed was made more comfortable by resting on bronze webbing.

An elaborate central heating system that sent hot air into his rooms was devised just to make Nero more comfortable. The silver service on his table was the most lavish the factories of Campania could make from the best of Spanish silver. His prize possession, however, was his great collection of gems that he inherited from Augustus Caesar.

All of Rome was busy with the task of rebuilding. Slowly the Christian community began to emerge from the catacombs with life in Rome gradually returning to normal. Christians were still being seized, nevertheless, and the prisons were filled to capacity with our people.

Reports came from Jerusalem of the maltreatment of the Jews at the hands of Procurator, Florus. The Roman governor forced the people of Jerusalem to give a public and solemn reception to the two cohorts of soldiers that came to the city from Caesarea. After much persuasion by the high priest, the Jewish people agreed to do what Florus demanded. When the soldiers failed to return the courtesy of the Jews, the people of Jerusalem turned all their hatred on Florus. The soldiers set upon the people. A battle was fought in the streets and the outcome was that the Jews succeeded in gaining possession of the temple mound and cutting connections with the Fortress Antonia.

Agrippa hastened from Alexandria, where he was at the time, and went to Jerusalem. From his palace, he pleaded with the Jews, begging them to abandon their rebellion. The people were ready to obey the emperor, they said, but as for Florus—they would not obey him. Soon the rebels proceeded to take over the Masada. When a decree was made to suspend the customary sacrifices for the emperor, it was a declaration of war.

What remained of a peace party in Jerusalem—the high priest, the representative Pharisees and members of the Herodian house—asked Agrippa to rescue them. With the help of a cavalry of three thousand, sent by Agrippa, they managed to take possession of the upper city of Jerusalem, giving the rebels possession of the temple mound and the lower city, as well, driving the troops of Agrippa out of the city, burning the palaces of the high priest and that of Agrippa and of his sister Bernice. Next the rebels proceeded to take over the Antonia, causing the Roman cohort to flee to the towers of the Herodian palace. The rebels burned the rest of the structure. The former high priest, Hannanian was found and murdered.

On the condition that they could leave the city unharmed, the Roman cohort agreed to lay down arms. The Jews agreed to this proposal, but no sooner had the soldiers of Rome surrendered than the Jews turned on them, slaying them all.

Apparently Nero was oblivious to all that was happening in Jerusalem or Rome, because he left the imperial city to compete in the Olympic games and make a concert tour of Greece. When at Olympia, Nero entered a chariot in the races. In the midst of the contest he was thrown from his chariot and was almost crushed to death. Undismayed he rose to his feet and reentered his quadriga and continued the race, but he had to quit before the race was over. Nevertheless, the judges gave Nero the crown of victory. Overjoyed, as recompense, he freed all Greeks from paying any tribute to Rome in the future. To further please Nero, the Greek cities agreed to hold the Olympian, Pythian, Nemean, and the Isthmian games all in one year. He took part in all of them as a singer, harpist, actor, or athlete. Nero was all courtesy in dealing with his opponents who lost, awarding each of them Roman citizenship as a consolation prize.

When Nero received the news that Judea was in revolt and that there were rumors of rebellion brewing in Gaul and Spain, he merely sighed and continued his trip through Greece and his amusements. When the Emperor sang in a theater, no one was allowed to leave, even for the most impelling reason. Some women actually gave birth to their babies in the theater during Nero's concerts. Some people pretended to be dead in order to get out of the concert hall, it was reported.

Reports of rebellion in the West and uprisings in the East finally forced Nero to cut short his trip and return to Rome. It was a proud emperor that entered the city in triumph, bearing the one thousand eight hundred prizes he won in Greece.

Meanwhile, Gallus, the Governor of Syria, took the twelfth Roman legion and marched into Judea together with two thousand men from other legions, six cohorts and four wings of cavalry and numerous other troops, including Agrippa's. Defeated by the Jews, they retreated, leaving behind supplies that served to strengthen the rebels. Joseph, son of Gerion and the former high priest assumed defense of Jerusalem. Joshua, son of Sappha, and Eleazar son of Hanniah were in charge of defending Jerusalem. Josephus was given the command of Galilee where it was assumed the Romans would strike first.

Nero, once more in Rome, was determined to rule the empire with an iron fist. It was early spring. The chief command for the planned attack on Judea was given to Vespasian who was tarrying in Antioch preparing for the war, while his son Titus was sent to Alexandria to bring up a legion.

We were making plans to celebrate the thirty-seventh anniversary of Christ's death and resurrection. Nero, busy with so many crises, was giving us a measure of peace. Christians were still dying in the arena—the prisons still were full with our people, but Nero no longer had his interest fixed exclusively on us. We felt that it would not be long before the dissatisfied Gauls or Spanish would march on Rome and provide the empire with a new Caesar. It was well known that the Gallic governor of Lyons, Julius Vindes, was very independent. Galba, the commander of the Roman army in Spain—it was rumored—hoped to rise to the purple.

As part of the celebration of the coming Pascal season, Peter duly consecrated Linus as a bishop in the church of God and acknowledged him as his appointed successor as Bishop of Rome.

"We are getting old," Peter said. "We never know how much longer we shall be here."

I approved of Peter's choice of Linus, who was young, strong, and had been assisting Peter for years. We were still using the catacombs as the public place of worship, not wishing to expose large numbers of the people of God to possible arrest by Nero's soldiers. One night as we were preparing to offer the Holy Sacrifice—it was just a short time before the feast of the resurrection—Julius came to me in my cell in the catacombs, very distraught and nervous, as he entered my presence. Even after I invited him to be seated he continued pacing the dirt floor. I knew that whatever it was that was disturbing him was serious.

"Out with it!" I commanded.

"Nero has decided to put an end to the murder of the Christians."

"So? That's good news, isn't it?"

"He plans to finish the persecution in a great finale. He is going to empty all the prisons of Rome of all Christian prisoners. He will do this on the Vatican hill on the anniversary of the crucifixion."

My heart sank as I realized what Julius was telling me.

"He is going to crucify them all. A forest of crucifixes will be erected. Men, women, and even little children will be nailed to the crosses."

"God forbid!" I could see that Julius was deeply agitated.

"Father Paul, I have been assigned to be one of the executioners. I am to take nails and drive them—into the wrists of my fellow Christians in whom dwells Christ. O God, Father," he sobbed, "it's awful—I am to nail Christ to the cross!"

"And if you refuse?" I knew the answer to that without asking.

His eyes met mine and held them fast.

"They will put me to death." He spoke bravely without flinching.

"They will kill our bodies—yes, but our souls they will never have! Listen, Julius, I will go to our people as they hang on the crosses and I will minister to them. I dare say, Peter will do the same. Perhaps some circumstance of God's providence will deliver you. Perhaps you will be given another mission and you will not need to refuse to obey the order that has been given you. No matter what happens, I, Paul, and Jesus—will be with you."

"I am not afraid, Father Paul, but human nature shrinks at the thought of death. Even our Lord suffered at the approach of the bitter chalice."

"You are very brave, Julius. If Jesus wishes you to die for him, he will give you the grace and the fortitude to do it well. Trust him, not yourself." He seemed to find comfort in my words.

Worshipers were beginning to fill the chamber of the catacomb where the Sacrifice was offered, when I sent Julius to Peter to relate to him what he had just told me. Later when Peter rose to address the people of God, it was with a very heavy heart that he passed the news on to them. Very solemnly Peter announced to them the impending crucifixion of their friends, relatives, and neighbors. After the reality of what Nero planned to do settled into the consciousness of all, Peter began to preach.

"What more fitting way is there for the Church of Christ to commemorate his passion and death than to be nailed to the cross with Him?" Peter spoke sincerely and from the heart. "And who is there to harm you," he continued, "if you are zealous for what is good. But even if you suffer anything for him, you are blessed. Don't be afraid. Don't be troubled. Cling to the Lord Jesus in your hearts. Always be ready to tell everyone why you have this blessed hope within you, but with gentleness. When they speak evil of you, know that Christ died for our sins, he who was just for those who are unjust, that he might bring us to his Heavenly Father. He was put to death in the flesh that he might give life in the Spirit."

Peter's face was radiant with faith, hope, joy, and love as he continued, "My beloved children, do not be alarmed at the fiery trial that is meant only to prove you. Rejoice that you are sharing the sufferings of Christ, because you will also exult when his glory is revealed in you. If you suffer for the name of Jesus, you will be greatly blessed beyond measure, for the glory, the power, and the honor of God will come upon you. The day is coming when the Lord will punish the wicked and ungodly—the pagans and the idolaters. And you, my faithful children in Christ, will receive a glorious and incorruptible crown in heaven."

I watched the faces that were turned towards their shepherd. It was easy to see that the lamp of faith burned brightly in the Church of God. We began a vigil of constant prayer that was to last until after the mass crucifixions were over and until the day of the feast of the resurrection.

The dreadful day of death dawned. I arose from my knees where I had spent the night in prayer. Putting on my toga and accompanied by Luke, I climbed up the stairs and emerged into the light of day. It was a bright sunny morning as we made our way through the splendid new Rome that had sprung up like a phoenix from its ashes. Stately homes with gleaming marble porticoes lined the streets, but we did not tarry, however, to admire the new buildings and their architecture. We were hurrying to the Vatican hill where a forest of crosses was waiting to receive their victims.

In the distance we saw some of Nero's soldiers leading a group of men, women, and children relentlessly to their deaths. Another group was approaching right behind them. Slowly the death march was beginning. The soldiers were armed with whips to beat and drive our people like sheep to the slaughter. It was an amazed bunch of soldiers and an equally amazed populace that watched as the people of God carried their heads high, marching, as if in triumph, to their deaths. They were singing, "Christ has conquered death, Christ reigns, Christ is king." With the hope of the resurrection emblazoned in their hearts, they continued on their way to their Calvary singing hymns of praise to the glory of the Lord Jesus. They were joyful! It was a miracle of grace I was beholding.

Other soldiers were arriving from various parts of the city with more prisoners. All Rome was turning out for the event with the streets lined with curious onlookers. Luke and I followed at a safe distance in a crowd of jeering Romans. I was concerned that the courage of the Christian prisoners might desert them when they were confronted with the nails and the executioners. I wanted to be there to encourage them to hold fast to the faith.

Holiday happy Romans were continuing to stream to Vatican hill. Nero, because he wanted everyone to witness the deaths of the Christians, had ordered that no work was to be done in the city that day—that it would be a great holiday for all.

Arriving on Vatican hill, we saw the first of the martyrs being stretched out on the wood of the cross. When the soft thud of the nails, as they pierced the flesh, gave way to loud hammer blows when the nail bit into the wood, I shuddered involuntarily.

I drew near to the prisoners who were waiting to be crucified. While the soldiers were engaged in the messy work of affixing their victims to their crosses, I whispered words of consolation to all I could. Luke went to another group and did the same. I began to go from one to another of those who were about to die for Jesus. The rows of crosses seemed endless. I was carrying Christ with me in the consecrated Bread of the altar. Whenever I was able, I gave him to everyone I could, strengthening them in their agony.

Peter was in the midst of the flock, the pastor they knew and loved. Few, if any of the dying knew or recognized me. I caught a glimpse of Peter as he fearlessly moved from cross to cross with his hand raised in blessing.

Nearby, I saw about ten soldiers having a heated discussion and making a great deal of noise. As I drew nearer and saw that Julius was one of them, I hastened to see what was happening. I saw a Christian lying outstretched on the ground with his hands on the wood of his cross waiting for the nails, while the officer in charge was bellowing orders like a mad bull.

"I command you," he screamed, "in the name of the emperor—pick up that hammer and nail the man to the cross."

It was Julius he was commanding. Just then Julius looked in my directions. I raised my hand and blessed him. He smiled a great joyful smile. Loudly he answered his officer. "I am a Christian, sir. We have committed no crime deserving of death. I cannot do what you order. It is wrong." Julius spoke with determination.

The captain of the guard drew his sword. He plunged it into the exposed heart of Julius who was standing waiting for the blow—his arms outstretched in the form of a cross. Each of the other soldiers took his blade and sank it into the dying Julius. They walked away leaving him lying in a pool of blood in the street.

As soon as they were gone, I bounded to Julius. He was still alive, but he was failing fast. I placed my arms under his head and held him close.

In his ear, I whispered, "Go to Jesus, my son." He opened his eyes for a moment, smiled ecstatically and said, "Father Paul, Jesus is here—I see him. His body went limp in my arms. I heard a soldier shout as he pointed at me.

"Seize him! He is one of them!"

I ran as fast as my legs would go with a soldier following in hot pursuit. He was gaining on me. I ran faster. I found a thicket of brush and dove into it. I held my breath when I heard the soldier walking close by me in the road. He went past. I was safe–for the moment.

When I was sure he had gone on about his business, I crawled from the brush. Once again I resumed my ministry to the faithful. I passed Peter in the road as he was surrounded by a large number of children who were to be crucified on nearby crosses that were waiting for the little victims. He was trying to comfort them, but at the sight of their faces as they clung to his robes, tears began to stream down his cheeks. He gave himself to the children without reserve. There must have been a hundred of them between the ages of eight and sixteen. When the soldiers began nailing the children to the crosses, Peter could no longer restrain himself. He drew near to them and began comforting them openly, promising them eternal happiness in heaven. The little ones, gladdened to see their holy Father Peter, began yelling his name.

Soldiers were standing by, observing the Rock of Christ ministering to his lambs, all set to pounce on him. Someone behind me gave the order, "Seize him! It looks like my plan has worked. The Apostle Peter has walked right into my little trap!"

As one soldier slapped a chain on Peter's wrists and another chained his legs, I turned my head to see who gave the command. It was Nero himself! I found myself looking him straight in the face. He had become horrible to look at with sores on his face caused by his debauchery. He was repulsively fat. Wearing a blonde wig, he was utterly grotesque.

"Hah," he snorted and observing my toga said, "If my memory does not fail me, I have also snared the Apostle Paul, the Roman citizen!"

"Spawn of Satan," I yelled at him. "You yourself will die before a year has passed!"

A wave of terror crossed Nero's face. "You are no oracle," he hurled at me with a curl of his fat sensuous lips.

From high up on one of the crosses a Christian yelled out, "You will die, Nero! You will pay for your sins!" A chorus of the dying martyrs repeated the verdict passed on Nero.

"You will die Nero!"

"Stop it! Stop it!" he screamed stamping his feet. "Kill them, kill them all immediately!" He pointed at the nearby Christians in agony on their crosses. The soldiers took lances and began piercing the hearts of the crucified.

Peter yelled at the top of his lungs for all to hear, "From this blood will spring a mighty church! Christ has conquered Nero! Christ has conquered death! Christ has conquered sin! Will you die in your sins, Nero? Repent of your sins, son of perdition! Christ will forgive you!"

"Silence him" Nero thundered. "Away with him! Crucify him! Now!"

As the soldiers began marching Peter to a large cross nearby, he called out, "Nero, crucify me upside down because I am unworthy to die like Christ!"

The soldiers glanced at Nero for his confirmation of the request. Nero laughed and said, "Yes, upside down. That will be great sport for everyone to watch. Peter, the head of the Christians, hanging upside down on a cross! Wonderful entertainment for a great Roman holiday!"

I studied Nero an instant and then took up where Peter left off. "Everyone in Rome knows your sins, Nero." Slowly I began to enumerate. "Agrippina, your own mother, Octavia, your wife—"

The crowd of martyrs, still in agony, took up the list. "Britannicus!" they screamed in a deafening roar.

"Poppaea!" I said boldly.

"Seneca!" roared the martyrs.

"Sporus," I hissed practically in his face.

Nero clapped his hands over his ears. "Take our Roman citizen to the Mamertine!" He climbed into his covered litter, and signaling for them to take me away, he left hurriedly in a cloud of dust.

When the soldiers were placing the familiar chains on me, I was distressed to see Luke approaching me, ready to speak to me.

"Go away!" I ordered. I didn't want him to be taken prisoner. He merely smiled at me. The soldiers grabbed Luke by the sleeve and said, "You are one of the leaders of the Christians, too, aren't you?"

"I am," Luke answered joyfully.

"Come with us!"

We were taken to the Mamertine in the heart of Rome, where I still wait for my execution by the sword. Weeks have gone by and still I wait. The rain continues. The prison is cold. Surely my hour will come soon. Nero has nothing to gain by keeping me alive. I have heard that Peter died a glorious death praising God. Now I recall something I once wrote to the Romans in a letter I sent them from Corinth.

What can separate us from Christ's love? Can troubles, difficulties, hunger, or nakedness, or danger, or persecution, or the sword, or death itself? Absolutely not. In the face of all these things, we are victorious through Christ who loves us. I am convinced that neither death, nor life, neither angels nor demons, neither the present nor the future, nor any powers that may be, neither height nor depth, nor anything else in all creation, can separate us from the love of God that is in Christ Jesus our Lord."

About the Author

Dr. Allienne Becker has a B. A. degree from Duke University, two M. A. degrees from West Virginia University, and a Ph. D. from the Pennsylvania State University. She is the author of several books published by Greenwood Press, including *The Lost Worlds Romance,* 1992, *Visions of the Fantastic,* 1996, among others, and *Eagle in Flight: The Life of Athanasius the Apostle of the Trinity,* Writers Club Press, 2002.

0-595-21321-9

Made in the USA
Columbia, SC
25 September 2018